Megan

Acknowledgements

Thank you for taking the time to read these acknowledgments. Without these people, and others, the journey would not be continuing.

My thanks to my wife, Julie, for her support with this story. For her patience, guidance and understanding, but most of all for her love.

As always, I am grateful to my parents and family for their love and continued guidance. Special thanks to Natasha Mostert for her valued friendship and belief. Her words of support always diminish the doubt.

Many thanks to the talented Marjo Klindenberg for the cover and the ideas, and thanks to Lesley Holmes for her support, the book trailer, and help with the promotional work. A large single malt is raised to Andy and Britt Waspe for their continued friendship and dark tales. Thanks to Kyle 'Wildheart' Vallis who always gives honest views. 3 -1 behind now Kyle, just like in Istanbul…

Collective thanks to those who have been with me from the start. Rachel O'Connel Hallums and Maribel Marrero across the pond. Here comes the silver bird again.

To Stephen, Ann Attwood and Brynne Corcoran-Openshaw for their support, points and corrections. To Teri Rowan, Bonita Parry, Jane Lomas, Stella Stafford, Christina Darby, Heather Gordon - Cotterill, and Vanessa Escalano for their belief in me.

A big hearted thanks to Anthony J. Langford and Sally Corvini who, despite being on the other side of world, give great support, guidance and friendship.

Grateful thanks to Nita Robinson of *Nita Helping Hand?* for her hard work editing and her guidance.

So readers, old and new, and those I've missed off, know your love and support is always greatly appreciated.

Here we go…

'Forgive me if I stare but I can see
the island behind your tired, troubled eyes…'

Chapter 1

Hellmanse Hotel, Tikrit, Iraq

Although he knew for himself that the large clock beside the stairway was accurate, the man disregarded the time it currently showed. Trusting his judgment, which had rarely let him down, he was working on the time shown on his wrist watch, as were the other two men close by. For nearly two hours the three of them had been waiting in the reception area of the former hotel where, in grander times, several heads of states had graced the many corridors and rooms the building provided. Several of the floor tiles on which Page Darrow stood were cracked and pitted, any gleam once held now gone. Little remained of the grandeur the place had once possessed, and Page doubted whether it could ever return.

Even within the pressure he found himself under, he was still able to feel something lingering in the air that told him that once upon a time you would have had to be someone of status merely to enter the building, let alone stay there. Now it was mainly used as a meeting place for several of the oil companies who were busy at work across the war-ravaged city.

Page thought little about why the people were engrossed in their meeting on the fifth floor of the building; his only current interest was getting the two company engineers under his protection safely away from the hotel and back to the designated areas under military control. Several times he had seen American forces move by outside in armoured vehicles, their eyes no doubt continually scanning the streets they moved along. Only the previous day, a loud explosion had shaken the nearby buildings, as more lives on both sides were lost.

It was seriously hot across the city today, close to forty-five degrees. The air conditioning no longer worked in the hotel, and though the drink machine they used offered them plenty of chilled water, the heat still took some handling. Every ten minutes or so the three men exchanged positions without speaking, only showing visible signs of communication when it was necessary. Page knew little personal details about the other two men, aside from the fact that they came highly recommended to the company that Page currently worked for. For the duration of their work, they were merely known as Jameson and Burnett, which to him sounded like the name of a legal firm in his home city of Manchester. With the heat threatening to overcome him, he imagined the people on the streets he knew back home running around in the cold and wet, wishing they were somewhere lovely and hot. He thought to himself, *Didn't life throw a nice irony every so often?*

A slight crackle in the earpiece he wore alerted him to a following message. All three of them then heard the news that the meeting up above had finished and the next stage of their work could begin. Jameson moved swiftly toward the central doorway of the building and spoke into an additional small, handheld radio. Page knew he was alerting the nearby driver. As Burnett joined him, he saw the illuminated panel beside him indicate that the lift was now descending.

A soft bell-like sound announced the lift had arrived, and as the lift doors opened, three other security men nodded in

Page's direction before they led the two men across the hotel lobby. Page couldn't remember which company the two engineers worked for; Mobil, Shell, Exon or something similar, and the truth was that he didn't care where they were from. What he did know was that they were here for the same reason as so many others. Aside from the acts of sheer humanitarianism going on across many parts of the country, the black gold deep in the ground drew many and offered far greater rewards.

Through the glass doors at the front of the building, Page could see crowds of people moving along the roadway. There were always so many bloody people around the crowded roads of the city. Their attempt to continue with some form of normality, even though everywhere around them had seen some sort of devastation, made Page admire the courage shown by many. But where on earth were they all going?

Ideally, he would have liked the vehicle to do another circuit of the building, but people above him had agreed they needed the men out as soon as possible. Page stayed close to the smaller of the two engineers, who was carrying about twenty extra pounds, causing him to be sweating profusely in the heat. Burnett moved in front of the group and waited for a signal from Jameson outside.

Despite the overcrowded street, an old man was pulling a donkey laden with boxes along the edge of the roadway, causing the oncoming car to slow down.

Burnett raised an arm to hold the two engineers back while the old man moved on, shouting what were obviously obscenities their way. With the car now parked up, Page and two of the security men emerged from the dimness of the building into bright sunshine with the oil engineers. Situations like this were never easy; with so many people milling about, every single person looked like a potential threat to Page as they moved toward the car. On the opposite side of the road, a row of vehicles moved by with more than one of the impatient drivers sounding his horn. Most of the vehicles were worn and dented, thickly dusted in the sand, so the white Mercedes that Page then spotted at the rear of the line seemed to stand out all the more as he looked across. While the increase of heat was to be expected as they moved outdoors, the confinement of the Kevlar body vest he wore for some reason felt more substantial than usual when he moved. Jameson was reaching for the car door handle just as Page's hearing began to alter. He could still hear the people around him talking, along with those in his earpiece, but it sounded as though they were somehow talking much slower. The edges of his peripheral vision began to expand, whilst at the same time other objects stood out with increased clarity. The line of vehicles opposite had now passed, with the white Mercedes soon slowing till it was directly in front of Page as he shepherded the engineers forward.

In the back seat of the car, he could see what appeared to be auburn hair pressed against the side window. A decorative scarf partially covered the face of the person who sat alongside, the eyes and top half of the nose the only parts visible. Page couldn't understand why the eyes seemed to stand out so vividly amidst the scene around him. It wasn't just the intense blue colour of them he noticed, it was the look of concern etched upon them. Looking directly at him, the eyes then appeared to sway from side to side as the head began to shake. The movement only causing the concern in the blueness to intensify, as did the feeling in

Page's stomach, both indicating that something was wrong. Very wrong.

More people emerged close to the side of Page. A couple of women carrying what appeared to be baskets of clothing spoke loudly as they passed. Two young children dragged sticks along the ground, making patterns emerge in the patches of windblown sand. Anxiously, Page now turned his attention back to the security car. He could make out the shape of the driver who sat at the wheel as Jameson began to open one of the vehicle's rear doors, the driver's arm held out straight in front of him, firmly holding the steering wheel. The sun caught the links of the watch strap, the glare making Page blink quickly. Something was causing Page to slow his movement at the same time he held onto the engineer's arm. The white Mercedes had now moved on with the other traffic, only glimpses of the roof of the car now visible, though the eyes remained active in his memory, as did the shaking head of the person whose age he could not tell. At the same moment, he looked back at the driver and realised what was different. When the driver had dropped them off at the hotel earlier, Page had taken little notice of his appearance but had confirmed the time with him and the other security guards. Page remembered the man had been right-handed like himself, but the watch was now on the other wrist. Different sounds came to Page's ear, mostly heavy breathing that seemed to make the still slow voices echo. The different sound that he could make out was a gradual, deliberate ticking.

In the moment of calling out to Burnett to stop, he saw the small eruption on the side of his colleague's head as a bullet entered the front of Jameson's skull. A large piece of the man's skull broke away as the bullet passed through, blood swiftly followed, spraying against the side of the car.

Page instantly pulled back on each of the two engineers, forcing them back toward the relative safety of the former prestigious building. As he did, Page pulled free his handgun, firing several shots into the vehicle. He thought that at least one had hit the driver, though he was unable to confirm this as he was busy moving the two men back inside. Some of the noise of the commotion outside seemed to disappear as the tall doors closed behind them, entering the building where only moments before had seemed relatively peaceful. Page saw a blood stain appear on the trailing leg of the taller of the two engineers where another bullet had found a target, just as he got them behind one of the vast pillars in the hotel lobby.

It was the massive change in pressure that shattered the glass doors of the building in the briefest of seconds before the fireball from the exploding vehicle spread across the hotel entrance, engulfing all around it. Page felt blood run down from one of his ears as the intense explosion ruptured the drum inside. He kept his face down and his arms outstretched across the oil engineers as the glass and debris continued to rain down on him.

Chapter 2

Present Day

The silence within the house was complete. Not the slightest draught attempted to break the still air. Any prospect of scurrying feet from a stray rodent seemed as far away as the cushioned sound of a moth fluttering by. Although moonlight streamed unchallenged through most of the windows along the front of the large building, the stillness within was graced by its pale shroud. There were other rooms though where the doors acted almost like a barrier to the nocturnal visitor, ones that remained perpetually in darkness. In these rooms that saw not even daylight, where only darkness held refuge, thick curtains covered many of the windows. Around the sections that lay upon the floors, as well as within the folds across the tops of the curtains, the dust lay heavy. Other rooms were windowless, the darkness within complete. Long since disturbed.

Wooden shutters were drawn across the frames of other windows, where the rust upon the securing bolts showed how long it had been since many of them had been opened. Outside, what paint remained upon them was badly cracked and peeling in thin strips. Crude wooden boarding kept other windows secure, yet in the narrow gaps around the edges, small chinks of light occasionally found their way inside. Whenever the sun or daylight faded, it gave the impression that it had retreated more out of fear than anything, allowing the shadows within to spread with ease.

Within the darkness of the vast cellar there began a slight movement. It had come from the furthest corner, perpetually held in night, long before the day's light had faded. Here it edged out, feeding on the confined shadows, darkening them further, increasing their density until only one option remained for the blackness. It began to spread.

Increasing both in shape and size, eager to disperse any forms of moonlight that now attempted to penetrate the darkened interior of the house, it began to creep up the wooden steps that gave access to the cellar. Its strength increasing so rapidly that it failed to pay any attention to the closed doorway. The series of locks that held the door secure failed to be disturbed as the blackness just seeped through the grains of wood around them.

Shadows increased elsewhere within the house as a thickening cloud began to obscure the final traces of moonlight, all drawn to the increasing darkness that probed and searched the rooms and corridors. Having long lost respect for the allowed time of daylight, the unseen presence had been drawn to someone who was close now. So close that the blackness began to form the shape of whispery hands that clawed and grabbed at the window frames in front of it. Now was not the time, and reluctantly it began to retreat, to diminish, holding back its power until its time would come. For now, it waited. The patience within strong, as was the intent. When that time happened, it would begin to probe the minds of visitors, seeking out secrets held deep within them. Then it knew it could spread easier, more purposely, and before long devour all in its path.

Chapter 3

The lobby of the Arlington Hotel was quickly becoming congested as a group of newly arrived Japanese tourists began to find their own luggage from a pile of cases stacked close to the entrance. Several of the group were already bombarding a young woman behind the reception desk with repeated questions, mostly in poor English, making the onlooking Page Darrow smile to himself as he saw the perplexed look on the woman's face. In spite of the stressful moment that the tourists were causing, the dark haired receptionist was somehow managing to keep a degree of composure, which Page greatly admired.

As a form of a queue began to assemble, several of the tourists were forced to step aside of an elderly couple who attempted to reach one of the hotel's two lifts.

Page glanced briefly at his watch which confirmed the same time as shown by an oval-shaped clock set opposite the main entrance where he now stood. When another member of staff approached from an adjoining corridor, Page spoke briefly to him before he pointed him in the right direction. As Page walked away, the man himself became a target for the troubled tourists.

Being one of the oldest hotels in Manchester, The Arlington still held onto the prestige and character that most modern buildings failed to capture. It seemed content in its city centre location, set alongside similarly aged buildings that showed the city's former status. *Another city, another hotel* Page thought to himself. Even though the streets of his home city often made headlines for the wrong reasons, there was a familiarity with certain parts of the city that had always given him a sense of comfort and security.

Page was twenty minutes early for his appointment, which suited him fine, as he would be able to assess the location first for himself. He followed the sign for The Deverre Suite as instructed, and as he walked, he pulled on the sleeves of the dark suit. Earlier that morning, Page had considered wearing a tie, but in the end had just chosen a blue shirt, the collar of which was left open. Passing a row of mirrors at the far end of the lobby, he thought he looked reasonably presented, although his thick, brown hair would have looked better had it been cut recently.

The suite he sought turned out to be a bland, open planned room filled mainly with circular tables. There were matching chairs set around a long conference-style table at the end of which sat a man. The presence of the two men flanking him indicated to Page that he was not the only person to be early. When he entered the room, Page noted that the only other people were three maintenance staff dressed in royal blue overalls showing the hotel's name, busy cleaning the windows at the far end.

As Page approached the long table, the two men in black suits with matching shirts and ties stepped away. Page noted that one stayed close to the seated man while the other walked over to the members of the hotel's staff. After a quiet word, Page noticed that they soon left the room.

'Mr. Darrow, I presume?' the man who sat at the end of the table asked as Page looked back. He looked to be in his late sixties, his thinning, silver hair swept back over his tanned head. Page noticed he looked to have been fed well beneath the expensive looking suit he wore. When he stood, he extended his right arm before adding, 'I'm Charles McAndrew, thank you for coming.'

Page felt a firmness to the older man's grip that belied his age as they shook before he sat in the seat adjacent to him. There was a warmness to McAndrew's welcome which eased Page a little; this was soon removed by a glance at the two other men. The one who had spoken to the staff now stood beside the door, which Page presumed no one was going to enter through. The other stood impassively nearby, and Page had already seen the earpiece each of them wore.

'Nice choice of venue,' Page told the man.

'Indeed,' replied McAndrew as he smiled again. 'Excellent rooms, I hear, but expensive.'

'Not as expensive as the high-class prostitutes I know who work here regularly,' Page remarked, keeping his expression still whilst noticing the other man's smile vanished as he seemed at a loss for what to say. Gradually the smile returned, but it appeared weaker as he continued.

'You obviously received our letter, and with your attendance, I presume you are interested in its contents?'

Two days ago Page had received a letter delivered by courier from a company called A.R Solutions. The man who had signed the letter now sat alongside him. The contents had informed him that any relevant questions would be answered if he would like to meet them at the time and date mentioned. The only other details were that his services would be required for approximately one week's work with the proposed fee alongside. Usually Page would have ignored the letter and placed it with several other similar letters he had received since terminating his latest work contract, but the fee and the fact that they had known his home address had caught his attention, as well as caused a sense of unease to settle within him.

'As stated in our letter, Mr. Darrow, we would like your services for a short while; I presume the fee is acceptable?' McAndrew added.

The fee is more than acceptable, Page thought, though he kept his face expressionless. It was equivalent to his total earnings in the last three years. The smell of money was masked by the stench of the large rat he sensed was lurking somewhere nearby. He was also amused by the reference to his work as services. Page preferred the term 'Close Protection'. Everyone else though, like A. R. Solutions, no doubt used the word bodyguard.

'You might be wasting your time though, I feel,' Page told the older man, 'as I no longer do the type of work you mentioned.'

'What you have done recently with your work, or intend to do in the future, Mr. Darrow, is of little importance to me right now. My current concern is getting you to accept the terms of the assignment we need you to work on. Maybe if you would permit me to be more expansive on some of the details, then the job might be of more interest to you.'

Page remained upright in his seat as McAndrew spoke. As he did, he couldn't help but notice that there was no paperwork or files on the table. Usually at such meetings there would be an array of items regarding the proposed work, but there was only a bottle of table water and two glasses. McAndrew poured an equal measure into both before he spoke.

'A. R. Solutions is currently working on a variety of projects across the globe, providing alternative remedies for the sort of problems that many of our clients have. The company has expanded widely over recent years, better than we could ever have wished for, and our services are in great demand. Occasionally, the work becomes varied, and a great deal involves, as I stated earlier, an alternative way than one would imagine. So much so, that some particular jobs require us to have a specialist member of the staff on board to help. Someone who, shall we say, has certain abilities.'

Page saw that McAndrew had lowered his voice slightly as he had mentioned the term 'certain abilities', and was forced to take a sip from his glass of water beside him before continuing.

'And this member of staff which you would like me to give protection to,' Page suggested, 'although I presume that you already have your security staff in place. Something like Tweedledum and Tweedledee here.'

The man in the suit directly beside him ignored Page's remark and continued to monitor the room with his colleague.

'A. R. Solutions has an extensive range of security, which, as you say, could deal with this,' McAndrew agreed, 'but the unusual nature of the job still requires you to provide close protection for this particular person.'

Shaking his head Page asked, 'But why me?'

Charles McAndrew had disliked Page as soon as he sat down. He had been informed that there was a coldness to the man which, given the type of work he had been involved in, was to be expected. But there was something else about him which he couldn't quite place. He did, however, have to negotiate with him, so McAndrew put the man's personal views and rudeness aside as he continued.

'Because, Mr. Darrow, the person involved asked for you herself.'

Now Page reached for the other glass of water on the table, despite the fact that he would have preferred something stronger. He was becoming more and more intrigued by the conversation, and his last comment had got him wondering who in particular had asked for him. He emptied the contents of the glass in a couple of mouthfuls before he looked directly at McAndrew.

'Okay, I'm intrigued and interested. I would, however, like to meet this member of staff first,' Page told him.

'Well, then, that can be easily arranged, as she's currently here in the building,' McAndrew told him before he stood and motioned for him to accompany him. Page's newfound friend in the dark suit stepped aside to let McAndrew pass, his expression still impassive.

'If you follow me,' McAndrew told him, 'I will try and answer most of the questions that are no doubt beginning to occupy your mind.'

Chapter 4

Surprisingly, only McAndrew and Page took the main lift once they had left the suite; the two security men remaining in the lobby. Page could see that the number of Japanese tourists appeared to have thinned out as the lift doors closed. Hopefully, for the under pressure hotel staff, their issues were now resolved. The two men stood in silence as the lift began to ascend, coming to a slow halt as they reached the fourteenth floor. Page was informed that this and the upper three floors were the private apartments the hotel offered, and were owned by A. R. Solutions.

As the doors opened, they were immediately met by further security, including a man who looked close to forty wearing a charcoal suit, who stepped toward them and enthusiastically shook MacAndrew's hand.

Page was not introduced, nor hand shaken. Instead, the man asked him to raise his arms out. With a sharp nod to two of the security men, they began to run a grey and yellow coloured scanner over Page's body. A couple of times it beeped, and, after removing keys and coins from his jacket pocket, he was told to step forward.

'We have to be thorough, Mr. Darrow,' McAndrew told him as he himself was then frisked. Once his mobile phone had been taken from him, Page was allowed to enter the apartment.

Page guessed there were almost a dozen people in the extensive room. It was the usual luxury apartment, with no expense seemingly spared. His feet sank slightly into the carpet as he walked into the room with McAndrew. His eye noticed the expense of the furniture and fittings within. He quickly scanned the people all at work around the room, some of which were busily working on various computers set against one of the side walls. These included six security men, all wearing what appeared to be the now regulation black suits, spread at strategic points around the room. Two women stood beside an open drinks cabinet, both well dressed. Neither of them looked across as the two men entered the room. Page quickly noted three doors leading off to the rear of the large room which he presumed could lead to a bathroom and bedrooms. To the side of where he stood, a double door led elsewhere; these were also closed. Whilst the two women had shown them no interest, three other men did look interested, one of whom now approached.

'Charles, I see you have found Mr. Darrow.' the man said, extending a hand for McAndrew to shake. Once shaken, he turned his attention to Page. There was an air of ex-military about the man's appearance, Page thought, brought initially by his posture, but now clearly evident in his manner alone. Though he appeared to be in his late fifties, he looked younger due to his strong physique. His hair was neatly cut short, with only touches of grey edging his strong features and jawline.

Dressed casually in a dark blue polo shirt and charcoal trousers, he still managed to look extremely wealthy.

'Mr. Darrow, I'm Anthony Rowlance. Thank you for coming at such short notice.'

He shook Page's hand and held the grip for a second longer than Page preferred.

'That would explain the A. R. bit then,' he told him before adding, 'Call me Page, if you would.'

'Very well, Page, please take a seat. Can I get you a drink? Scotch maybe? I'm sure Charles has been on his usual bottled water.'

'That would be good,' Page replied, noting the touch of humour that the man attempted to force upon him.

Whilst McAndrew moved elsewhere in the room, one of the two women came and took note of the drinks required. Her hair was cut short, almost boyish, but it added immense character to her already beautiful features. She held a smile behind her stern expression which made her eyes widen slightly as she caught Page's stare. As she walked off, Page watched the shape of her legs below her neatly fitted skirt.

When their drinks arrived, the two men sat down in the corner suite close to where a large collection of cactus plants stood. They seemed oddly out of place within the room and gave him the impression that they had been merely been added as an afterthought. When his drink arrived, Page turned his attention back to Anthony Rowlance.

'I'm sure Charles has given you a brief reason as to why we require your time.'

'He told me you have a project going on, which you are having difficulties with, and that you want to look after some woman you have brought in to help you out,' Page reiterated, knowing he had interrupted the older man.

Rowlance looked at him for a moment as if thrown by his bluntness. If he was annoyed, he didn't let it show as he continued.

'Due to the company's security agenda, I can't discuss specific details with you, but I will do all I can to tell you about what we would like you to do. You are correct when you say we want you to provide protection for someone over what we expect to be no longer than a week. Should we overrun that timescale you will be compensated accordingly, but I very much doubt that will happen.'

'Tell me more about your projects and, in particular, about the relation of the woman to them,' Page requested using his usual direct approach. He hoped it would actually help to ease any tension that could be growing. The method of building a foundation between himself and the person attached to him had worked in the past on several occasions, and at that moment he saw no reason to change his ways. When Rowlance gave a gentle nod, he seemed to be taking a moment to compose himself before he spoke.

'The natural resources of our planet, as I'm sure you will no doubt be aware of, Mr. Darrow, are a constant problem for all countries now. For too long now we have gorged ourselves on them, and the need and wish to control them over the last thirty years has made the world an unstable and frightening place. Whilst we pamper some countries with these precious assets, our futile governments have taken us into conflicts with many others. The lasting effects of our actions we can barely begin to imagine. We have all seen the slow switch to forms of alternative energy and, in particular, harnessing that energy, as we attempt to break our reliance on commodities such as oil and gas. I'm sure you would agree that countless lives would have been spared had the once huge reserves been more fairly distributed around the globe when they had first been discovered. This is one of the reasons why my company is used; to find energy sources in the least likely of places.'

As Rowlance continued to speak, Page took another refill of his glass and found his interest increase as the man began to get closer to the actual point that he himself wanted to hear. He knew that he had to keep up his level of composure, if only to settle the security team in the room, aside from the fact that he was on the fourteenth floor of a building he knew little about.

'We have had considerable success recently with ongoing work extracting a material called sand oil, which, given time, could solve many of our energy problems. At present though, the cost of such work is astronomical. There is also the limiting problem that this method of work creates a huge amount of added waste. The woman you are concerned with has been extremely busy on this side of our work, and without her skill, we really would be behind many of our competitors. Sadly, we had to pull her out of a project a month ago when another problem much closer to home appeared.'

The man in the charcoal suit that Page had noted on his arrival on the high-level floor now came over and apologized for interrupting Rowlance. After speaking silently in his ear, Rowlance raised a hand as if he had understood what had been said before the man retreated elsewhere in the room.

As Rowlance composed himself again and gathered his thoughts, Page glanced across to the two women and again ran appraising eyes over the woman who had brought his drinks, as well as the other woman. She wore a beige two-piece suit.

Page noted the height of the woman's heels as she looked over at him, her long brown hair just covering one of her eyes before she brushed it back. As she did, Page noticed a ring on her left hand.

The more Anthony Rowlance spoke, the more Page became intrigued. True, he thought he could trust Rowlance and the rest of them about as far as he could throw them, and still had doubts about what he was exactly doing here. He drained the contents of his glass again and declined another offered him when the shorthaired woman came across again. As she removed his glass from the table, Page was aware that her eye contact only broke from him when Rowlance spoke.

'So anyway,' Anthony Rowlance continued, 'There is a property close by in Cheshire called Ravenscroft, owned by myself, within which we believe we have located an incredible energy source. This source is stronger than anything you could ever imagine.'

'What sort of energy?' Page asked

'That will become clearer to you in time,' Rowlance told him. 'I know that this must all sound extremely vague to you right now, but as I said, later on you will realise what I mean. It is within the grounds of this property that you will be based, and in doing so, help to protect our member of staff.

Anthony Rowlance stood when he had finished speaking and suggested Page do the same when he moved his hand. To focus his mind and eye, Page adjusted the cuffs of his suit sleeves as the woman who had served him his drinks approached.

'Page, this is Collette Logan,' Rowlance told him. 'Colette has many roles within the company, one being my P.A. She will be working alongside you at certain times, as will other staff members who she will introduce to you in due course. I suggest though, you don't worry too much about Miss Logan's welfare whilst on the project, as she can more than look after herself.'

The woman smiled at the older man's comment, as though amused, and remained silent as she ran appraising eyes over Page. As she did, Rowlance looked at her with concern showing on his face for the first time since they had been introduced, then added, 'Now I feel it's time that Page got to meet who he will hopefully be keeping a close eye on.' Anthony Rowlance turned his direction directly to Page now, who saw that the concern he had noticed in the older man's eyes had been replaced by a weak attempt at ease. Rowlance then added, 'It's time for you to meet Megan.'

Chapter 5

Anthony Rowlance led Page to the right of the three closed doors that he had seen earlier, and gave the door a slight knock. Page expected someone to answer, but instead noticed Rowlance himself appear almost hesitant before he opened the doors without waiting for a reply.

The most noticeable thing that Page found when the two of them entered the room was the change in light. The area which they had just left had been filled with natural daylight that the many windows provided, yet in this room there appeared to be none. In the seconds that were needed for his eyes to adjust, Page found both he and Rowlance bathed in a pale blue light. It was what the room contained that threatened to overload his mind.

The best way he could think of describing what he saw was that it was like an enormous glass tank. The height immediately gave Page the impression that part of the ceiling of the room must have been taken away, with considerable structural work having been undertaken at some point just to fit the tank within the room. He recalled how Charles McAndrew had told him that the floors above the fourteenth were owned by A. R. Solutions, so alterations were more than possible without prying eyes. The glass tank was at least ten-foot square, and the area around it was filled with a pale blue light. White light brightly lighted the insides of the tank, but Page failed to see where the source came from, plus how it failed to ignite elsewhere in the room was a mystery. It was what the container held that made Page struggle to comprehend.

A figure of a woman hung within. Her arms were outstretched either side, while her legs hung down with the ankles overlapping. Dressed in what looked like a white surgical gown, it failed to conceal her thin, almost gaunt frame, the muscles and sinews around her arms and lower half of her legs disturbingly noticeable. Around the wrists, soft hands gave the joints an almost deformed appearance, and with her hair hanging over her bowed head, it was hard to see just how old she was. How she was supported, Page had no idea. The only thought that he could come up with was that she gave the appearance of having been crucified. When Rowlance stepped forward, the blue light across his face turned almost white when he tapped gently on the glass in front of him.

'Hello, Megan,' he said softly, making the suspended woman slowly lift her head to reveal her face partly. 'How are we today?'

Surprisingly, the woman's face didn't hold the gaunt appearance of the rest of her body. Despite the strands of hair that attempted to conceal her face, Page could see that she looked no older than eighteen, possibly twenty. Her high cheekbones gave her features a striking look, whilst her full mouth added a stronger form of character. However, it was her eyes that caused Page concern. He could just make out the edges of her eyeballs in the top of her almost white eyes, and it looked as though she was highly drugged when they failed to respond to the words that she had heard.

'What the hell is this?' Page asked, taking a step back towards the door they had come through.

'Oh, please don't worry,' Rowlance said in a tone that was meant to reassure him, 'This is only a temporary state that she is in.'

'What the hell is the tank all about and how on earth did she get up there?'

'This is what we call a cleansing tank. It is something that Megan helped to design herself. It helps her to cleanse and gradually re-focus her mind. The special light that you see inside is apparently filtering away any bad energy that she will have picked up recently. We can't sense it from here, but I am aware that the entire thing is quite harmless.'

Page stepped forward again and began to walk around the edges of the tank, failing to hide the alarm that his face showed.

'She is suspended on a thin frame which you will just make out when you look around the rear of her,' Rowlance added. 'The position may look strange, I agree, but like most things concerning Megan, it's done to her wishes.'

Sure enough, Page could make out two thin strips of a material that were as clear as glass, hooked under each of her armpits. By the time he had walked around to the front of the tank, the girl's head was bowed again, her features lost, and any sign of response or reply had only been seen by Rowlance. Page was now, for the first time, beginning to doubt.

'You've got to be kidding me,' Page said finally. 'How the hell am I supposed to look after that?'

'Oh, this is only temporary, as I stated. She will be out of here in another hour or so and she will appear quite different to you. Megan has an ability to locate things, Mr. Darrow. By that I don't just mean, say, items hidden around a room, but much more detailed and complex than that. This ability is used as one of the solutions my company can offer.'

'I've seen enough,' Page said flatly and headed for the exit door. Rowlance looked down slightly and stood with his hands in his pockets, still facing the cruciform figure of Megan. He did not attempt to stop him.

When Page pulled the doorway open, he half expected to be met by at least two of the security men. Instead, the people in the room continued about their business as though he hadn't even stepped into the room. The visible security was back at the entrance and they also appeared unfazed by his appearance. Behind him, he became aware that Rowlance had now joined him, and he could feel his anger rising as he turned to face him.

'I appreciate that this must all look surreal to you at the moment,' Rowlance called after Page, 'but after a while, I'm sure you'll see things differently.'

Although the urge to leave was threatening to make him lose control, there were too many questions fighting to be heard, and he exhaled deeply and looked at the people in the room as if for answers. None came.

'Downstairs,' he finally said, 'your man said that I was here because she had specifically asked for me. How, exactly?'

'I'm afraid I can't give you an answer to that question.'

'Can't or won't?' Page rasped.

'If you want to know why she asked for you, the only person who can answer that is Megan herself. Though she often takes a while to answer questions, so at a later time may be better.'

'You seriously think I'm going to hang around to play twenty questions with some dumb kid?'

The comment must have been heard across the room as a silence fell as people paused or stopped in their work. As usual, Page cared little about who he had upset with his blunt manner.

'I think I shall ignore that comment, Mr. Darrow. Mainly because of your ignorance around Megan at present.'

'And I think I'll ignore the whole bloody thing,' Page interjected and began to head for the door once more. He noticed that none of the security men were moving to try and stop him, and he was wound up enough to take on anyone who wanted to stop him. Only the words that Anthony Rowlance said stopped him.

'You can't afford to leave though, Mr. Darrow, can you?' Rowlance told him in a quiet voice that was heard by all within the tension of the room.

Chapter 6

Page had caught something else in the man's comment, and not just about his financing. He sensed that Rowlance had intentionally meant more by his comment, as though he was holding back more than he knew. Turning back to face the room, Page saw that Rowlance had raised a hand over to one of the security men who now walked over holding two document-style files.

When they were both placed down on one of the free tables, Page approached cautiously before sitting down to view both files. Each was about two inches thick, bound with security tape, both showing the company name as well as a decorative letter 'R' wrapped around an 'A', what he guessed was the company logo.

'What if I'm not interested in what you want to show me?' Page asked as Anthony Rowlance joined him. 'Whilst the fee you offer is good, I don't necessarily need the money.'

'On the contrary, Mr. Darrow, you do need the money,' Rowlance interjected, picking up one of the files off the table. After pulling off the tape it was also bounded in, he removed several of the contained papers.

'You are at your limit on six of the seven credit cards you own. Your overdraft at your bank has been breached countless times in the last six months. There are copies of the many letters from your bank and other finance companies within here, which are all demanding money from you.'

The papers handed to Page showed the mentioned items as well all his latest bank statements, along with the 'This requires your immediate attention' letters he had mostly ignored or just not opened. He was about to ask how they had come by this information when Rowlance spoke.

'Even though you have been earning good money in recent years, you still owe nearly sixty thousand pounds, Mr. Darrow. A sizeable amount. Acceptance of our offer will see these debts cleared immediately, and the fee which we offered you in our letter will remain the same. I fully understand how costly care can be these days.'

Page's mouth felt dry as he tried to swallow, the air in the room around him now seemingly lost. He wanted to challenge the comment that Rowlance had made, especially the last few words, but he swallowed profoundly and somehow managed to control his anger.

'In just over a week's time you will be, 'sitting pretty', I think the term is.'

When Page stacked the papers back together, unable to bear to look at them any longer, he pushed them away from him.

'How do I know you will clear that lot?' he asked.

'Accept the job offer, and it will be done,' Rowlance told him flatly.

When Page looked across the room towards the staff who sat beside several computers, he noticed a young woman with wavy blonde hair watching him. Page heard the question asked again and realised that the woman was awaiting instructions from the elder man.

'There's something else, isn't there?' Page asked, looking back at Rowlance. 'You meant something else by your comment.'

Rowlance smiled, touched his upper lip with his tongue, and looked downwards before he reached eye contact.

'Excellent, Page,' he told him. 'Megan was right about you, that much I can see for myself', his face took on an expression which took Page by surprise.

'Megan chose you for a reason that I am currently unaware of, and I can give you my word on that. From my previous dealings with her, I firmly suggest you take up our offer.'

Page had twenty minutes to look through the other file, after which he was informed he was unable to take it with him. The data was split into two parts; the top half containing necessary details of what was required of him and ran in a similar pattern in terms and conditions, which he was used to, but it was the other paperwork that surprised him most. Assembled in about thirty pages were details of his most recent work. There were a series of photographs taken of him on various assignments, some so detailed that he was shocked anyone had gotten so close without him being aware.

Dates and times had been listed among the drawings and documents, which he thought only he was aware of. Towards the back of the file he saw the edge of a building on the part of a photograph that the paperwork partially obscured. Page knew without looking that a line of olive trees stood in front of the building as he had seen them so many times. Before his eyes fell on the rest of the photograph, he looked away and closed the file.

During the time he was reading about what he thought had been securely locked in his mind, the woman with the short hair tapped frenetically away on a laptop on one of the other tables. Her expression seemed almost severe as she typed at a ferocious speed on the laptop keypad. After forcing himself to stand, Page walked over to one of the windows and looked out over the city.

While they waited for the woman to finish, no one spoke. Several pigeons flew past the window Page looked out of, one soon breaking free of the leading group, deciding to land on a row of aerials fixed to the side of rooftops, where chimneys pots in chess piece style bore traces of previous visits by the birdlife that often went unseen within the city.

When his attention was required, Page was told the time and location to be at the following morning. Anthony Rowlance took the completed stack of papers from the woman, which showed him the new statements for each of his credit cards. Her eyes, which up until that point had remained expressionless, now looked intensely at him as she smiled. He disregarded her sudden interest in him by looking down at the papers which showed his balances were showing as zero, and on most of the cards, his credit level had been increased to much higher levels.

'Payment of your fee will be paid directly to your bank when the week is over and Megan has been safely returned,' Anthony Rowlance informed him as Page turned to leave the room. When he reached the door, Page looked back when the older man spoke again.

'One more thing, Mr. Darrow. Should you decide to change your mind, things revert back to as they were. Furthermore, this meeting never happened.'

Chapter 7

The three Mercedes S-Class saloons had stuck to a steady seventy miles an hour for most of their journey. Each of the security members within the car that Page Darrow closely followed hadn't appeared to move for most of the drive, giving him the impression that they were merely cardboard cut-outs on an unusual fairground ride. In the passenger seat beside him, Charles McAndrew had remained mostly silent during the hour-long drive, only commenting to confirm the route the vehicle in front was taking. Behind, another security team followed with Page's new employer.

As the cars slowed slightly to negotiate a couple of sharp bends in the road, Page thought that he needn't have bothered with instructions, relayed via a small earpiece that Page wore, as he had already memorised the route, along with two alternative routes that they could take if needed. With the bends safely negotiated, their speed was soon restored.

For the fourth consecutive day, early May remained dry. Whenever the breeze dropped, it felt relatively warm. Cirrus clouds danced across an azure coloured sky high above the patches of lower white cloud which only occasionally passed by, their partial shade taking a slight edge off the temperature.

Collette Logan sat directly behind Page, alongside Megan who sat with her head out of sight either sleeping or just resting.

Collette had been watching intently for most of the journey, impressed at how attentive the close protection officer was being. Whenever traffic had increased on their journey, Page had moved closer to the vehicle in front, intentionally she presumed, to prevent another car from getting in between them. Now on quieter country roads, they remained close to the other Mercedes, far closer than she would have even dared to drive. Despite the speed, Collette felt entirely at ease.

Page regularly checked his position in the mirrors and spoke only to McAndrew when he needed to. Even when Megan stirred and slowly rose, Collette noticed Page's eyes check the girl's position in the rear-view mirror. Strands of the girl's hair had fallen across her face, masking her sleepy expression, but rather than push them away, the girl left them where they had fallen and looked blankly out of the side window. Ahead, a turn off was approaching, and another message was relayed to him moments before the red brake lights confirmed Page's thoughts that they were almost at their destination.

Thankful that the headache pills he had earlier taken were kicking in, Page tried hard to keep his mind both bright and alert. For some reason, strands of a dream he had the previous night kept filling his mind. He had woken early that morning, having thought that he had slept well, but after meeting up with Rowlance at their designated meeting place, curious images had begun to fill his mind.

There was no clarity on any scene, or any trace of meaning to the unknown views, many of which refused to leave him. As he tried to refocus, he was thankful that the only two other security men that had been sent were in the vehicle in front with Anthony Rowlance, along with another man who Page had only met that morning. No details of his purpose within the company or what his duty was had been revealed to Page yet. The only thing he knew about him was that he was called Toby Connor. His thin features seemed lost under his mop of light brown hair, and Page had noticed the trace of a deep scar across one of his cheeks. Although appearing to be in his late twenties, he had seemed nervous at being introduced and had gotten inside one of the cars before Page could attempt to shake his hand.

As the lead vehicle took the turn, Page glanced in the rear-view mirror to check that the rear car was still close. They continued at a slower speed now as the road began to skirt along a stone wall. Standing over seven feet tall, the boundary wall prevented Page from seeing anything of the estate that they were soon to enter. He gave a cautionary glance across at McAndrew as the lead car continued just past where the wall opened up to a large entrance gate.

'Drive inside when the other car passes the entrance,' McAndrew told him, to which Page did as instructed, passing through a set of large metal gates. The arched gates appeared to have recently been restored, with the ornate metalwork capped by gold-painted spikes. Page brought the Mercedes to a halt once inside the gateway as further instructed through his earpiece. The rear vehicle pulled up close by.

A small lodge house stood next to the entrance, which appeared not to have been inhabited for a considerable time. Wooden boards covered all the visible windows, and most of the sand coloured stonework had become lost beneath thick ivy. Sections of the roof tiles were missing next to the thin chimney, close to where two large crows pecked at moss in the weed-filled guttering.

'This is where we lose our escort,' McAndrew announced as he and Page stepped out of the car. Positioning himself close to the door beside where Megan sat, Page looked along the driveway running from the gate, which soon became lost in the shadow of a section of woodland which stretched across from the wall. Taking a quick glance around to familiarise himself with the area around him, he glanced inside the vehicle, noticing that Megan was leaning forward, her hair masking her features. Returning his attention to the scene around him, he heard the sound of a vehicle approaching along the driveway which, until that moment, had been concealed within the shadow of the woodland.

Page noted that the two security men who had accompanied Anthony Rowlance and Toby Connor now retreated to the gateway, no signs evident of the weapons they no doubt carried. Anthony Rowlance wore a broad smile as he approached, somehow managing to lift the mood his black suit gave him, and he seemed more than pleased that they had reached their destination.

'Are they not joining us?' Page asked him, looking across to the gateway as one of the security men spoke into a mobile phone.

'No,' he answered, 'no need for them here, Page. We are quite safe here.'

Now standing beside Anthony Rowlance, Toby Connor gave the impression of a nervous rescue dog about to be handed over to a new owner. He nodded at him briefly before removing his glasses and wiping them on a cloth he pulled from his trouser pocket.

'You can lose the earpiece now,' Rowlance continued, 'and there will be no need for the weapon you are carrying.'

As Toby scuttled away to the rear of the Mercedes where he opened the boot, McAndrew waited for Page to remove both items, placing them inside a black case which he had kept with him during their journey.

Page was unimpressed, even when he was informed that the items would be returned in due course. He looked around him as a shadow fell across the estate entrance, surprised how the lower cloud was now encroaching, beginning to take away the morning brightness. He felt an increasing sense of unease creeping over him, still unsure of the size of the estate due to the obscuring woodland. The approaching Range Rover had now stopped, and a woman who Page felt he had seen before, stepped out and gave a slight kiss on the cheek of Charles McAndrew. The older man smiled almost nervously with a touch of emotion before the woman then embraced Anthony Rowlance.

Dressed more casually than when he recalled seeing her at the Arlington Hotel, the blue jeans and grey, woollen sweater suited her better, while her hair tied back in a decorative clasp made her high cheekbones stand out all the more. Her knee high boots gave her an extra sense of height but kept the touch of elegance she owned. When her eye caught Page's, she offered a hand out to him as she came closer.

'Hello, I'm Charlotte Wareham. You must be Mr. Darrow.'

'Yes, but I prefer Page,' he told her, feeling the softness of her skin as he shook her hand.

'Page it is then,' she replied.

'You were at the Arlington Hotel, if I'm correct.'

'Yes, that's right. I'm sorry we didn't get to speak, but I couldn't interrupt all that man talk,' she answered, the lightness of her comment strangely appealing amid the tension between the assembled group.

To one side, Rowlance and Toby Connor were joined by McAndrew and were in conversation with one of the two security men who had re-entered through the gateway. Their words remained unheard by Page even though he tried to listen in. Megan and Collette stayed inside the car, which Page preferred.

When Charlotte spoke again, he noticed her look across at the group of men and thought that he saw a touch of unease in her eyes. Trying not to emphasise this, he brought Rowlance into the conversation.

'Anthony Rowlance seems to know a lot about me,' he went on, 'especially when it comes to my, shall we say, poor finances.'

'You must forgive my father; he has this thing about always being in total control.'

'Your father?'

'Afraid so,' she said, returning her gaze toward him. 'My father has his moments, I can assure you, but to him, business is always business.'

'I didn't realise,' Page told her.

'That's okay; you should have been told in the first place. I did ask my father to inform you of who you would be meeting, but as usual, he had other, more pressing business to attend to.'

The conversation was broken when her father returned. Page noticed Toby Connor look across at him as he got inside the Range Rover that Charlotte had arrived in, whilst McAndrew stood beside the car that Page had driven, appearing to be speaking through the window with Collette Logan.

'I see you two have met,' Rowlance said, pulling Page's thoughts toward him.

'Your daughter was just filling me in on the unknown family connection,' Page told him intentionally, making his voice sound mocking. Whether the older man was annoyed by his tone or comment, Page was unable to say, and when he held a hand up and made a weak apology for not mentioning it, Page was less than impressed.

'Would it have altered the way that you offer close protection?' he asked, to which Page shook his head. 'Then no harm has been done, Mr. Darrow.'

Page couldn't help think that at some point the two of them were seriously going to fall out. They held a stare for a few seconds before Charlotte intervened.

'Come on then, let's go and show you Ravenscroft.'

Chapter 8

From the sudden gloom of woodland, the driveway of the Ravenscroft estate opened up to vast green fields on either side. Where the grounds were exposed to the strengthening southerly breeze, patterns were readily formed in the longer sections of grass, already giving Page an impression of energy across the estate.

The driveway was undulating to begin with, making Page struggle to take in exactly how vast five hundred acres of grounds were. As the drive straightened further, smaller trees began to line either side, many of them young and flimsy enough to require wooden frames to support their early years and wire fencing to keep off hungry deer. On his far right, Page could still see sections of the perimeter wall he had passed on the way in before it got lost in a thicker section of woodland that appeared to run across a vast part of the grounds, falling short of a set of buildings surrounding a much more extensive property.

As the two cars got closer, the main house of the Ravenscroft estate proved to be somewhat of an anti-climax to Page. Though as impressive in stature as the photographs he had seen in the folder shown to him at the hotel, it appeared somewhat subdued and in far worse condition than he expected. Tall chimney stacks stood at each end of the house, while two further, much shorter sets topped a raised central section where the grey tiled roof looked weathered by time. Page noted that the rows of Georgian style windows which ran the length of what appeared to be the front of the house were equal in size and stature on both floors. Even at a distance, many of the glass panes looked dis-coloured, and he could also see a dozen or so broken ones on the upper level. More black crows spiralled around the rooftop; their ungainly aerial battle crowded enough for some to turn away, choosing to fly closer to where sections of the property were covered in a mixture of Virginia creeper and ivy. There was evidence of the extent that this had once grown where large sections had been cut back at some point, leaving behind only a spidery outline of its former glory. The persistence of both plants continued, with new shoots already beginning to cover the boards which covered some of the lower windows.

When the Range Rover they followed turned abruptly away from the house, the movement caused dust to swirl up from a gravelled area at the front of the house, partially obscuring a large doorway reached by three steps that stood in the broad central column of the building.

The change in direction took Page off to the left of the property underneath a large stone archway, arriving at a courtyard area where the Range Rover then parked beside other vehicles, in front of a row of smaller outbuildings. In stark contrast to the main house, these were in excellent condition.

What he presumed had once been the coach house and stables for the main house, these had each been lovingly restored. The grey stonework had been professionally cleaned recently and only helped to emphasise the poor condition of the rest of the main house. The three-story building was adjoined to the main building by a single floor section which was topped by decorative stonework that matched part of the stonework set on most of the visible corners of the main house. Turning his eye away from the building, Page noted that the courtyard had just the one entrance, making him manoeuvre the Mercedes around to face the exit before finally stopping. He was first out of the car and stood to flank the door next to Megan. Rowlance had already gotten out of the vehicle with his daughter and was walking across to him. Opening the car door, Page checked around him, keen now to have the young girl safely inside the main property.

'Please relax, Mr. Darrow,' Rowlance told him. 'I appreciate your professionalism, but you don't need to be so attentive here.'

As he opened the car door fully, Megan stepped out, her eyes partially closed as the sunlight seemed to dazzle her. When Charlotte approached her, Page remembered how he had not seen anyone actually touch the girl so far, so he was surprised when the woman embraced Megan, holding her close to her. Charlotte brushed back the strands of hair that remained across Megan's face and gently kissed her forehead, making her pull even closer to her. Page was surprised by the affection and how young and innocent the girl looked compared with the figure who had bizarrely hung with her arms held out in a tank which filled the hotel room. He noticed that Colette had to have seen the tender moment and held her stare upon them as they all headed towards the doorway of what Rowlance informed him was indeed called The Coach House.

In the main hallway, Page was able to get his first proper look at Megan. She was dressed in brown jeans and a slate grey top which was mostly concealed by a loose-fitting grey cotton jacket. Multi-coloured laces on the white plimsolls that she wore gave the only sense of colour. She wore no makeup on her face, which was revealed when she pushed her long hair back behind her ears. When she caught him looking at her, she bit nervously on her fingernails and averted her eyes away. They were far removed from the zombie-like eyes that he had first seen within the cleansing tank, and even though her thin frame looked almost too painful for her to carry, he could see an awkward kind of beauty in her. The time he had expected to have to talk with her at the hotel had never materialised, making the working relationship he was to have with her, unknown.

As explained to him earlier, the Coach House was to be their living accommodation for the length of their stay. Set over three floors, the upper two bedrooms were already being used by Charlotte and Megan, whilst similar rooms for himself and Collette were on the floor below. Page was initially concerned about the positioning of Megan's room, as he would have preferred to have had a quick escape route for her if he needed one, and thought the room next to his would be more appropriate. The stairway gave the only access, yet this seemed of little concern to Anthony Rowlance as he again stated that there was no need for protection in the estate's houses and grounds.

After insisting on checking the positioning and layouts of the other bedrooms, Page finally returned to his own. He soon welcomed the privacy the room offered as he closed the door behind him. Leaning back against it, he closed his eyes and exhaled deeply, the carefree and haphazard approach to security around the estate more than unnerving him.

As he attempted to relax, he recalled his impression of the upper floors of the building, which must have been converted into bedrooms due to the shape of the room. The tapering of one wall in the room in which Megan was using was quite evident from where he had stood, yet the work had been skilfully done and it was difficult to notice the unusual shape when he had stepped closer to the single bed. In contrast to Charlotte's room, which held personal belongings such as photographs in frames by the bed and clothes dotted around the room, Megan's room was pale and as uninviting as a prison cell, with no similar items evident. The bed looked as though it hadn't been used for some time. Only a half-filled glass of water on the bedside cabinet and a pile of clothes gave any indication the room was actually being used.

Page's room was tastefully decorated. The muted colours, with the help of the two lit table lamps set on a low wardrobe and table on the far wall, gave the room a warm, comfortable feel. A taller closet stood in the right-hand corner, the edge of which just touched the side of the bed. On the opposite side to where he stood, Page saw some tea and coffee packets beside an electric kettle on the cabinet. Right at that moment, he thought a well-stocked mini-bar would have been more appealing. On the other side of the room, Page noted a door, which, when he walked over and tried it, led to an ensuite bathroom. He had initially thought that it was an interconnecting door and had been pleasantly surprised to see his reflection in the bathroom mirror. A shower was fixed over the bath, on which stood various soaps and shower gels. The fittings around the room looked expensive, as did the thick towels hung on the rail. *You've stayed in worse,* he thought to himself as he ran some cold water in the sink and rinsed his face. He looked older to himself when he studied his reflection. The dark rings that had once always been under his eyes seemed to have faded now, only to be replaced by more than enough lines on the side of his eyes. In less than two months Page would be thirty-eight, the prospect of turning forty did nothing to improve his mood.

So out of the habit of fully unpacking, he left one of the two bags he had brought with him on one side of the bed and placed the other on the chair beside the room's only window.

The view looked out over the landscape where several birds pecked for worms on the neatly cut lawn. A row of new saplings stood at the end of the grass, which he guessed in time would help shelter the main house. Judging from the condition he had witnessed on his arrival, it seemed a little futile. No-one was visible as he looked around the garden or in the area below, close to the building.

Page unpacked only a few of the belongings he had brought with him, preferring to use the back of a chair to hang his clothes. From a concealed section of the bottom of the smaller of his two canvas bags, he took out a small handgun. It was a Glock 36. The single-column magazine held twelve rounds of ammunition, which, when checked, he found already loaded. Page felt happier with the weight of almost 220g in his hand. He had carried it with him on his previous four jobs, using it each time. Taking extra magazines out of the concealed compartment of the bag, he slipped the weapon inside his jacket. Page had been surprised to have been asked to hand over his main firearm earlier, even with the curious ways of A. R. Solutions becoming accepted reluctantly. The spare weapon he always carried with him now seemed more appreciated as he again felt the reassurance in his hand.

Close to the bedroom door, a narrow mirror showed him his reflection again, making Page recall the last time he had fired the weapon. For some reason, the face of the bearded Latvian man he had fired three shots into failed to come to him as he stepped closer to the mirror. The longer he stared at his own reflection, the more his features appeared to change. The colour of his eyes remained the same, but the pupils were larger, emphasising the sunken, shaded skin around it, the ravaged expression across his altering face, brought on by his imagination, making him close his eyes and turn away.

Page placed his right hand inside his jacket, running his fingers over the top of the pistol within the concealed holster before heading downstairs, keen to focus his mind and even keener on getting the job done to enable him to leave.

Chapter 9

When he returned to the hallway, Page found Charles McAndrew in conversation with a man he had seen at the hotel in Manchester. Now the man had exchanged the charcoal suit for a loose-fitting grey jacket and trousers which made him look less severe and more comfortable. When the two men heard him approach, they brought their conversation to an end and faced him.

'Ah, Page, let me introduce Alex Sutton to you,' McAndrew told him, stepping to the side to allow the Page to shake the newcomer's hand. 'Mr. Sutton is usually in charge of some of our security team away from the U.K., but I've asked him to come along and assist you in any way he can.'

After their introduction, McAndrew excused himself and left the two of them alone. After checking on the whereabouts of Megan as well as Charlotte and Collette, each apparently back in their rooms, they walked out of the front door into the restored bright sunshine. The breeze of the day appeared to be lighter and more comfortable now, allowing the warmth of the day to be more appreciated. All this helped to lift Page's mood.

'There seems little threat to Megan here,' Page suggested as he and Sutton walked leisurely across the courtyard, 'even though a place this size should present a nightmare of opportunities for her to be abducted.'

'On that, I would agree with you,' Sutton replied, 'but within the grounds and outbuildings she is perfectly safe, as you will see in time.'

They walked underneath the archway that he had driven through earlier and made their way until they stood to face the main building of Ravenscroft. The clouds had retreated slightly and broken to allow the late afternoon sunshine to attempt to add some warmth to the appearance of the building that looked as sombre as a grey November day. It failed. The dark windows gave the impression of recently dug graves. When Sutton reached into his pocket and brought out a packet of cigarettes, Page declined one when offered. As he watched the other man draw on his lit cigarette, Page felt unease within Sutton. His grey, short military style haircut added a few years to him, but only on initial appearance, which his lean build and dress sense more than compensated for. Page felt his initial untrusting reaction to him might have been harsh, yet he was wise enough to make a valid judgment of him in the time he stayed at the Ravenscroft estate. For now, he used the trust no-one policy.

'You say that she is safe here, as did Anthony Rowlance, but I still don't get your meaning,' Page said as they slowly walked across the face of the building. 'They ask me to give close protection to the girl, then bring along one of the main people in the security team in yourself, but leave the only security you brought us at the entrance gates, yet everyone tells me that there is no threat to Megan here.' Sutton gave a wry smile as he continued his cigarette and blew out a stream of smoke before replying.

'You need to be patient,' he told him. 'The company does things their way. There is no threat here, simply because Megan says so.'

'You can't be serious.'

'Deadly, I'm afraid. You have no idea what Megan is capable of. What I have seen is apparently only part of it. Once you've spent time with her, you will begin to understand some of what I'm saying. You'll soon discover her, shall we say, moody and awkward ways. But don't let her give you the impression that she's dumb; she's smarter than you could ever imagine.'

Sutton took a final drag on his cigarette before dropping it and stubbing it out with his foot. 'The only threat to Megan comes from within that damn place.'

Page watched as the security man's gaze looked towards the main house, the unease on his face now sharpened. He appeared nervous in view of the building, as though under scrutiny, and welcomed Page's suggestion that they walk on. They took a path to the side which led through an ornate garden where boxed yew bushes surrounded well-kept rose gardens.

'What sort of threat?' Page asked.

'If I'm honest, I have no idea. But no one now steps inside the place without Megan.'

'Anthony Rowlance told me about a belief he had that the house contained an energy source.'

'That's what I hear,' Sutton assured him. 'Though what exactly, I know little or nothing about.'

As they passed through the rose garden, they disturbed a group of crows similar in size to those he had seen on the driveway, which had all now landed and began feeding on one of the lawns. One flew gingerly onto the top of a wooden post supporting a weak looking wire fence that attempted to separate the front lawn, its purpose unknown to the current owners. The birds protested loudly at their intrusion before flying up to high nests in nearby trees. Though questions were now stacking up in Page's mind, the conversation between the two of them waned, and by the time they had walked around to the rear of the property, neither of them was speaking. When he eventually stopped, Sutton lit another cigarette, as though his nerves needing calming further, before they began to retrace their steps. Sutton walked on, looking down at the pathway beneath him before stopping again and flicking his still lit cigarette away.

'Between you and me, I think this whole so-called 'project' is bollocks. I see no need for you to be here, any more than I see the need for me to be here to assist you. There's something going on within the house though, and I suggest that you watch your back. Me personally, I trust no one and that includes yourself, a view I suggest you adopt. If you haven't already.'

'Fine with me,' Page told him. 'The sooner I'm done here, the sooner I can leave,' he added before walking off. Sutton had increased his pace now as if keen to be away from the edifice of the large house, which, even to Page, felt as though it would topple over onto the two of them at any moment as they walked away.

Chapter 10

The dining room of the Coach House was set back from the main hallway and was by far the biggest room in the property. Like most of the ground floor, it had been extended some years before A. R. Solutions had acquired the property, with the dining room benefiting most from the alterations. While sections of stonework on the exterior failed to match the existing building, and in some areas was in need of urgent repair, the interior still showed the full benefit of the work.

Wooden panelling lined the walls along which ran a series of paintings. Page Darrow was no art critic but thought that the landscapes added a welcome sense of character to the room. The main window had at one time held shutters, but now modern blinds had been hung. In the centre of the room, a glass chandelier hung over an oak table, large enough to seat ten people. It was here where Page sat, surveying the other guests around the table.

He sat alongside Toby Connor who had eaten little and spoken less over dinner.

Only Alex Sutton occupied one of the remaining seats on Page's side and had, for the most part, spoken only with Anthony Rowlance and Charles McAndrew alongside him. Charlotte Wareham faced Page, with Megan close beside her.

Page had been reflecting on the brief tour of the group of buildings that the Ravenscroft estate held that Sutton and

Rowlance had given him. From the area around the Coach House to the outlying cottages within the grounds, many of the buildings were unused, even though the stable block and adjoining cottages had also been renovated at some point. Too many places held risk to Megan for Page's liking, yet he kept his thoughts more and more to himself as the three of them walked around. By the time they had finished, Page was at least a bit happier knowing more about his surroundings. A meeting was then planned for eight o'clock in the morning. Till then, it had been suggested that everyone should relax and settle in.

During the meal, the conversation had been relatively muted, all down to the welcome taste of the pork, pheasant, roast potatoes and assorted vegetables that Charlotte had kindly cooked. Anthony Rowlance naturally took a great deal of pride in his daughter's culinary abilities, but Page got the feeling that she thought he was exaggerating slightly. The meal had been welcome after what he felt had been a tense and challenging day, and he thanked Charlotte as she began to clear plates away.

Whilst occasionally commenting on questions directed towards him, Page had chosen to keep quiet, using the time to sometimes watch Megan's odd behaviour over the table with interest. The seat alongside Page, opposite to where Megan sat, was unoccupied. More than once the girls had stared across at it as though they either sensed something or was privy to something that Page and the others were unaware of. Megan had eaten little to begin with, but as the conversation started to pick up towards the end of most people's meals, she had suddenly started to eat so quickly that Page thought she ran the risk of choking.

When Charlotte asked her whether she needed more time to finish her meal, she abruptly stopped eating and pushed the plate away from her, spitting out the last of her full mouth into her serviette. Then she sat with her head lowered, declining the offer of dessert, and remained silent. Keen to continue to watch her behaviour, Page declined dessert himself.

The more he viewed Megan in Charlotte's company, the more he noticed how she preferred to stay close to her. Each time Charlotte left the table, Megan looked more vulnerable, even though from what he understood about the company's work, she had spent a lot of time with them all.

Charlotte soon began to dominate the table, her warm nature now more evident in the way she both spoke and acted. Page found her quite alluring and relaxing given his recent months of worry. Whenever her father brought up work issues, she politely changed the subject, each time Anthony Rowlance conceding graciously to her. Charlotte occasionally included Megan in the conversation, yet she often chose to comment on the girl's behalf. Page thought it was an act of kindness in many ways, as Page knew she was protecting her from awkward questions.

Over coffee, Rowlance and McAndrew excused themselves, informing Page that they would meet up with him in the morning. One of their seats was then occupied by Colette Logan who arrived, giving no explanation for her absence during dinner, dressed in a silver coloured blouse, which hung loosely over her black skirt.

'So, have they all been entertaining you?' Colette asked Page as she poured herself some coffee from the large pot that Charlotte had brought to the table.

'It's been a riot,' he replied, holding the eye contact she had on him. She broke it almost reluctantly, and then only to wave hello across to Megan.

'Bet old spooky down there has been the star of the show and never stopped talking,' Colette suggested, making Megan look at Charlotte as though for a response.

'Maybe she prefers to let you do all the talking,' Charlotte remarked, causing a slight twitch to show on Colette's temple. One that Page noticed.

Page sensed that Alex Sutton had himself noticed the increase in tension within the room following Collette's arrival, and wondered what the relationship was between them. It seemed one of irritation on Sutton's behalf, yet held with a touch of caution.

'So tell us about bodyguarding,' Colette then suggested as though she was disinterested in replying to Charlotte's comment.

'It's close protection, actually,' he reminded her before he accepted another coffee when Charlotte offered.

'How close?'

'Close enough,' Page told her, making a point of not elaborating.

'Oh come on. You must have seen some exciting things,' she suggested, again holding eye contact, 'things that could impress us all.'

Page became aware that everyone around the table was looking at him intently, which Collette herself was well aware of.

'Most of the time, the work can be dull and uninteresting, quite routine,' Page replied. 'You are often around to give an impression of protection as much as anything, but at the end of the day you're there to take a bullet or more, if required. The protection of the client is what you're paid for, after all.'

A slight pause in his words made the feeling of compassion that Charlotte felt for the man suddenly increase. When he looked at the table for a moment, she thought he had said all that he wanted to say, but a sterner expression fell upon his face as he looked back up at Collette.

'Having said that, I've seen close hand the horrors of the actions of those close to who I have had to protect. I've seen a stray missile take out a whole market crowd, where only moments before innocent people were simply trying to make a living from buying and selling their goods. I've heard the screams and pain of the dying, while at the same time been grateful that the person under my protection had remained unharmed. A couple of months back, I drove away from a street where a ten-year-old child strapped up with explosives then detonated himself, in what is, in some people's eyes, honour. If you want to call these sorts of things exciting or impressive, Miss Logan, feel free, but in truth, you have no idea what you are talking about.'

When she broke away from his stare, Page saw a slight pulsing on the side of Collette's neck. Pleased that his comments had both hit home and annoyed her, as well as not caring about the feelings of those who sat close to him, he drained the last of his coffee and found Megan looking at him. Whilst Colette switched tactics and began to talk with Sutton, Page watched as Charlotte stroked away strands of hair that had fallen across Megan's face. When her young face was fully revealed, Page thought he saw traces of humour in her eyes, even though her mouth remained unmoving.

For the next ten minutes Colette ignored Page, which suited him fine, and when Charlotte said that she and Megan were having an early night, he stood and told Sutton he would see him in the morning. He saw the humour had returned to Colette's face as he headed away from the table.

Chapter 11

Moonlight bathed the open countryside. Across a broad expanse of field, a sheen of pale light gave an impression of a gentle snowfall. Ruts of earth across recently ploughed fields caused shadows to lie like scars upon the landscape. Only remnants of clouds now challenged the three quarter moon's dominance, even though the newly settled weather was set to change. This was of little interest to the barn owl that had spent most of the night preoccupied with a constant search for food.

The clear conditions had helped the creature in ways, but it had found prey hard to find tonight, at times almost sensing the unease across the land. As it flew low over a section of woodland that concealed the boundary wall of the Ravenscroft estate, it called out, allowing its eerie cry to help to dislodge particles of bone from the previously digested rodent. The stone division across the land meant nothing to the owl as it considered further food lay on either side of such things. A gnarled branch, which had suffered severely in the storms of the past winter, offered a perch which the bird eagerly accepted. It remained motionless for a while before using the moment of rest to preen feathers on one of its wings.

The stillness of the woodland felt unusual even to the owl, the regular sound of life failing to come to its usually sensitive hearing. The unique conditions were enough for the owl to take flight once more. Flying higher now, the dark shape of the main house and outbuildings came into view, and the owl considered landing again as it felt a sudden weakness overcoming it. No moonlight appeared to have even touched the darkened building, and when an invisible pulse emitted from within the large structure, the owl's flight was almost brought to an instant end. It struggled under its weakened condition to maintain its height, the edge of one of its wings seeming to fold back on itself, making the bird fear that it would break. Only by losing altitude did it manage to level out finally. A rush of fear threatened to overcome the bird, a feeling it had rarely known. Calling on what appeared to be the last strands of its strength, the wings were beaten harder, allowing it to turn away from the power it sensed below. A final cry, as much out of relief as it was fear, would have been heard by anyone who had been present below, but the departing owl had been alone in its plight, the only witness to the changes happening in the darkness below.

Chapter 12

The following morning just the three of them ate breakfast together. In contrast to the previous evening's meal, Charlotte seemed preoccupied with something and spoke little, while Megan held her monk-like silence throughout. Page was surprised to find he had a keen appetite and ate the full English breakfast that Charlotte had prepared. Megan barely ate, sitting hunched up in her seat only using her spoon to push the cereal around in her bowl occasionally.

'You okay?' Page asked when he helped Charlotte to clear away the table after they had all finished.

'Yes, thanks,' she replied. 'I didn't sleep very well, that's all.' He followed her into the tastefully decorated kitchen which benefited from a large amount of light in the mornings. Dark wood cupboards lined two of the walls, with glass panels of some of the doors showing the displayed contents behind them. The main cooking area was concentrated close to the doorway, giving enough room for a round table and chairs to stand next to the patio doors leading to the rear.

'A change of scene always affects my sleep pattern,' Charlotte told him as she ran some water in the sink to clean the used dishes. 'I've been here a few days, but find my mind drifts at the same time that I feel like I need rest.'

'I take it, it also affects Megan's moods,' he suggested.

'Oh, that's normal. She's always up and down like a roller coaster,' she told him as she began to prepare some coffee. From one of the cupboards beside where he stood, Charlotte asked him to pass her some mugs. After doing so, Page looked into the dining room and checked on Megan who remained at the dining room table, her arms folded and head bowed as if she had fallen asleep. When he returned to the kitchen, he found Charlotte had sat at the table with their drinks. A slight breeze now filled the room from the small gap where Charlotte had apparently opened the rear doors.

'So what's your relationship with Megan?' he asked as he sat. 'She seems close to you.'

'There's only me that she is happy being with. My husband, Greg, is one of my father's chief engineers. He's currently out in the North Atlantic working on a deep water drilling project. It was on a similar type of job that my father first brought along Megan.'

Making sure that Megan had not walked in and joined them, she continued.

'The type of work that Greg was working on at the time had been plagued by endless problems. The location points for the drilling points that they had been provided with were causing problems, and there had been some expensive mishaps. The project was one similar to ones which Megan had had amazing success elsewhere. Greg was opposed to what he called interference, but my father insisted that she was brought on site. Within days he ran into difficulty with Megan. There was an instant clash of personalities, she began acting volatile, and Greg insisted that she was taken away from the site as he felt that she was putting everyone at risk.'

'In what way?' he asked.

'Megan's abilities are varied; they can be from a simple act of memory, finding a missing item in a house, to locating the exact spot for where engineers should drill. Greg thought all this was nonsense. I know it sounds pretty weird, but the amount of money she can save is too enormous to even think about. You will have seen the results that mistakes can make with the B.P. disaster in the Gulf of Mexico. The cost of that is incredible, let alone the risks to the environment. So anyway, Megan said the particular areas in which they were working were wrong. The energy was not being respected, which was resulting in the severe damage to drilling rigs. She told Greg to shut down the whole site as she felt the danger to his crew was too great. Greg refused, ignoring her suggestions, confident enough to rely on the technology that they had available.'

'When my father forced them to use Megan's locations, they were perfect. The company has some of the most advanced technology available, but sometimes Megan's information is far more accurate.'

'So what happened between her and Greg then?'

'Once things were put back on course, my father reluctantly took Megan away and brought her to our family home for a while until she calmed down. My husband is constantly away with work, so there was no real risk of them meeting up. During that time, I developed a kind of friendship with her that has strengthened. Occasionally we do stuff together, see a film or something similar, but Megan hates crowds so we have to go at a quieter time. Before we came here, I was teaching her to drive. But her patience is pretty poor at the moment.'

When she stopped talking, Charlotte held a stare as though she had recalled a memory or something. It was only a fraction of a second, but Page felt there was sadness contained within it. 'Anyway,' she continued, losing the look, 'now I tend to go wherever Megan goes to work. She usually insists that I am close to her.'

'I take it Megan's abilities are used in a lot of places.'

'You wouldn't believe it,' Charlotte confirmed. 'I've lost count of the number of places we have both been to in the last year alone.'

'And your husband's view on this?'

Charlotte lowered her eyes and clutched her now empty mug. Page thought that he had said the wrong thing straight away and for a moment she failed to answer.

'Sorry, that was too blunt,' he told her, to which she shook her head.

'No, that's okay, you're right. Greg distrusts Megan, as do many of the people she is in contact with.'

Deciding to change tack, Page asked about whether Megan had any family. 'Not now; her father was one of my father's employees some years back. That's how he first came across her. He was killed in an accident at work, somewhere in the Middle East. I'm afraid I know little about the details, but my father insisted on looking after his daughter.'

'And acquired the skills that she has.'

'You learn quickly,' she replied with a wry smile on her face. 'Cynical, maybe, but true. There are a lot of things about Megan which you will soon discover for yourself. Her moods and changes of personality are just some. She hates gadgets like mobile phones, as she says certain frequencies apparently irritate her senses. Even certain types of music can affect her moods. I think the most noticeable thing about her is that she doesn't like to be touched.'

'Yet the two of you embraced when we arrived,' he reminded her.

'We did, but that was only because she allowed it, and the fact that it was me.' Her face took on a more serious look as she released the mug and leaned back in her chair.

'Don't let her get to you though. Let her show off in small measures if you wish, but use your judgment with her.'

'Thanks for the advice.'

After they cleared away the breakfast pots, Page told Charlotte that he had to meet up with her father and Sutton, and had to take along Megan. When he stood, Page got the impression that she had liked talking, even though the subjects had been a bit on the intense side. When he reached the kitchen door he turned and asked. 'How long since you last saw your husband?'

'Six months and three days,' she replied without looking up.

Chapter 13

Before starting the meeting with Rowlance and Sutton, Page told Megan that the two of them were going to take a walk outside and get some fresh air. When he went to inform her that the walk was non-negotiable, his words were met with a shrug of her shoulders and an unenthusiastic look. Reluctantly Megan followed him, stopping only in the hallway to collect a black coat from the small cloakroom beside the stairs.

The rain had evidently fallen overnight but had cleared to a mainly hazy sky. The forecast suggested light showers later in the day, even though the grey sky on the horizon threatened a more imminent one.

From the side of the Coach House, they took a long gravel path that ran for the length of the rear of the main house. At the place where he had stopped with Alex Sutton the previous day, the trail split into two directions. The smaller path carried on towards a row of outlying cottages visible against distant trees, while the one that Page and Megan walked on stretched across the garden towards what could have initially been the main gates to the house. Looking back towards the main house, Page could see that the entrance door to what he still believed to be the rear of the property was not only larger than the one on the opposite side but had a grandeur appearance, which was more in keeping with the rest of the building's design. Large sections of this side of the building were slowing being covered by thick, unkempt ivy.

Given the extent of how overgrown many of the upper windows on the left-hand side had become, it showed that it had been some years since many of them had last been used. Several small birds could be seen flying back and forth from the thicker sections where the undisturbed leaves gave plenty of shelter to unseen nests. Even in the short distance that the two of them had walked, the weak brightness held by the sky had faded, with light rain now being carried in the increasing breeze. While Page turned up the collar of his jacket to at least keep the chill out, Megan ignored it. Her head remained slightly bowed, her mood more than matching the deteriorating weather. Since leaving the Coach House she had not spoken, nor had she since he had first met her. If he had not heard the occasional word from her, which she made on the journey to the estate, he could readily have believed that she was a mute. In an attempt to create a bond between them, Page asked her to sit on a wooden bench which they now approached. Set beneath entwined yew trees, the seat remained dry, the thickly packed branches offering them shelter from the lightly falling rain.

'You know, it would help if we could at least talk to each other,' he told her, noticing how she failed to even face him when he spoke. Had he not already seen her face he would have had no concept of her features beneath the hair that hung down over her still drooped head. 'It could help to build a bond between us.'

His comment had some effect, though quite what he was unsure of. At least she raised her head now and pushed back her hair.

'The house will test you,' Megan said, breaking her silence, her voice barely a whisper.

When he asked her to repeat what she had said, she looked across the garden, her expression as dark as the shadows of the yew trees behind her.

'I said, the house will test you. She always does. She likes to play tricks and games.'

'Is this what this all is, Megan, a game?'

'Do you have a wallet on you?' she asked, ignoring his question as well as the larger drops of rain that began to fall as Page nodded, feeling inside his jacket. He passed it towards her, interested to see if she would make contact with his hand. Instead of taking it from him, she told him to place it on the wooden bench beside her.

'Why did you ask whether I had that?' he asked, curious what her intentions were. If you can find things easily, surely you knew I already had one on me.'

'I'm making an effort to create that bond you wanted,' she told him, the first glimmer of warmth on her face he had seen as she looked up at him. For a moment she held her stare on him, her scrutiny a little unsettling to Page before she closed her eyes and then smiled. The effort of smiling appeared to sap strength from her. When she looked at him again, he thought her eyes looked tired, as though sleep had been hard to find.

'In your wallet, you have thirty-five pounds in notes,' Megan told him, 'three tens and a five, oh, and four credit cards. Plus there's a torn photograph of someone. She looks pretty.'

Page was not only surprised by Megan's comment but somehow unnerved by it. He didn't need to check for himself; he knew the amount of money was correct. It was the only money that he had brought with him. The only reason he did open his wallet was to confirm what she had said about there being a photograph in his wallet. He was convinced that she was wrong on that point as he had emptied the former contents before he had left. In one of the inner pockets was indeed part of an old photograph which he thought he had removed months ago when he felt he had removed the last trace of her.

'How did you do that?' Page asked, his voice now sounding weak.

'It's easy to see stuff like that. With other things, it's kind of different.'

'How?' he asked.

'Sometimes it happens when I touch things. With your wallet, I simply had to see it and the image appeared to me. Others…' she let the words trail off as she stood. Stepping out of the protection of the yew trees, the falling rain soon began to wet her upturned face. With her eyes closed, she allowed the drips to run freely down her face. Then, as though something had broken her train of thought, she lowered her head to look straight at him. The carefree expression that she had as she let the rain fall across her face had been replaced by a more pensive look. She clutched her arms around herself as though she had suddenly caught a shiver.

'She knows you miss her,' she said softly before turning to walk back up the path.

It was rare nowadays that Page was shocked, but now he felt it. There was a coldness about Megan that he didn't like, an uneasy feeling within him even though they had only recently met. Entirely how she had known about the contents of his wallet, he was unsure of. He would like to think that it had been removed from him without him being aware, but Page knew that wasn't possible as he was adamant that it had never left him at any time since arriving at the estate.

By the time he caught up with Megan, a rumble of thunder could be heard, as if to announce the heavier rain that the distant grey sky had promised. Large drops began to fall as they re-traced their steps, passing in silence once more underneath the archway that had first led Page to the Coach House.

Chapter 14

Page met with Anthony Rowlance and Alex Sutton in the main dining room where they had taken their evening meal the day before. Rowlance wore a well-fitting black shirt and matching trousers, occasionally fiddling with one of the silver cufflinks. In contrast, Page thought Sutton looked as though he had dressed quickly, the collar of his jacket folded over on one side. Within the room, the table had been cleared, with most of the chairs having been moved back to the edges of the room to allow free access around the table upon which a full-scale drawing of the plan of the Ravenscroft Estate had been laid out. On the drawing, various markings of coloured ink had been made around the area of the main house, where, in places, all connected with a series of unexplained lines. None of what he looked down on made any sense to Page, but to Sutton and Rowlance they now seemed the primary focus of their conversation.

At the far end of the table, Megan had slumped herself down in one of the pulled back chairs, her hair as unruly as her clothing. Her grey jeans still held damp patches where the rain had run off her coat, the crimson shirt, the colour of which somehow didn't suit her, now only made her skin appear paler. On one of her thin wrists were several coloured friendship bracelets, which now appeared to be her main focus of attention as she set about rearranging them in order of size.

From a side door, Collette Logan entered. Page noticed that Sutton looked up from the table at her while Rowlance continued to talk. The two-piece suit that Collette wore fit her well, in contrast to Megan's attire, the pale green of the outfit giving her an added look of confidence. Not that she needed it, he thought as she said good morning to everyone. When Page spoke to her, she smiled widely, and he became aware that the skirt Collette wore was a little too short to be appropriate for work, while at the same time Page already knew that was the intention.

'So, Megan, have you any intention of joining in today?' Rowlance asked as he looked across at her, his displeasure with her attitude more than evident when she shrugged her shoulders without replying or looking up.

'Maybe you would like to share your thoughts with Mr. Darrow?' Sutton suggested. 'Or let him know where we stand on the project, give him an insight into our work here so far.' His words made Megan stand abruptly and glare back.

'Maybe I'd like to show him shit,' Megan said sullenly, her words seemingly directed to all around the table before she stood, pulling on the bracelets as she did so, slamming the door behind her as she left the room. Page took in the expressions of everyone around, varying from surprise at her outburst to frustration. What he noted most was the gleam that held in Collette's eyes, even though she kept her expression perfectly calm.

Anthony Rowlance sat down slowly in one of the remaining chairs and rubbed the bridge of his nose between his fingers whilst Sutton attempted to restore some order again by scanning the paperwork below him. Whether Rowlance was aware of the intent behind Megan's comment Page was unsure of, but when he suggested that he go after her, Rowlance looked appreciative at his suggestion.

Page found Megan huddled on a long settee in the main sitting room of the Coach House. Had it been under different circumstances, he would have been taken by the room which was by far the cosiest room of the building. The long settee on which Megan sat was matched by a smaller one set close to a table under the main window of the room. Despite the rainy conditions outside, light still held steady within the room, highlighting other items of furniture. Rugs of varying sizes filled the floor space. On one, a square table held an unused glass vase on which the daylight highlighted the decorative markings upon it.

'So, they sent you to calm me down then, did they?' Megan asked, drawing her legs underneath her body. When she cleared her hair from her face, he was surprised to see her face appeared brighter, the sudden mood change surprising.

'No, it was my idea.'

'To offer close protection and keep me from all harm,' she said mockingly.

'Maybe I just like your charm,' he told her, noting the smile that now attempted to return to her face.

'They piss me off at times,' she told him as he sat at the other end of the settee, 'and that stuck up cow Logan drives me up the wall.'

Page had been surprised at her words and by the direct comment about Collette. It was the first time that she had expressed any real personal emotion towards anyone. When she looked blankly across the room, Page could see that her anger appeared to be waning. For a moment she reminded him of an Iranian woman he had worked with the previous year. She too had made the same impulsive comments about people she had around her soon after their initial meeting. Her greatest concern later turned out to be the main threat to her outspoken husband's political views. A year later they had been confirmed and silenced by a snipers bullet.

In the stillness of the sitting room, Megan now looked on an entirely different planet to the Iranian woman, her face so young and innocent looking, showing no trace of her previous mood. When she stood, he thought she was about to say something but instead walked over to a display cabinet where she knelt down and began to search through one of the lower drawers. She brought back a blue box which appeared to contain a game, the name of which was obscured by her hand.

'Let's play a game,' she then implored him enthusiastically before moving across the room to pull a chair back from the table close to the window.

Megan began removing pieces from within the box. Before he could suggest that they return to the dining room where he presumed Rowlance and Sutton were still waiting, Megan began spreading the pieces on the table. Keen to both humour her as well as to begin to know her behaviour, he agreed, moving glassware placed on the table out of harm's way.

When Megan had first begun to unpack the pieces, Page had seen various pictures on the small cards which were about two inches square. He continued to watch as she started lining up the cards into rows of ten until they were all face down.

'It's a dead easy game, all about memory,' she told him, smiling awkwardly as he sat on the chair opposite her. 'What you have to do is match the pictures. If you guess right, you keep them and get another go. There are eighty cards, so forty pairs. The winner has the most cards at the end. You go first.'

Page was taken aback by her sudden enthusiasm, yet went along with the game, interested to see where her mood change was leading. Turning over one of the cards, it showed a small, green fir tree set against a black background. Megan lowered her face close to the table, her smile much broader now as he turned over the next one. The cartoon figure of a smiling horse looked back at him.

'Ah, hard luck,' Megan told him as he turned the two cards he had chosen face down again. Looking down at the cards, Megan reached over and turned the horse card back over once more. Then, biting gently on her lip, she put on an exaggerated frown and scanned a hand over the top of the remaining cards. When she finally stopped, she lowered her thin hand and turned over a matching horse.

'Well done, that was lucky,' Page told her, his unease now growing, the feeling that she was teasing him almost annoying.

'Did you not listen?' she said to him, her face now more serious. 'It's about memory. It has nothing to do with luck.'

Before he could say anything else to her, she looked him straight in the eye whilst her hands began to turn cards over. Each successive card she turned matched with the previous one. Five pairs, six pairs, eight pairs and onwards, her hands moving so fast now that they were becoming a blur. What did remain were the exact pairs she turned over. In less than ten seconds she had correctly matched all forty pairs. Throughout that time her eyes had never left his.

'I win,' she triumphantly told him, punching the air. 'You're pretty shit at this game.'

'Maybe you were too good for me,' he told her, trying hard to hold her stare when she looked at him again. It was Megan that broke the stare as she began to turn the cards back over until they lined up in eight rows of ten again. Page felt his mouth go dry as he watched her expression change, expecting the dark mood of earlier to return. Instead, she pushed her seat back until she was about a foot away from the table. Holding her hands in her lap, she was silent for a while before she held his stare again.

'I'll go first this time,' she told him just as two of the cards flipped over by themselves. Not surprisingly, the two images matched. Still unsure what had just happened or how the cards had moved, Page watched as cards began to turn over quickly, each time revealing matching pairs. While the initial cards had turned over close to the table so the speed increased, some spiralled around in the air before dropping down onto the table whilst others appeared to move in slow motion. In around the same time that Megan had won the first game, she had won again, yet her hands had remained in her lap all the time and her eyes had never left his own. As the last card landed, Megan began to laugh, the sound seeming to taunt him as he moved back from the table, still in shock at what he had witnessed.

'Megan!'

The voice startled Page. As if he had woken from a dream, he looked down at the table and found that the matching pairs remained on the table. Megan continued to laugh even though Charlotte now held her by her shoulders.

'What do you think you are doing?' Charlotte asked, holding the girl now by the sides of her head looking directly at her face. She failed to answer and continued to laugh, the sound ringing in Page's ears as he left the room, wanting nothing more than to be away from the strange, unsettling girl, and even more desperate for some fresh air.

Chapter 15

When Megan refused to return to the dining room, Anthony Rowlance decided to call a halt to their meeting, stating that he preferred Megan was in attendance when they began to explain the house better to Page. The drawings which had made little sense to Page had been cleared away with the large, clear space on the dining table only seeming to emphasise the area in Page's mind since coming to the estate. Expecting them to regroup later that day, he had been surprised when Rowlance told him that they would start again the following day. His suggestion that they could at least take a look inside the main house only seemed to agitate the moment more. Megan, and only Megan, he was informed, would show him what lay within the house when she was ready to do so.

So, while Megan spent the afternoon sulking alone in her room, Charlotte used the change in arrangements to spend time with her father. Page had wanted to talk further with Alex Sutton about his reservations about the Ravenscroft Estate, but Sutton got called away, along with Collette Logan, leaving Toby Connor and Page on their own.

Page wasn't disappointed when Toby excused himself, stressing that he had work to do, as he felt he needed to use the time himself to try and clear his head, to try and make some sense of what had happened since they had arrived at the estate. After changing his light jacket for a waterproof raincoat, he took a walk back along the driveway to get a better sense of the main building's area from a distance. No one challenged or queried his movements, and although he cautiously checked behind him as he left, he appeared to go unnoticed.

The breeze had now strengthened, causing the rain to drive straight into his face, making him angle his head slightly to compensate for it. After looking back on the distance he had walked, Page found that he was forced to leave the driveway behind him to enable him to obtain the view he wanted. The wet grass he stepped into soon soaked his shoes, as well as the bottom of his trousers, but he tried to ignore this as he made his way up a small incline to where a single tree stood. Underneath the extensive beech tree, Page welcomed the small amount of shelter that the large branches provided, the thick roots exposed in places as though they sought the rainfall that had yet to touch them.

The main house looked shrouded in sadness from where he stood. He supposed that in its day, the vantage point which he had chosen would have provided an impressive view. Now though, the appearance of the property more than matched the miserable weather. The first sign of the tree canopy beginning to fail began to show as larger drops occasionally found a way through, several catching the edges of Page's coat as they fell. The prospect of there being some form of a power source within the decrepit building seemed remote as he watched the rain drive across the open estate. The water no doubt penetrated further into the nooks and crannies of the house, adding to the damp and decay, making the building unappealing. As he left the shelter of the tree canopy, there was something about the property that held his mind, something that he failed up to this moment to see, but something that became increasingly familiar the more he watched the house.

Chapter 16

Toby Connor enjoyed rainfall. He liked the concealment that it brought, the way even the slightest of falls made crowds scatter, forcing people to seek shelter, making them individual, like himself. Since being a child, he had taken walks out in the falling rain, from windswept hills and moors to the greyness of rain filled city streets. Uncomfortable in company and worse in crowds, Toby welcomed the solitude that rainfall gave him.

As an only child, Toby Connor had always struggled to be the perfect child that his parents had so wanted. With no siblings to compete against or to be beaten by, Toby had excelled in his schooling, and studied economics at Manchester University where he strolled through his degree. While other students took endless pleasure in all that student life offered, Toby lived an almost solitary life. That was, until the day he met Abby Lawrence. The two of them had come from differing backgrounds; she came from a relatively poor background and was one of five children. Despite this, they soon formed a friendship which strengthened into what Abby believed to be love. She was the first person to notice that there was a more appealing side to Toby Connor than the one he usually gave off, and she had also been the first to see that he had an unknown gift. It was something that once he was made aware of, soon enthralled him completely. Computers.

He had initially taken them for granted, almost unaware of just how quickly and easily he adapted to the quickening pace of the technology. A further degree, much to his parent's disgust, was abandoned as his passion for technology increased. His parents had, by now, become concerned about his newfound love and told him to put his ability to use if he was going to ignore his academic qualifications. One night, over a specially prepared meal, Abby had spoken from the heart about the distance that she felt was appearing between them. Toby dismissed her comments, reacting harshly to her claims. Before he had stormed off, she had given him an ultimatum between choosing herself and his bloody computers. He took a flight to Geneva the following morning to attend a large computer fair without even saying goodbye to Abby.

It had then been a chance meeting with a complete stranger in the airport terminal, where even then the rain had been falling, that had changed the course of Toby's life. It was a direction that he still followed. The stranger had been Anthony Rowlance, and the conversation that had built between them while they waited for the same flight had led to talk of the problems that Rowlance was having with his company's computer system. By the time they had boarded the plane, Toby had provided the solutions to the other man's worries, at which point Anthony Rowlance offered him a job there and then within his company, a position that he still held.

Raising his face to the falling rain, Toby continued his walk across the grounds of the Ravenscroft estate, the last remnants of daylight now having almost faded. Ahead of him, he could see the warm light cast from the two cottages that stood close to the most extensive patch of woodland the estate held. The yellow glow of the cast light highlighted the vehicles parked outside. When the rain fell heavier, he allowed the hood of his coat to fall back, the rain soon beginning to flatten his unruly hair and causing large drops to form on his glasses. The gentle drumming of the raindrops against his head and body brought him comfort, one he knew the others around him failed to notice.

The cottage he was staying in was the smaller of the two. Set slightly back from the other, its position seemed to match the manner of Toby, making him wonder initially whether that had been the intention of others within the company. Those who he knew cared little about him.

Nearing the buildings, he heard voices coming through the slight gap of one of the windows of the adjoining cottage. The voices of Anthony Rowlance and Charles McAndrew were easily recognisable. The two men had been close ever since Toby had started with the company, and he was grateful that it was they who he was nearest to on the estate. Toby had little time for Alex Sutton and his dumb security team, and he thought that the newcomer, Page Darrow, fit into the same category.

In recent months, Toby had worked in far more interesting places than the estate they were currently based, and he longed for a change of scene. He felt his talents were being underused here, and whilst the input of programs running elsewhere in the company's work kept his mind busy, he found the so-called 'project' of the house both disturbing and unnecessary.

For the time being, Toby tried to take what pleasure he could take from his walks in the rain and hoped that the unsettled weather would continue. Toby increased his pace as expectation filled his mind, ignoring the fact that his face and hair were entirely soaked by the falling rain. Making his way across the tightly packed gravel outside the front of the cottages, he trod carefully so as not to be heard. There was no need to use the key that he had for the front door of the cottage as someone had already let themselves inside, someone who brought a smile to Toby's face. Someone he was keen to speak to and spend time with.

Chapter 17

The overnight rain had left several large puddles scattered around the entrance to the main house where, over time, the ground had become uneven, allowing rainfall to collect. Page saw different images of the property reflected in the pools of water, the condition of the property appeared to look even darker in many. The rain that had soaked into the gravel suppressed the sound of footsteps upon it, the cloud of dust that the Range Rover had made when Page had first followed it down the driveway towards the house now feeling so far away.

A stream of smoke drifted across Megan's face as Alex Sutton continued to draw on his cigarette, but she ignored this as her face remained focused on the steps leading to the doorway which she now approached. Since Page had met with Megan, Rowlance, and Sutton almost an hour ago, Megan had, as usual, barely spoken a word. He had been told by Anthony Rowlance that Megan would give him his first tour of the main house at Ravenscroft as she wanted him to view the house without any prior knowledge. In a way, he was grateful that it was to be just the two of them as he hoped without others around her, Megan would at least be more communicative. The comments about Megan being the only person that now stepped on the property were given little if any thought as he watched Megan now stand facing the main door. Her arms stayed by her sides as though she was reluctant even to knock, and she remained almost huddled in the long black coat she wore, the bottom of her jeans showing slight tears where they rested on top of her scuffed trainers.

'So, this is where she needs my protection?' Page asked as Anthony Rowlance stood beside him while they both looked up at the property.

'That's correct,' he stated rather than replied.

'And your security team still can't do this?'

Rowlance looked put out by Page's comment. He glanced across at Sutton, who finally stubbed out his cigarette on the wet gravel before turning to face him once more.

'All that has already been made clear to you, Mr. Darrow,' Rowlance added, his annoyance at Page's comment quite evident. 'Give her the protection she needs inside the house and assist her in any way that you can.'

With that, Rowlance moved away from him and stood with Sutton once more. When Page walked himself over to the entrance, he found Megan waiting, holding a cloth bag. He was about to ask whether she had brought it with her as well as what it contained when she withdrew a large door key. The young woman looked at him as though she was about to say something, but her expression held her comment back and the moment passed as she inserted the key and began to open the lock. Page was curious as to why a building of such poor condition would need to be under lock and key. The privacy and remoteness of the estate seemed enough.

It took several attempts to move the mechanism of the lock, the friction causing flakes of paint to work loose on the door panels around it. As Megan continued to struggle, Page noted other traces of the paintwork nearby, tucked against the side of the property, which he presumed had come from previous visits. Finally, the lock freed and Megan pushed back the door which Page was intrigued to find then opened easily, the hinges remaining silent. As Megan stepped inside, Page looked back across to where the two other men had been standing and found that they were no longer there. He reached inside his jacket and brushed his fingers across a reassuring weight within the hidden holster before heading inside himself.

Page was surprised to see that the condition of the property didn't mirror that of the outside. What looked as though they could be the original floorboards lined the hallway, their surface almost perfectly smooth. There were several marks upon the ones he watched Megan stepped onto that gave evidence of the age of the timber as the imprint and scars of time had passed upon them. A wide staircase with elaborate balustrades was set to one side, the newel post at the foot almost oppressive in its design, even against the extent of the width of each of the steps. Brass carpet grips were fitted to each step, though there was no trace of any carpet that had once graced the elegant stairway. To the side of the staircase, the hallway narrowed on either side, leading to a closed panelled door, the design of which matched the four doors on either side of Megan. She stepped forward, her caution noticeable to Page since he had followed her in. She eventually stopped at the bottom of the staircase where she turned to face Page before looking at the large light fitting that hung from the ceiling. Upon this, dozens of pieces of carved glass hung down, each one catching the brightness that the main window above the staircase offered.

Page watched on as Megan kept her face upturned as she stepped into the middle of the hallway and slowly began to spin round in a circle. Stretching herself almost onto the tips of her toes, her feet barely made a sound. As she came to a stop, she wrapped her arms around her chest before she lay her head over to one side and closed her eyes. Then she began to circle again, much slower, as though she was held by an unheard tune. When she finally stopped, her eyes seemed to snap open, the bulging of them only weakening when she spoke.

'The house is watching,' she said so softly that her voice was almost a whisper.

'What do you mean?' Page asked, moving forward to take on the scale of the hallway.

'She's watching,' Megan told him. 'She's watching you and dreaming of the past.' Moving closer to him, she leaned forward and whispered in his ear, 'She knows you.'

A passing overhead cloud sent the hallway into shade, highlighting the shadows underneath Megan's eyes. There was no doubt that she was disturbing him, getting under his skin just like he said that she wasn't going to do, and Page knew that she wasn't going to answer any questions he wanted to ask. He decided to play along with whatever game she now herself wanted to play.

'I'm starting to know you now, Megan, and some of the games you obviously like to play yourself,' he told her. 'So come on, let's stop talking in riddles and let's look around. No more games. Just give me the grand tour.'

Megan let out a slight giggle as though he had said something that amused her. She bit on the broken nail on one of her fingers and winced as though she had bit too low on it. Rubbing her hand over her mouth seemed to change her mood, and again and she became bearable, if only slightly. As they approached the first door to his left, Page noticed the number '1' written on one of the door panels with a series of markings underneath. Pointing at them, he asked her what they signified.

'It means its room number one,' she told him, pulling a simple expression. He thought that she was playing with him again at first, but as if sensing his thoughts, she moved against the door and pointed herself at the markings.

'Most of the rooms in the house are numbered. You'll see numbers on nearly all of the downstairs rooms, but some of the upper rooms have none as we haven't been to them yet.'

'We?' he questioned.

'I mean me, sorry,' she quickly corrected herself, though he sensed that he had heard her right the first time. 'The thick line underneath means that we have checked the room. The circle means there was activity and the angle line shows I was not alone.'

'Okay, I got the numbers bit, but what do you mean by activity and not being alone?'

Shaking her head slightly, she smiled weakly at him.

'It's a bit too complicated for now,' she told him. 'Let's stick to numbers and rooms, shall we?'

The first room they entered was to the left of the hallway and was about fifteen feet square and bare of furniture. Again, the wooden floorboards showed to be in good condition as were the walls that were, for some reason, down to what looked like the original plaster, even though there was no sign of any renovation work having taken place. The size of the room surprised Page, who thought that it must have been a storeroom at some point, or maybe a form of a cloakroom. A single cord flex hung down from the ceiling with an old style lightbulb in place, which Page was surprised to see lit when he flicked on the switch beside the door frame. Little difference was made to the general light within the room as the window on the opposite side gave most of the light to the room, even though the glass was marred by dirt and grime.

'I wasn't sure whether the electric would be on or not,' he told her as she headed for the door opposite to where they had come in.

'Most of the time it is, but sometimes it just goes off by itself,' she told him as she paused with her hand hovering above the door handle. Pointing to a number two on the door, he guessed that she was sticking to a form of a plan as she then opened the inner door. Passing through, Page noticed other markings on the door when Megan passed through, ones that she didn't comment upon.

The room they stepped into appeared to be a sitting room. Here the furniture had been shrouded in white sheets, of which many held deep shadows across them. Page was unable to tell what style of furniture lay hidden beneath the layers or what age they could be. In contrast to the small bare room they had first entered, most of the furniture appeared to remain in the places that he would normally have expected them to be. Facing the large fireplace was the shape of a settee with three smaller chairs huddled alongside, the bottom of the legs adding to the impression that all the items matched. Framed pictures of differing sizes which had no doubt once graced the walls of the room were stacked against two dark, wooden display cabinets which still showed some of the contents remaining inside. A small collection of books, along with several ornaments, were just visible through the dull glass doors. On the pale blue walls, Page could see faint marks where the pictures he had noticed may have hung. There was no suggestion as to why these had been removed, and when he asked Megan about this, she didn't seem at all interested.

'I don't know,' she told him, running one of her fingers over the top of them, disturbing dust that gathered on the tip of her fingers. Puffing out her cheeks, she blew out slightly, watching as the particles fell away silently to the floor, momentarily highlighted by the returning sunlight outside. It puzzled Page as to why he took such interest in the room, despite its shut down appearance. The room appeared that it may have been quite appealing in another, more welcoming time.

'The door at the far end leads to a corridor which runs the length of the house with other rooms off it,' Megan told him. Instead of leading him that way, she began to head back the way they had come, pointing upwards. 'There's a similar corridor upstairs, but it's much wider, as you'll see.'

'Were not going through there?' he asked, to which she shook her head and led him back through, into the hallway. Once there, she seemed hesitant on which way to take him.

'We could just split up and I'll find my own way around,' he suggested, hoping to help her decide. The glaring look that she threw at him told him otherwise.

'No!' she snapped at him, her voice echoing around the hallway. 'You don't understand! You stay with me or…'

'Or what?' he asked, holding his hands out as though the house itself would answer. 'I thought I was here to protect you.'

'Doesn't matter,' she replied sullenly, though her voice was more measured and controlled. 'Look, it's not right today. I've had enough and want to go.'

With that, she headed towards the front door like a petulant child, motioning for him to follow. Page could think of no reason for her sudden outburst or why suggesting that they separate would raise her anger. Instead, he followed her across the hallway where her heavy steps sounded loudly before she passed through the now open front door where he caught sight of her shivering as she stepped into what was still a warm day. She remained silent as she locked the door behind them, not waiting for him as she walked eagerly away from the house. Page watched her leave, wondering what on earth was going on in her warped mind. He had been brought here to offer her protection, but from what? Not from any apparent risk in the sprawling grounds of the Ravenscroft Estate, but from whatever the house that they had briefly been inside held. He walked slowly across the gravel-covered front of the house and looked back at the sombre building, the neglect of it never failing to hold his attention.

On one of the tall chimneys, a couple of birds landed, far too small in size for him to recognise their breed. As soon as they had landed, the birds took flight again, making Page feel that they felt no welcome there and he was beginning to feel the same. Whenever a passing cloud created shadows across the building, the upper windows appeared to darken until an impenetrable blackness stared back. The lower windows didn't fare much better, the boarded ones giving an impression that they were merely a temporary bandage over wounds that would still take a length of time to heal. The warmth of the late morning seemed to be fading fast as Page shivered involuntarily before moving away in the direction that Megan had abruptly left. All that time, he had the strangest feeling that he was being watched.

Chapter 18

Alex Sutton decided against another cigarette. His mood and nerves repeatedly called for one recently, making Alex wonder whether it was something else altogether that cast a shadow over him lately. *Too much partying and shagging exotic women,* he mused to himself as he poured himself a fresh cup of coffee. *All are going to wear you out mate,* he thought as he tasted his drink, enjoying the rich aroma as well as the strong flavour.

Leaving the kitchen behind him, he returned to the sitting room where the paperwork he had been working on remained. He felt pleased that he had managed to kill the craving for a smoke with another drop of caffeine, and thought back to his recent medical. Always conscious about his general fitness since his days in the Army, he had undergone a full medical examination after taking out a complex life insurance policy. Not that he had much to leave behind. His small, two bedroom house edged one of the less salubrious parts of Manchester and came with a list of repair jobs which constantly needed tending to. But it was something. Something which he hoped might help one day. Another mouthful of coffee enabled him to focus on the paperwork where he had been sitting. Mostly routine work regarding the security teams on various projects, he was surprised at how long it had taken him to get this far into it.

Grateful in some ways that the day's activity in the main house had been halted, he used the time to catch up on other work. After signing off several papers and finishing his coffee, Sutton leaned back in his chair and closed his eyes, rotating his neck slowly to help ease the tension that had gathered around his neck and shoulders. God, he felt tired. Aside from being easily irritated nowadays, Sutton wondered whether his doctor had been correct in telling him that his health was in good order. True, you smoke too much, his doctor had told him, and the drink could be toned down a little, but in general, he was in good health. *No policy to cash in yet then,* he thought as he re-opened his eyes. His line of work had prompted the need to cover himself financially. There were too many incidents where he felt that he had been lucky to have escaped so easily.

As he stood, Sutton tucked his hands in his pockets, walked over to the window, and wondered how old Caitlyn and Diane were now. *Pathetic,* he thought to himself. *No wonder you failed to keep your marriage together, when the simple act of remembering the age of your own children was beyond you. A cigarette would help you think,* he joked with himself, but there was little humour felt within him. Had it been three or four years since the twins' sixteenth birthday? Again, the actual dates eluded him. It was the last major event he had been involved with. *God, they could be twenty now, grown women finding their own way in the world with no help from you, you useless bastard. No-one but their dumb mother to guide them and warn them of all the psycho's out there.* The thought cut through him like a knife, making him reach for his cigarettes, inhaling deeply as soon as he lit one. *Clear your mind,* he told himself, *concentrate on the here and now.* Maybe Rowlance would complain that he had been smoking inside the house. Or perhaps that weirdo Megan had already sensed his discretion and was informing on him at that very moment. Sutton blew smoke out again as he collected his paperwork, planning to finish it later.

Leaving one of the table lamps on before he left the room, he pulled the door partly closed to enable the light to cast into the hallway. He retrieved his coat from the small cloakroom close to the doorway. Within the shadows opposite, a figure remained as still as possible, only moving out of the place of concealment when Sutton had left the building.

Chapter 19

Collette Logan moved her face closer to the bathroom mirror that had held her reflection for almost ten minutes and ran the thin pencil eyeliner carefully under her right eye. The tip of her tongue brushed along her bottom lip as she studied both her eyes now that she had almost applied her makeup. The eyeliner added an extra touch to the dramatic grey and silver eyeshadow that she already wore. Her short hair had been swept fully back, held in place by the wet-look gel she preferred to use in private. After choosing a deep grey lipstick, which she deliberately took her time to apply, her facial transformation was complete.

Still in her black silk underwear, she had not chosen an item to wear only because she had no intention of leaving her room for the rest of the evening. She walked through into her bedroom where the two table lamps cast a warm glow around her, and drained her glass of wine. Before she poured herself another, she found that she was smiling as she noticed how little now remained in the bottle. After taking another taste of her drink, she lay down on her back across the bed and stretched out, her smile far broader than before. Staring at the ceiling, she wondered if Megan was sleeping in the room above where she lay. She wondered what the girl's thoughts were and if she dreamed, where those journeys took her. Was her mind too tired to do so by the time night came? Or was she also troubled by her thoughts when she attempted to sleep? Collette wondered if the events and sights that she had witnessed over the last few years were now beginning to take their toll on her. Megan's moods were becoming darker by the day.

Earlier on, Collette had stood with her ear to one of the doors, listening to Anthony Rowlance ranting about Megan's behaviour. At one point, Alex Sutton had suggested that they call a halt to the project which had surprisingly made Rowlance refocus his mind and begin to settle. Like some naughty schoolgirl, Rowlance had then ordered Megan to her room, insisting that Charlotte stay with her for most of the evening.

Collette stretched an arm upwards and pointed out her fingers wondering, or possibly hoping, that she could pick up some of whatever abilities the stupid, sickly thin Megan possessed. She would never look as good as she did, Collette thought as she ran her hands across her shapely figure, pausing as one of her hands rested above her heart. Relaxing her breathing failed to decrease the quick rate of her heartbeat, a pace that always overcame her whenever she felt herself gaining control.

Collette Logan had loved taking the lead role ever since being a child. For some reason she recalled an evening close to her last few days at university where she had first felt the excitement that could run through her body when she made an assertive decision against somebody. Then it had been Amanda Talbot or had it been Thomas? She couldn't recall now and to be honest, she cared little. Her failure to remember the name of the girl who had dared to challenge her in the popularity stakes couldn't prevent the laugh that escaped her as she sat up and reached once more for her drink. How many times had she told the stupid cow to keep her distance? Too many, for sure, yet Amanda still had the front to smile at her and start some banal conversation with her at a party to celebrate graduation. When Collette stood and walked over to the tall mirror fixed to the bedroom wall, she recalled holding Amanda firmly by her immaculate blonde hair as she repeatedly rammed her perfect face into the mirror in one of the bathrooms. Collette smiled as she remembered the sound of the other girl's nose shattering, the cracking of her perfectly chiselled front teeth, and the pathetic attempts at screaming as she continued slamming her head backwards and forwards. So many other memories had come to her in the short time that she had stayed on the estate. Some she could barely recall at first, but once she allowed her mind to open, they came flooding back.

The face of Gerry Mellwood came back to her. Their so-called relationship had lasted for six months, taking in some of the best hotels and restaurants that she had ever seen. It had given her the expensive taste that excited her as well as strengthening her darker side. Six months had been how long it had taken to extract all the information she had wanted from him. The additional blackmail money which Gerry had stumped up to keep his affair with Collette private had been a real bonus. The levels that Chris Acomb, the man who Collette had hired to threaten and blackmail Gerry, had gone to had impressed her to no end. He had made a video of Mellwood's two young children leaving school, going to friends' houses or even pictured inside their own home. He took cuttings of their hair without them even noticing, posted items of their clothing, along with a piece of his wife's underwear, which he claimed to have taken from their home.

A photograph of the couple's bedroom had all but convinced Mellwood of how close the man had gotten to him. The panic-stricken businessman had turned to Collette Logan for help, even though it had been Collette, or Breda Jenkins as he knew her, who had supplied most of the items. After taking over a hundred thousand pounds of blackmail money off Mellwood, Collette had then handed over the business details of her alleged lover to various competitors, making five times the amount by the time she planned to leave with Chris Acomb. Many were the times that Collette had wondered how long Acomb had waited at the airport before he realised that she wasn't going to show, how many times Gerry Mellwood had tried to contact her, finding no trace of Breda Jenkins wherever he looked, and how Gerry's wife, Catherine, would have collapsed when she opened the post one morning to see what her precious little husband had been up to. All at the same time Gerry grasped at the fragments of his crumbling business.

Aside from the money that Collette was building up, her level of cruelty was intensifying. She had kicked a reporter unconscious close to a railway station and blackmailed countless other people. She bought and sold hacked I.T. systems. She set fire to a homeless shelter simply because one of the tenants had the audacity to ask her for some spare change when she was busy trying to shop for new shoes. When the fire and resulting deaths made the front page of the Daily Mail the following day, she had bought two copies, pleased with her sense of achievement. A year ago, though, had come her most significant break, when she accepted a job offer with what she believed was a consulting company. A. R. Solutions had presented her with all she could ever want from a job and the P.A. work that she did for Anthony Rowlance allowed her to live what she considered a perfect life.

Reluctantly pulling her mind away from her memories, Collette moved against the bedroom door and considered unlocking it and knocking on Page Darrow's bedroom door. What reaction would he have to the way that she was dressed? She considered whether he would like her make-up and her hair or would it be too direct for him? There was a darkness about the man that she wanted. It matched the strange surroundings that she now found herself in. His ways and manner were etched with scars of the past, scars that she knew could and would easily be opened. For the moment, she would leave him alone, and she returned to her bed where she sat and pulled open her bedside cabinet, taking out a mobile phone. Sliding open the thin cover, she pressed down the list of contacts until she found the name she wanted. Despite the warmth within the room, she felt a chill catch her skin, the sensation exciting enough to cause goose bumps to appear across her upper arms as she pressed dial and waited as it began to ring.

Chapter 20

The pot of coffee that Charlotte made over breakfast helped to clear Page's mind. The caffeine was as welcome as her company.

The previous evening he had dined alone with Megan in another attempt to get closer to her. While she had eaten more than he had seen her eat before, she had spoken little, especially about what had disturbed her within the main house. She was withdrawn again, her hair partially masked her face from time to time as though she had lost a part of herself that she was searching for within. All Page's attempts to get her to speak more than a few words failed, and he was relieved when Charlotte came and joined them.

Charlotte herself failed to get much response when she tried to speak to Megan. The biggest conversation she got from her was when she said that she was going to have an early night. Megan looked like a child when Charlotte laid an arm around her as though she was being comforted after a nightmare rather than somebody about to go to bed. Soon afterwards, Page found himself within the darkness of his room where he lay awake for what seemed like hours before he finally drifted off. The small amount of sleep he had managed seemed to hold him still as he accepted another coffee from Charlotte.

'You look tired,' Charlotte told him as she sat opposite him at the small kitchen table, her words breaking him from his thoughts.

'That obvious, hey?'

Smiling, she nodded before taking a sip of her drink.

'What size feet do you have?' she then asked, her sudden question surprising him.

'My feet? Elevens. Why?'

Before answering, she stood and walked over to the far corner of the room and opened a cupboard where she knelt down and started rummaging through the contents. Moments later she reappeared holding a pair of walking boots.

'You're in luck. One pair, amongst dozens, that's just your size.'

'I presume they're not for use inside the main house?' he asked her.

'No,' she replied, the return of humour showing in her eyes, 'it's to get you away from this place for a while.'

'Any reason I should know about?' he asked.

'Can't tell you that, I'm afraid. Maybe it's so we can leave hideous and cunning traps for you to fall into.'

When she tried to hold a severe expression, her eyes quickly gave her away. She brushed back her hair, holding it for a second while she waited for a reply to her comment. Page found the smile came readily to his face, which was unusual for him. He knew that her company was helping him relax but knew he needed to keep focused as well.

'So, where are we actually going then?' he asked as he kicked off his shoes and began putting the boots on, impressed at the comfortable fit.

'For a walk. I need some exercise, and you need to wake up.'

Charlotte took him easterly from the main area of buildings to where the pathway soon became surrounded by woodland. The shaded cover of the newly leafed canopy occasionally concealed the walkway which narrowed as it made its way through the trees. Many of the species were deciduous, but there were several types of trees which Page couldn't identify. Charlotte soon pointed out the unknown types to him when he asked, as well as several species of unusual plants. Where the occasional conifer tree broke the natural pattern of trees, it added a form of strength that, far from looking out of place, only appeared to add to the appeal of the woodland. Charlotte's knowledge of the woodland and nature, in general, was interesting to Page, and without making him feel ignorant about it, helped him to relax more than he had been in months.

'Somewhat different surroundings to some of my recent work,' he told her as they paused to take in the surroundings.

'Me too, to be honest,' Charlotte replied. 'It's nice to see so much greenery. Megan and I have been on enough boats recently to last a lifetime.'

'You're not good on the water,' he suggested.

'I am, actually. I've done a lot of sailing over the years. But there's no escape from the work out there. Plus you should try spending two or three weeks cooped up with Megan in a confined space.'

Page held his hands up and conceded defeat to his comment, his actions making her laugh gently before they walked on.

'How long have you been coming here?' he asked, hoping that the question wasn't too intrusive.

'Megan's been coming here on and off for a couple of months, though I've only been here for a few weeks. Usually four, five days at a time. There's little to do work-wise here, so when Megan's busy, I tend to get outdoors as much as I can.'

Where a low branch attempted to block their path, Charlotte herself held it back as Page passed through first.

'And Greg being away for so long hasn't helped,' she added as she tucked her hands into the pockets of the grey jacket she wore.

'So other than your father's business, have you ever worked elsewhere?' Page asked as he lifted a low branch to allow her to continue along the pathway.

'I worked up until a couple of years ago. But getting married sort of put a stop to it, along with a viral illness I had at the time. Then my father asked me to come on board with the company to help with Megan.'

'What sort of work did you do before?' he enquired as the pathway opened up more, beginning to leave the constraints of woodland behind.

'I taught English in a sixth form college. Nothing glamorous, I'm afraid.'

'Don't knock it,' he told her. 'You're braver than I am doing that.'

Charlotte smiled appreciatively at his comment, welcoming the calmer side of Page that she was now seeing. The walk was a simple thing that she wished she could do with Greg, and a pang of guilt rose in her as they walked on. Deciding to hide her guilt, she continued.

'My teaching has helped Megan in many ways. She has had a fair few of private teachers, but none have stayed long enough for her to get her full education. She has taken the necessary exams and passed with top marks, but I get the feeling that she cheated in her own way.'

The sun broke through above them, making Charlotte turned her face upwards, enjoying what warmth it held on her skin. They walked in silence for a while, making Page think that she had other thoughts on her mind. In the trees to their side, crows circled above a concentration of nests as each fought for space.

'You know, Greg wouldn't do this,' she told him.

'Do what?' he queried.

'Walk and just talk. It's nice.'

'Tell me more about Megan,' Page then asked, steering the conversation away from her apparent resentment of her husband being apart from her. *Does it remind you of anyone?* a voice cried within him.

'In what way?' she asked.

'Is there not something else she could be doing? Could she not use her ability to say, find missing people instead of being carted all over the place to make money for companies like your father's.'

If Charlotte felt that his words were too blunt, she failed to show it. She did, however, suggest they sit on the trunk of a fallen tree while she adjusted one of her boots.

'She could, I guess. But where would she start? And how long before she was being paraded around like a freak show or being used exclusively by the highest bidder? How long before she was being used to locate enemies of already corrupt governments? The possibilities are endless. Within the company, I feel she is more secure, and at least she has some privacy.'

'You said that her father worked for the company in the past?' Page asked as she took one of her boots off, shaking out a couple of loose stones.

'He did. Mainly on the rigs in the North Sea as an engineer. There was an accident some years ago, where her father and two others workers were lost when a gantry collapsed during a severe storm.'

'Has she no mother?' he asked, thinking this company seems to have more than their fair share of accidents.

'Not that she knew of; her mother died when she was just a child.'

'So who was looking after her at the time of the accident?'

'The company,' she told him, finally pulling her boot back on.

'I'm sorry, I'm missing something here,' he told her.

'The company was already looking after her long before the accident. Megan was on the rig at the time, helping to find and match drilling samples to the places she had located herself.'

'But how old was she then?'

'Fourteen,' Charlotte told him as they resumed their walk. Page remained silent, too stunned to be able to comment on what Charlotte had told him. As the buildings around the main house of Ravenscroft came into view, crows filled the increasingly grey sky, the noise of their calling appearing to make Charlotte pause.

When she caught Page's stare, she asked, 'Do you believe in God, Mr. Darrow?' the change in topic throwing him further.

'At times I have, but... '

'Well, sometimes I think he fails to see,' she interrupted, a vacant look filling her eyes before she turned away and walked off.

Chapter 21

The relaxation that the walk with Charlotte had brought faded by the time Page met back up with Megan. Her mood had worsened, and for some reason, a section of her hair had been cut away. The fringe had been severely hacked, presumably by herself, so it was now only an inch from her hairline. When he asked her about it, she sullenly told him she had cut it because it had been irritating her. She wore the same black coat and jeans, though her footwear were now brown boots, the toes of which were also badly scuffed. She seemed edgy, and chewed on several of her fingernails while she appeared to wait for Anthony Rowlance to finish a conversation with Collette Logan. The two of them stood just inside the Coach House hallway where, although their voices gave off a slight echo each time one was raised, Page failed to catch a single word.

When Collette broke away from Rowlance, her face was screwed up in annoyance, a look she didn't bother to conceal as she stormed past Page.

'What's wrong with her?' Page asked as he faced Megan.

'Don't know, don't care,' she replied shrugging her shoulders. Page could see that one of Megan's fingers was now bleeding from where she had pulled away part of a nail. She began sucking on the finger as Anthony Rowlance joined them.

His expression looked sterner than usual, no doubt due to his conversation with Collette.

'So, Megan, are we in a better frame of mind today?' Rowlance asked, his question answered with another shrug.

'I'm ready if he is,' she said, nodding toward Page before sucking on her sore finger again. As they began to walk towards the main house, Toby Connor walked over to them holding a file of papers bound by a strip of tape bearing the A. R. Solutions logo. His floppy haircut seemed as agitated as his manner.

Page stepped aside as Toby began to thrust the file at Anthony Rowlance, demanding his immediate attention. He dismissed his request by stepping aside from the younger man. When Toby pulled back on his employee's shoulder, Rowlance reached out and grabbed him by the shirt collar.

'Later,' he snarled at Toby, who dropped the file, the impact with the floor causing the contents to spill out.

'Our main work is more important than this nonsense,' Toby told him as he attempted to reach an arm out and keep the glasses off his face. Anthony Rowlance pushed him away, the amount of force exerted sending Toby falling backwards. When he steadied himself, Rowlance stood over him, stepping on top of the spilt papers.

'Our business is here for now,' he told him, his temper now more controlled.

'Because Megan says so?' Toby asked, pushing back his hair, his rising chest showing his breathing was coming hard. Page couldn't help but give him a small amount of credit for his stance against Rowlance. When Anthony Rowlance failed to respond to Toby's accusation, Page felt his stare directed at himself almost as though he was supposed to answer. Thankfully the sound of Megan walking off broke his stare, and Page watched as Rowlance disregarded Toby Connor and walked after her. For a moment Page considered helping Toby back on his feet, who was now busy collecting the spilt papers. It was the first time Page had seen Rowlance lose his temper, and he had the feeling it had little to do with Toby's interruption.

It took nearly an hour for Megan to show Page the whole of the lower floor of Ravenscroft. They went methodically from room to room, spending different times in each. There were fifteen other rooms in the whole of the downstairs, not including the small room that Megan had first led Page into, along with the hallway. Aside from the sitting room which Page had previously seen, there was another, more formal room which at one time would have graced guests, a large dining room with eight chairs placed around a dust-covered table. The dining room led to the kitchen, which could also be reached from the hallway and rear corridor. There was a morning room off the main sitting room, the scale of which was hard to tell because the light failed to illuminate with the windows being boarded up. There were two other rooms of similar size, one of which had previously been used as a study. Piles of discarded papers lay upon a desk, along with a box containing pens and pencils. The other was now a storeroom with open shelving, set close to the side of the kitchen. The final part of the downstairs, which Megan informed him was technically a room, was the cellar of the house. It stood at the end of the rear corridor, set back in a slight recess, where three good sized padlocks were attached to the frame, the amount of dust upon them suggesting that they hadn't been opened in a long time.

In each of the rooms that they walked through, nothing untoward happened and only in the morning room did Page notice Megan react to something that made her stop abruptly and turn as though she had heard a noise. Eager to ask her what she had felt or heard, he turned his head in the same direction and listened. He heard nothing.

Megan showed him other symbols on the doorways, as well as some on the walls of the larger rooms, but she failed to enlighten him as to what their purpose was. He allowed her to take her time, never attempting to question her actions in each of the rooms. By the time they returned to the hallway, boredom was setting in within him.

'Megan, we have been in here nearly an hour now,' he told her as she sat on the base of the stairs. When she pushed her hair back and made the odd-looking fringe disperse, she looked almost serene. 'There's nothing here.' He continued, 'Where's this power source that you claimed to be here?'

She remained silent as she watched Page hold his hands out and call out loudly, 'Hello!' his deep voice echoing slightly before the hallway fell silent again.

'Nothing. Why don't we at least look upstairs?' he asked her, exhaling as he watched Megan shake her head. When she stood, her hair fell forward again, and the badly cut fringe could be seen once more. Now standing almost directly underneath the hallway light fitting, she appeared to be listening.

'What are you doing?' Page asked, his curiosity for her actions with her increasing.

'I don't feel or hear anything,' she replied.

'What do you mean?'

Moving back towards the stairway, Megan sat on the bottom step and drew her legs together, angling one of her feet whilst scrapping along the edge of her other one as though she was thinking how to respond.

'The house speaks to me,' she told him without looking up. 'She tells me things. There are times when the house changes and she leads me through the place as though it wants to show me things.'

'What sort of changes? How can…'

'Changes that you wouldn't believe, or want to,' she said, interrupting him. 'Did you know the house was calling to me long before I even stepped inside here?'

Sitting on the step beside her, Page tried to control his breathing, if only to keep a hold of reality. He asked her how somewhere can call to her. His patience appeared to be working as she kept eye contact whilst she spoke to him.

'I get flashes, images of things that at first make no sense. Some drift away and I fail to see them again. But there are others, like the ones with the house, that won't leave me alone. For some reason when I first felt this place, I knew it was not far away. So I got a stack of maps out and let my mind drift over them.'

'And that's how you found this place?' Page asked as he stood and looked around him.

'Pretty much.' She continued, 'it was when I got out a map of Cheshire that I felt like I wanted to puke. I pointed at the exact spot on the map without even looking.'

A week ago Page would have dismissed such talk, like what he was listening to was deluded rambling, but as he looked around him and listened to the near complete silence, there was something about the place that, if he would only be honest with himself, was getting to him.

'And does it work the same when you find things for the company?' Page then asked.

'At times, but this is something else. With this place, I heard it talking to me, words I couldn't make out at first. Creepy sort of whispers. But when we first came here, they sounded so clear…'

Her words trailed off as she stood herself, pulling her coat tight around her as though she had felt a chill. She scratched the side of her face and watched as Page positioned himself at the bottom of the stairs, looking up to where sunlight now showed across the upper steps. During the time that she had spoken about the house and her abilities, Megan had appeared totally focused. She could, of course, have been entirely delusional, but Page detected an honesty about her that belied her usual appearance.

'So, what has this to do with me?' he asked as he turned to face her. 'Why bring me here if the place is talking just to you? It makes no sense.'

Page thought he saw something in Megan's eye when she looked directly at him, a slight change in colour that must have been caused by the loss of the bright sunlight as cloud cover returned outside.

'One of the things the house asked me was to find you and bring you here,' she said as the chill that he thought had briefly caught hold of Megan seconds before wrapped itself tightly around him.

Chapter 22

Despite it being late morning, Anthony Rowlance had little guilt at pouring himself a glass of whisky. Apart from a half-empty bottle of vodka, a bottle of lime cordial, and a couple of measures of tonic water, there was little choice but Scotland's finest, he thought as he stepped away from the small drink cabinet. He added a generous amount to his glass and moved it in a circular pattern, helping to agitate the liquid before walking over to the seat placed close to the window.

Before he sat, Rowlance opened the blind slightly, allowing extra light to filter into the dining room. He felt tired this morning, even though he considered that he had slept for most of the night. *More than you used to,* he thought as he took a mouthful of his drink. Stiffness at the base of his back had held longer than previous days, a legacy of a former back operation, and he hoped that it would have worn off as the day passed. The darkness his closed eyes brought seemed almost as comforting as the sensation of the whisky, as it etched its way slowly down his throat. Although his eyes remained closed, he noticed the room around him brighten temporarily as the sun attempted to break through again. When he finally opened his eyes, he had to squint until his eyes adjusted and the familiarity of where he was appeared again. God, he was beginning to hate this place. The broad expanse of the estate's grounds did little if anything to help him lose the claustrophobic feeling he felt being here. He knew that others were feeling it too, especially Charles McAndrew.

Aside from Charlotte, Charles was the one person he felt he could open up to now. Strange, he thought, how many similarities they had. With Charles, he knew that it was his work within the company that was helping him to keep sane, allowing him to keep hold of a small fragment of hope.

And your hope? he asked himself as he finished his drink. *What faith do you have in that? A reliance on a dysfunctional young girl whose judgment you've rarely questioned, but whose theories and beliefs of late were leaving a greater sense of doubt within you?* The sound of a knock at the door pulled him away from his thoughts. To his surprise, he found Charles McAndrew stood there.

'What are you doing knocking?' Anthony Rowlance asked as he stood to greet him.

'You looked lost in your thoughts…' McAndrew suggested, letting his words trail off as he watched his colleague pour himself another drink. He declined one when offered.

'Just thoughts, Charles. Just thoughts.'

Sometimes that's all we have, McAndrew agreed. His friend looked weary as he pulled a seat over to the window where Rowlance had sat again. Despite the relative warmth of the room, he kept his coat on, preferring to hold onto what warmth he already had.

'I presume they are now within the house?' he finally asked.

Anthony Rowlance nodded before staring at the contents of his drink. He remained silent for a moment before draining the contents in one go.

'This will work,' he said.

'Will it?' McAndrew questioned, doubt showing on his face. 'Are we any closer this time? Or any time previously, come to think of it.'

'I have to believe that we are,' he answered.

'And if not? What then?' he asked, his uneasy manner beginning to unsettle Rowlance. 'How do we even know what Megan is thinking? I need…'

'I know what you need, what we both need,' Rowlance interjected, knowing his words were inadequate. 'Hold onto what you have for now at least.'

'At least?'

When they both stood, Anthony Rowlance rested a hand on McAndrew's shoulder. He knew that the harshness of his words may have seemed inappropriate, even between them. The look he gave him was enough to ease him for now, but he knew that words would eventually not be enough. Turning to leave, Charles McAndrew stopped and looked back, recalling why he had come looking for Rowlance.

'Toby's harping on about some figures he wants you to see.'

Rowlance gave a short laugh as he looked back out of the window.

'I'll talk to him,' he replied as he heard the door close behind him. Closing his eyes once more, Anthony Rowlance wished his backache would return, if only to clear his mind from his present thoughts.

Chapter 23

They had been inside the house for close on thirty minutes now. In contrast to the previous visit, Megan took no notice of the numbering system for the doorways and had gone through the downstairs rooms as if she was trying to recall a former route she had made. Several times she re-visited rooms, and each time Page queried her actions, Megan held a palm out to him as though he had interrupted her thoughts or she was trying to hear something. By the time they returned to the hallway, it appeared gloomier than before, the inclement weather no doubt the reason. After suggesting they take a look upstairs for the first time, Megan began chewing on one of her fingernails. To his surprise, she hadn't objected when he started to climb the stairway.

Thickening cloud cover brought with it more significant drops of rain which fell upon the window at the top of the stairs. He had the curious feeling that he was meant to climb the stairs, and as he did so, all sound around him faded away until only the increasing beat of raindrops could be heard. In what seemed like an instant, Page found himself looking down a wide corridor that ran either side of him.

When Page turned to see where Megan was, something appeared to brush his ear. Flinching slightly, as though a small fly or insect had flown close to his ear, he thought he heard someone whisper. The voice was faint, barely heard, but when Page looked around, he found himself alone. He considered calling out to

Megan to see whether she had heard anything, but before he could, the whispering returned, increasing all around him as though dozens of voices were spiralling around him. Then as quickly as the voices started, they diminished until he could hear only one, the single word was spoken enough for him to back away to the top of the stairway.

By the time he was able to see Megan again, beads of sweat were gathering across his forehead, enough to make one run down his temple. Page felt as though all breath had instantly been sucked from his body as he attempted to rest his hand against the top of the bannister, fearing his legs would weaken and that he would suddenly fall. With the drop of the stairway too close for his liking, he somehow managed to move back enough to enable him to lean against the edge of the window frame. Page wondered what the hell had just happened. Below, at the foot of the stairs, he could still see the gaunt figure of Megan who stood facing him, wondering why she hadn't followed him and what had caused the concern etched across her face. She mouthed words which he failed to hear, making it seem impossible for her to have been the voice that had spoken in his ear. As she began to run frantically up the staircase towards him, his mind filled with a single word that threatened to open scars that had bled too much pain for him, ones that he had prayed were now long healed. It was the word, Emma.

Page felt his body jolt as though he had been shaken from a dream as Megan reached the top of the stairs and grabbed him by his jacket collar. His hearing appeared to have returned to normal, but his body filled with growing anger that now threatened to consume his body. Had it been under differing circumstances, Page knew that in that split second he would have fought back against Megan's actions and immediately drawn his weapon. In another second, it would have been thrust straight at her. Instead, all he saw was the wild face of Megan pushing him back further down the corridor, her face and hair looking as disturbed as he now felt. He wanted to grab her by her shoulders and shake answers from her but bizarrely remembered in time about her not wanting to be touched.

'What?' Megan asked, her voice trembling as he stopped inches from her face.

'You know what!' he now screamed back at her. 'How did you do that and who the hell do you think you are to say her name?'

Megan was speechless and backed away, releasing her grasp on him, fearing that he was about to strike her. When one of her hands touched the side of the wall, she pressed herself against it as if needing support.

'I didn't do or say anything,' she told him, running her free hand through her jagged fringe. The simple action eased her enough to attempt to reassure him. 'You have to believe me.'

'Then what happened?' he asked as he saw her move her hand out towards him as if to attempt to silence him. Megan tilted her head now as though she herself had heard or sensed something. When she raised her head again, he saw more than concern filling her eyes.

'We have to find a marking,' she told him, her voice noticeably more serious. 'One of the door numbers or one of the larger drawings.'

'What the hell are you talking about?'

'Because something is about to happen. You asked what I meant by the house being able to change? It looks like you're about to find out.'

Chapter 24

Megan led him quickly down one side of the corridor, the increased pace almost making her stumble at one point. When she finally stopped outside one of the bedrooms, Page found his breathing came hard. A panel upon the door showed a number nine with a small triangle that had two diagonal lines through it.

'Remember the number and the symbol,' Megan told him, her voice now falling much quieter. 'It may be the symbol that we have to find if they try to separate us.'

Opening the doorway, they both stepped through into a dimly lit room.

'What's going on?' Page asked as her growing agitation now seemed more of a threat. He knew no specific details of what was about to happen, and the uncertainty was making him more than uneasy.

'You're making no sense,' he continued, but before he could ask her anything else, he felt a sudden drop in pressure as though the air was being sucked out of the room. Just the effort of reaching into his jacket and removing the Glock 36 felt so draining, the feeling of light-headedness beginning to overcome him as he stepped in front of Megan, wary of an unknown threat to her increasing. He scanned the room that they had entered, but only saw the weak outline of a bed, the cover of which showed traces of the small amount of daylight the partially covered window offered. Page recalled the ivy-covered section on the rear of the house and tried to get a quick bearing as to where they were. Managing to remove the handgun had done little to reassure him, and in the poor light Page struggled to see Megan's features clearly enough for his liking. He cursed to himself and regretted her decision to restrict their position by entering one of the bedrooms. The thought was removed from his mind when there was another sudden drop of air pressure that only levelled out when he became aware of a change in his hearing. When he adjusted his position, the sound of one of his shoes scraping against the floorboards below it seemed distinctively clear. When Megan spoke, he heard the tiny puffs of breath that accompanied each of her words.

'It's happened.'

Page was about to query what she meant when the answer unfolded before him. The door that the two of them had been standing against had somehow completely gone. They found themselves standing back in the corridor where faded yellow flock style wallpaper now covered the walls. Where the bedroom entrance door had previously been, an ornately carved mirror hung, the glass too discoloured to offer much reflection. The scale of the corridor around them was unsettling now as its length stretched much further than before. On each side, the shadows were more pronounced, highlighting the edges of a row of picture frames along the nearside wall. Any light that reached the corridor came from the run of windows where the light was partly held back by thin, discoloured curtains that hung from them. Some of the curtains further along the corridor appeared so long that they draped onto the aged carpet that now covered the floor.

'We need to keep moving,' Megan told him, her voice still sounding strange in his altered hearing state.

'What's happened?' he asked her as he found himself moving forward with her.

'The house is playing games. It's taunting us. It's done it before, many times, and it wants us to play along,' Megan answered, the unease in her voice becoming stronger by the minute. They had now moved forward about thirty feet when Page sensed movement ahead. He moved instinctively in front of Megan, shielding the girl with his left shoulder, motioning her closer against the wall while he aimed the weapon ahead at a suspected threat. Ahead of them, a much larger window offered a shaft of sunlight held strong across the corridor. While it helped in one aspect, it only helped to darken the shaded area behind it. It was here that Page saw what he thought was movement.

'Don't believe everything you see,' Megan told him, as out of the shadows a figure slowly emerged.

Chapter 25

Page felt the familiar tension across his right shoulder as his raised arm rested just against the side of his face as he directed his aim. Shielding Megan, he adjusted his position, enabling him to at least move her back close to a doorway which they could use as a quick point of escape. He had no idea how long the corridor ran behind him anymore, and when he glanced over his shoulder there was no sign of the window above the top of the staircase to give him any bearings. The wall nearside just seemed to continue onwards into more shadows. He needed an escape route. Maybe a bedroom, though the last time he tried that he had felt trapped. If he chose one, it would have to be one of the rooms which he hoped would at least have interconnecting doorways, like the downstairs of the property seemed to favour. Maybe from there he could gain access to part of the lower roof, if needed. For now, though, his main concern was what was about to appear a short distance from them. When Megan attempted to speak, he told her to be quiet while pushing back his free arm closer towards her.

The figure that emerged was a man who appeared to be his late forties. His build was painfully thin, more so than Megan's, his weight only accentuated by the fact that he was bare-chested. The sunlit area that he had stepped into caused shadows to form across his rib cage where the skin clung tightly. His stomach looked almost convex and reminded Page of the horrific images seen towards the end of the Second World War when the prisoner of war camps had been liberated. In the area above his collarbones, two deep pits made it look as though they were struggling in their attempt to form a base to hold up the man's thin neck and face. The trousers he wore hung from his hips and only the occasional glimpse of his bare feet was possible. What concerned Page the most was the man's features. He looked completely terrified. Countless tears seemed to have fallen from his swollen eyes, the bloodshot parts giving his face the only amount of colour. Dirt and grime marked parts of his chest, with similar amounts more evident across the man's cheeks and forehead where some had caused his unkempt hair to lay stuck on it. Spittle ran down the side of his mouth, so strong that the man struggled to control it. Page's concern increased further when one of the man's bony hands began to appear, clutching a handgun within it. Until the figure's frame had been illuminated fully, the weapon had not been noticeable. The man's arm appeared so thin to Page that the weapon looked far too heavy for him even to attempt to raise. Page was taking no chances.

'Drop the weapon, now!' Page ordered, his words echoing all around them.

As though only now aware that he was armed, the man looked down at his hand that clutched the weapon, making Page repeat his instruction. Instead of obeying his command immediately, the man hunched his shoulders as though he had begun to sob, his arms trembling and making the weapon sway slightly. Page decided that he couldn't take the risk with the unstable nature of the man and prepared to fire either a warning shot above his head or to one of the man's legs to immobilize him.

There appeared no need though when the man released his grip, allowing the weapon to fall to the carpeted floor with a dull thud. The thin man began to shake his head and raised his hands to cover his face. Page could hear the sobs that escaped him and struggled to decide on his next move. Again, there was no need, as the man slumped to his knees and lowered his hands to reveal the extent of fear upon his face.

'Nothing m…m…matters anymore,' he said weakly, breath now seeming hard for the man to find. 'It's too late, all too late,' he added before Page registered the change to the man's features.

When the figure angled his head, Page saw that a section of the side of the man's skull was missing, traces of where the blood and fluids had escaped ran down the side of his neck and onto the top of his back. One of the now lifeless eyes continued to look at Page as the man continued to shake his head, each part of its motion helping the wound to weep further. By the man's side, Page could see traces of smoke rising from the weapon, the familiar smell of cordite from the recently fired weapon sharp in his nose, as was the coppery scent of blood. Page didn't doubt that the wound he could see was an exit wound, the single entry mark on the opposite side no doubt lost within his unruly hair.

'Megan, back up now,' he ordered over his shoulder and began to step back himself. Still bathed in what appeared to be natural sunlight, the sobbing figure collapsed face down upon the carpet, the action only adding to the surreal scene in a way that failed to entertain him. With the figure now motionless on the corridor floor, Page took full advantage to retreat. Keeping the Glock 36 pointed down the corridor, the two of them retreated, with Page hoping that they could reach the doorway he had seen earlier. Megan tried to speak, but again Page gestured for her to be quiet. The sounds of the man's anguish, for some reason, appeared to echo louder than ever around them as Megan forced him to listen.

'Not this one,' Megan was eventually able to say as she saw Page reach down for the handle whilst moving further down the corridor. Cursing her choice, he hurried after her, thankful that she had at least opened the next one that, until that point, had been concealed within the shadows. She paused by the doorway and pointed at the circle and line markings on the door as they stepped through into one of the bedrooms, its contents unknown to him. When Megan began to speak again, Page held a hand out to stop her.

'Leave it,' he told her moving across the bedroom. 'You can try and explain everything later,' he continued, grateful that she was at least following him. 'For now, I'm getting you out of here.'

Thankfully the room Megan had chosen did have a connecting door which they quickly passed through, entering another bedroom. Here a double bed still for some reason held onto its boxed up towels and bedding, as though long forgotten guests were due. Again Page scanned the weapon across the room, pleased to at least find it clear. Struggling to comprehend what had happened back in the corridor, he cursed his lack of knowledge of the house as he began checking to see if any of the windows would open. To his relief, Page found one of the windows could give him access to the lower roof, yet his instincts told him the choice would be wrong. Beside him, he saw that Megan had raised her head slightly as though she had heard something, and then moved across to the room's doorway. There she rested her ear against the door and listened. He was about to pull her back close to him when she raised her hands and wiped them down her face, her shoulders slumping as if in relief.

'It's gone,' she told him quietly.

Still clutching the weapon in his hand, Page moved beside her at the doorway.

'What do you mean?' he asked, his patience almost exhausted.

'The change. It's gone.'

Page took a step forward and motioned for the girl to move behind him again as he slowly turned the handle and opened the door enough for him to look out. He saw nothing untoward, but still held his nerve as he widened the door opening, enabling him to lean out and survey the corridor. In a mixture of relief and amazement, the area had somehow returned to normal, with no trace of the yellow walls or the carpet spread out along the wooden floorboards. No anguished figure greeted him or even called out as he motioned Megan back into the corridor and quickly headed along towards the stairway.

The only change he could see as they hastily descended the staircase was that the light had faded rapidly in their journey from the bedroom. As they walked past the room that they had taken refuge in, sunlight still held across the corridor, even though the intensity of the sunlight showed that the sun was lowering. As they reached the bottom of the stairs, deep shadows filled the hallway, the changes in light making no sense to Page who tried to dismiss the doubts from his mind as he urged Megan towards the doorway. There was no sound, no noises or anything untoward as they exited the main house of Ravenscroft. Thankful to be out of the place, he felt shut off from the horror of what he had seen, even though only a single doorway stood between him and what the house had held. He looked back to see Megan staring back at the house, her face becoming lost in the shadows that fell around her.

They had entered the house in the late morning, where the warmth of the day had attempted to raise his spirits, but now the daylight had all but faded. For a moment Page recalled rain falling at one point, the sound against a window drumming in the back of his mind. All concept of time appeared lost as he saw Alex Sutton and Charlotte approach. His breath continued to come in short bursts as Charlotte took hold of Megan's arm and began leading her away. Images of the thin, anguished man filled Page's eyes. The smell of cordite was strong enough to recall, as was the thumping noise against the carpet as he watched the weapon slowly fall from the thin hand. When Sutton approached him, Page failed to hear his words directed at him. His mind showed a doorway opening and screams sounding within the darkness, ones that Page knew could only have come from the thin man they had encountered. Another face filled his mind, one much loved, whose laughter and warmth had, over time, been replaced by a ravaged look that bore deep into his heart. As Page felt his body temperature rise, his face coated in sweat. When he tried to speak, the simple effort was almost impossible. He began to sway and faintly saw Sutton reach for him before his vision became too distorted for him to hold onto and he eventually blacked out.

Chapter 26

Charlotte Wareham ran the tap for several seconds, ensuring that the water ran as cold as possible before running the small hand towel underneath it. While the cloth absorbed the water, Charlotte opened the bathroom cabinet and looked for any painkillers she could find. Apart from a small glass and a bag of cotton wool wipes, the cabinet was empty. The only trace that the bathroom in Page Darrow's room was in use was the small toiletry bag placed on top of the toilet cistern. Guilt at first prevented her from looking inside the bag, only looking when she finally decided that he wouldn't be offended. She found only deodorant and shaving gear. After turning the tap off and ringing out the towel, she remembered that she had some painkillers in her room as she began to fold the towel into a small compress.

Thankfully, Page had settled into a deep sleep by the time she returned. The restlessness that had come to him when she and Alex Sutton had brought him back to his room had now subsided, the mostly illegible words that he spoke having fallen silent. Sitting gently on the edge of his bed, Charlotte placed the towel across Page's forehead, hoping that it would help to ease his high temperature. If he were to wake, she would then consider getting further help if she felt it was needed.

It was Alex Sutton who had helped her to remove Page's jacket, revealing the holster and weapon beneath. Neither had commented on this as they went on to remove his sweat-stained shirt, this act allowing her to see a deep scar running across his right shoulder. The small indent where the wound had been deepest caught the shade that had been cast by the bedside light, the healing on the surface now complete. After Sutton left, Charlotte tended to Page. He had stirred at one point, attempting to rise, but soon had fallen onto his side, allowing her to see other scars. These were less prominent, but each one held a memory no doubt now contained within. Pulling the bedclothes over him, Charlotte felt even though he still wore his trousers, she had at least returned an amount of privacy to him. Turning the towel over to the cooler side, she rested it back across his head for a few minutes longer. Page's eyelids no longer flickered, and his breathing had thankfully become more settled. When she rested the back of her fingers across his forehead, the burning sensation seemed to be easing.

Charlotte remained with him for another hour, during which time she thought mainly about Greg. She wondered whether he too was sleeping, whether his mind was as occupied as her own, and when she would next see him. Maybe she would try and ring him when she got back to her room, not caring whether she disturbed him should he be working. She longed to be held, to be reassured that the paths that they were taking were not only right in their choices, but that they would lead back to each other. As she stood looking back at Page now peacefully sleeping, she felt a growing sense of compassion towards the man. She had seen glimpses of the man behind the blunt, objective manner he gave off. Charlotte knew that her father would be holding something back from Page. She knew he always did. It was another of his ways of keeping control of people. Leaving the door slightly ajar, she descended the staircase, deciding to make herself a drink of tea. Sleep for herself seemed far away. As she reached the bottom step, she wondered what the real reason was that Page had been brought here.

Chapter 27

He recalled hearing the name somewhere before, but as he scooped up another hand full of cold water, Alex Sutton failed to remember where on earth he had heard it. To dream the same dream for the second consecutive night seemed impossible, yet even the latest blast of cold water that he had tried to wake him from his nightmare failed to help. After turning the tap off, Sutton gripped the edges of the sink, his head bowed, too fearful to see his haunted face again in the mirror in front of him. Turning away, he returned to his room and lay back on the entangled sheets of his bed, the wetness of his hair and face soon dampening the pillow he sought comfort on. Thankfully his heartbeat was slowing and his breathing had become more measured, even though the strain across his chest remained.

In his dream, he had been running. At first it had seemed blind, with no sense of purpose. When he had stopped to try and catch his breath, he recognised a figure stood further down the street. Even though the man's hair was much longer and his face now showed a full beard, there was no mistaking his brother, Michael, but he knew inside him that it couldn't have been. It had been ten or eleven years since the accident, a day not passing when he didn't wish that things had been different. The difference now was that Sutton had locked away the memories in a room within his mind and had learned as the years slowly passed to resist the urge to try and unlock it.

When Michael had turned away and fled, Sutton resumed what he now realised was a chase. It mattered not that the streets they raced through were deserted, only discarded contents from overturned rubbish bins were taking refuge there. Sutton knew that he had not been to blame for his brother's actions, but had he forced him to hand over his car keys, or at least found his brother another way to get home, he would never have had to hear the coroner's report, read the police reports, or struggled to stand at his funeral, seeing the shattered lives around him. It had mattered not whether he had been three times or a hundred times over the alcohol level, or whether Michael had even seen the articulated truck that he had ploughed into the back of, the result had been the same.

Further on in his dream, Sutton had reached a road junction where he collided with the door of an abandoned car, catching the same mirror as he had done on the previous night. His chest pulled tighter as he attempted to increase his pace. Fearing that Michael would soon be out of sight, he pumped his arms as he ran harder in an attempt to improve his speed. As the buildings around him began to lessen, trees started to overhang the pavement where he found himself almost catching up with Michael. A stone wall alongside him opened up to a roadway which led into a large cemetery. Sutton recalled calling out to his brother, begging him to stop. Around him, large tombs and gravestones, many gothic in design, were so aged that Sutton began to worry that if he shouted too loud, the sound of his cries could cause some of them to topple over. If they did so, it would prevent him from ever catching up with Michael. To his relief, the daylight increased as the cemetery increased in width, the graves growing smaller and more personal, the spaces between them further apart. Though free of the constraints of the oversized tombs and lavish resting places, a chill set in deep within him, not helped by the gathering of figures that now showed on the raised ground above him. He recalled passing a sign that read Wingate Cemetery, and even in the midst of his dream, he felt shame in not recognising the name of the resting place for his brother.

Although the mourners could easily have obscured his view, Sutton found that when he approached them, they began parting almost apologetically, allowing him easy access to where his brother stood. The pile of earth that awaited the end of the service seemed to add an extra sense of harshness that he now felt as he stood beside the open grave. There seemed no sign of exertion on his brother's face following their long chase, even though Sutton found his breathing ragged and every part of his body seemed to ache. He wanted to ask Michael why he was now dressed in worn, almost threadbare clothing. His eyes were being drawn to the other mourners around him, their sombre faces all looking at him with a mixture of confusion and disbelief. Why, he had no idea. Again, he wanted Michael to offer him an explanation. Instead, he watched as his brother reached across and took a handful of the cold earth before tossing it into the opening. There was no sound of the soil breaking against the hard surface of a coffin, giving him the impression that the grave was deeper than it should have been. It made Sutton step closer and peer down below him. Somewhere deep inside him, he almost expected there to be no coffin since there hadn't been when he had dreamed the dream the night before, yet the horror of what he witnessed seemed as strong. He had woken with a start and attempted to scream, but parts of the soil that his brother had thrown down still appeared to fill his mouth, while the remainder had scattered itself across his own lifeless body that had filled the open grave.

Chapter 28

The clarity of the morning light seemed to add an extra dimension to the private garden area of the Ravenscroft estate. Set apart from the extensive gardens where the yew trees offered greater protection from wind and frost, it had initially been designed for a previous owner who was now barely remembered by anyone. The lawn area had long since been divided into three separate areas, each being surrounded by much smaller and neatly boxed yew bushes. The yews had been trained and shaped over the years to a height of almost a foot, and although they showed signs of growing uneven now, they still gave some order as well as a sense of shelter to the beds that edged the lawn where roses were close to flowering. Whilst the lawns had recently been tended, some of the rose bushes looked as though they needed care bestowed upon them. Shoots had been allowed to grow wild, and on many, greenflies were busy gathering. The day was already warm but unnoticed by Page Darrow who sat on a wooden seat overlooking the rose bushes, their thorns as sharp as the feelings he still held within him. Sometimes during his disturbed night a dream-filled sleep had found him, though he failed to remember anything about it. Daylight had brought no rest to his mind and what sleep he had gotten had left little if any comfort. Despite the increasing warmth around him, Page wore a jacket fastened over his open neck shirt, his hair still wet in places from where he had just run water over his face and head in an attempt to wake himself fully.

In contrast to Page's need for warmth, Charlotte Wareham wore a thin, loose-fitting white blouse over her jeans. The breeze, although welcome upon her skin, caused her hair to fall across her face occasionally.

'You spoke in your sleep a few times,' she told him as she pushed her hair back behind her ear once more.

Charlotte had come looking for Page when he failed to come down for breakfast. The one place where she found some peace and quiet at Ravenscroft was the private garden of the main house. It had seemed strange to discover him there. Further back from where she had come across him, Charlotte knew a more mature section of woodland with several footpaths would have given him more privacy. Seeing his troubled look, she had not been surprised to hear that it was an incident with Megan that had affected him.

'When I spoke, did I make any sense?' he asked her eventually, still surprised to hear about how she had cared for him until his body had settled.

'Not much of it did, to be honest,' she told him, 'but you did say the name Emma more than once.'

The directness of his stare made Charlotte instantly regret her words. She only seemed to have caused the concern showing on his face to increase. When he allowed his gaze to fall across the gardens, she thought that he might walk away from her, but instead saw his face brighten as though holding onto a better, brighter memory than recent ones.

'Emma was my daughter,' he told her as he let his stare stretch across to one of the yew hedges on which a male blackbird landed and began surveying the grounds.

'At one time she was everything to me,' he continued as the memories came flooding back, and despite the increased temperature the strengthening sunshine now brought, he felt a shiver run over him.

Emma Darrow was born eight months after Page had married Jayne Claremont. Jayne had been the first person that Page felt he had truly loved. The arrival of their daughter, Emma, had come as a complete surprise to the couple, about who tongues were still talking, even after their wedding day had passed. They had only known each other less than a year, so their decision to marry had surprised their few close friends. With no family of his own, Page's choice was never questioned, but more than once Jayne's parents had warned her against marrying someone who they openly disapproved of, let alone the fact that Jayne had only known him for what seemed like five minutes. Ever since those early days, Page had known that it really was their unease of someone serving in the armed forces that really got to them.

Page had often thought that it was the disruption of their daughter's life due to his work that they really cared about, rather than their own plans for her that were no doubt now destroyed. Far from causing strain between the two of them, the arrival of Emma only served to deepen the bond and love between him and Jayne, as though her tiny frame served as the final link between them that could never be broken. Time away from his family on military missions put a different perspective on his home visits. He began to see changes that both shocked and captivated him.

The inevitable time came when he became torn between the Army life he loved and his more immediate duties at home.

One August day when Iraqi helicopters and boats had begun deploying commandos into an unprepared and nearly defenceless Kuwait had changed everything. A year later, as Emma had laughed and played with friends under summer sunshine at her tenth birthday party, Page had stood under blackened skies as Kuwaiti oilfields burnt out of control. The skies were so dark that it appeared that there was now no difference between night and day.

Those chaotic first days of invasion instilled in Page the need to strengthen his military commitment, causing further cracks to appear in their relationship. Each time Page returned home over the next few months, Emma had grown more and more and the divisions between himself and Jayne were wide enough for all to see. Jayne and others never questioned his dedication to his country and job, but his inability to handle problems at home caused endless confrontations between them. By the time Page had finally arrived home following his last tour of duty and had then left the Army behind, Emma had experienced her first overdose on heroin at just seventeen years old.

'Standing in a hospital watching staff attempt to save her life brought home to me where, over the years, I had failed her,' Page told Charlotte as a passing cloud began masking the sunshine, the shade pleasing in the coolness it brought.

'How did she ever get on that stuff?' Charlotte asked, taken by the honesty and openness with which Page spoke.

'Far too easily,' he told her, his voice edged with emotion. 'Most people still believe that addictions only find the weak, the poor and vulnerable, those wasting life away in tower blocks or run down council estates long forgotten about by society. But Emma's home life was good. Okay, so I wasn't there much, I confess, but she lacked for nothing, she got everything she ever needed. The final grades that she got at her private school were excellent and the staff there spoke of a caring, loving girl who seemed so full of life.'

Yet the dark side of Emma's life had been kept hidden for over a year. Only after she was discharged from the hospital did the truth begin to surface. The vast amounts of money that she had borrowed or stolen from friends to feed her habit had shocked us, her parents. Late one night, whilst Emma slept, I sat with Jayne looking through countless photograph albums, looking for changes in her appearance or attitude, a small clue to offer them an explanation. Never had she lost her manners or let her behaviour or respect for her parents wane, even though she was allowing herself to be ravaged inside by her addiction.'

'So we set about trying to get her cleaned up. Jayne's parents were so horrified that they refused to help, demanding that their daughter leave what they called her loveless marriage, which, although she now hated most of it, she clung to in an attempt to save Emma's life. We spent a fortune on rehab and counselling, amounts you couldn't believe.'

'And did it work?' Charlotte asked.

'For a time it did,' he answered, 'and for a time Jayne and I came close again, but one Christmas Emma failed to come home from a friend's party. Three days later, the police found her body in an alley behind a row of shops close to where we were living. She lay amongst the discarded rubbish with an amount of heroin in her that was way beyond help.'

Charlotte sat numbly beside him now as he leaned forward and held his hands together as though in silent prayer. Strangely, when he looked at her he seemed brighter, as though he had spoken about his loss and pain for the first time.

'You know, I've been back to the place where they found her, and watched the refuge guys clearing the streets, and saw what I had let her life become. She ended up as a piece of garbage that someone would simply walk past.'

'No one can be there all the time,' she suggested, her words meaning to hold comfort.

'I guess not,' he told her as he stood. She paused, then rose and they walked across one of the lawns where the cloud had now passed, bathing them in the sunshine once more. 'A week after her funeral, Jayne and I split and I've never seen her since. I took most of the debts we had with me and have worked ever since to try and repay them.'

'I see why you took the job my father offered given your finances.' Her words, far from sounding too blunt, actually brought a smile to his face.

'And there's you thinking I spent it all on whisky and wild women,' he joked as he reached into his trouser pocket and removed his wallet. From one of the sections, he removed part of a photograph.

'That's Emma, sometime around her sixteenth birthday,' he told Charlotte as she took it from him 'We went on holiday to

Tuscany and stayed in a villa surrounded by olive trees. Looking back now, I can't remember us being happier.'

'She's beautiful,' Charlotte told him, returning his weak smile and resting a hand on his own as she handed back the photograph. She was pleased when he didn't pull away. They remained in silence for a while, their hands gradually parting, only moving when he agreed to her suggestion of getting something to eat. They slowly began to walk back towards the main house, the warmth of the day still failing to touch Page.

'Page, I have no idea what happened to you yesterday, any more than I know what you've told me about Emma has got to do with here?' Charlotte stated, breaking the silence just as the breeze caught her hair again. Page slowed his pace for a moment, kicking at a loose stone laying on the pathway before replying.

'You know, I saw something in that house I could scarcely believe.' For a moment he considered telling her about the figure they had seen, and how the house had changed, but it was the voice he had heard that he wanted to speak of. It was when I was all for leaving the house with Megan that I heard someone call Emma's name.'

'That could simply have been Megan playing her games again,' Charlotte suggested. 'She could have heard about Emma through my father. He does know plenty about you, as you said so yourself.'

'Initially, I thought that, but I could tell that Megan was surprised herself by my reaction to having heard her name spoken. I believe that she was as shocked as I was.'

'Remember, Page, how Megan likes to play games,' Charlotte said as they neared the archway close to the Coach

House. Page couldn't help but smile to himself at Charlotte's choice of words but declined on explaining the irony. He found himself walking ahead of her now and had to slightly pause when Charlotte asked him to slow down.

'I know what you mean, Charlotte,' he told her as he turned to face her, 'but right now I need to hear what both Megan and your father have to say.'

Page left her alone as she watched his uneasy walk over to try and find the answers he sought. She folded her arms around herself and closed her eyes, wondering what the hell the rest of the day would bring.

Chapter 29

Alex Sutton remained quiet for several minutes, continually checking through sheets of paperwork that he had placed beside the laptop which he now busily typed upon. Occasionally, images of graphs and charts were displayed and altered as the data that he had entered began to change relevant pages accordingly.

Another laptop close to where Page Darrow stood had earlier been used, though the screen had long since gone to standby in the time that they had been waiting, the A. R. Solutions logo drifting slowly across it.

Collette Logan sat close to the doorway on a high back seat wearing an immaculate black suit, her legs tightly crossed with the skirt high enough to have caught Page's attention. She had her usual confident look, as though she knew more than she was letting on. Collette had long since learned the art of using her looks and body to her advantage, but Page was less than impressed. He had the feeling that if he were to shake hands with her, he would have to count his fingers when she eventually let go of his hand.

On his return, Page had headed straight for the kitchen where he sat in silence for a while before pouring himself a glass of orange juice, half of which remained in the glass he still held.

He had tried to hide the thoughts running through his mind, forcing the usual, professional way of thinking to the surface. The doubts had resurfaced when he had seen the tired and troubled look which Alex Sutton wore, and wondered for a moment what had caused this. Elsewhere in the room, Megan sat in a wicker chair close to the window. She still wore the same clothes from the previous day. Her hair lay flat against one side of her head as though she had just woken from sleep, the remainder looking lifeless and lank, with parts having become entangled. Her hands were not visible due to the sleeves being pulled down. She looked pensive as she continued staring out the window. Page noticed that she failed to look across when the door opened and Anthony Rowlance walked in with Charles McAndrew.

'My apologies for the delay,' Rowlance announced to everyone as he handed over a computer disc in a clear plastic case to Sutton, along with a couple of small envelopes. 'I trust you are feeling better, Mr. Darrow?' he then asked as Charles McAndrew nodded across to Page before becoming engaged in conversation with Collette.

'Yes, thanks,' Page lied.

'Excellent,' he replied before turning his attention to Megan. 'So, are you not going to join us, Megan?' Rowlance asked as he stood close to the table with his hands resting on the edge of the drawings. Acting as though she had failed to hear him, Megan continued her watch outside. Rowlance failed to react to her manner as though her insolence was normal.

'Maybe Mr. Darrow will be more enlightening about your visit,' he suggested as he focused now on Page himself.

The stillness of his room when he had woken had done little to ease his mind. Now standing with the man who could provide some of the answers to his questions, Page struggled to find the words to begin. He felt the focus on him appeared to increase as he stepped closer to the table and studied the main drawing of the house, regretting not taking in the details beforehand. His plan of leaving that to Megan seemed a poor lack of judgment. Not like him at all. So he began to follow one of the marked lines on the drawing, explaining the route that he and Megan had taken when they had stepped inside Ravenscroft. The careful look on Megan's face when he caught her eye held him back when he spoke.

'We ended up in the upper corridor which, as you know, runs along the rear of the house,' he told them, noting the keen interest shown. Sutton took notes on a small notepad whilst Rowlance stood with his arms folded, listening intently to his words.

'And from there?' Rowlance prompted while Sutton typed information he had noted into the previously unused laptop.

'We retraced our steps back downstairs and left shortly afterwards,' Page finished.

'You were in there for nearly seven hours,' Sutton informed him as he looked across at him, his words the first confirmation of the distorted time that he and Megan had experienced. 'There must be more than that you could tell us.'

'He knows you're lying to him,' Megan then interjected, making everyone turn to face her. She had stood but remained preoccupied with what had held her gaze out the window. Her thin arms were once again visible as she attempted to straighten her hair with her fingers. When her hand caught on a tangle, she winced and pulled harder, becoming frustrated when it wouldn't clear.

'You've told him a crock of shit to get him out here in the middle of nowhere and you can't tell him the truth if you tried.' Trudging over to the table, she added, 'We had major activity, Anthony. One of the best.'

Megan didn't try to conceal the smile that was beginning to widen, and by the time she approached Sutton, she looked close to laughter. Sutton kept his expression passive as she leaned against him and playfully blew in his ear.

'We saw Thomas,' she told him gleefully, to which Sutton's chest rose more noticeably at her comment. When she stepped face to face with him, his obvious annoyance with Megan began to show further when she added, 'He was, oh, so pissed off.'

Grabbing one of the marker pens that Rowlance had brought to the table, Megan pulled the main drawing over to herself, causing the sheets to crumple in places before she marked an 'x' where Page presumed they had been in the house.

'What's he doing upstairs?' she asked aloud as laughter burst from her, adding a more lunatic touch to her appearance than was necessary. Rowlance reached out and pulled Sutton away from the table, fearing a confrontation between them, whilst at the same time looking over to Collette who seemed more than amused by the sideshow unravelling before her.

'Go and get my daughter. It may help to get her to calm down,' he ordered, making Collette quickly stand. As she left the room, her smile was hard to contain as she made her way into the hallway, the sounds of Megan's laughter still audible above the strong beating of Collette's own heart.

Chapter 30

Toby Connor removed his glasses and rubbed the bridge of his nose as he leaned back in his chair, hoping that the simple action would help ease the strain he felt within his eyes. In front of him, three computer screens were running, each carrying various levels of information for the projects he'd been working on. As he looked back at the most central of the screens while still holding his glasses, his poor vision made the figures and wording unreadable. He laughed silently to himself at the irony of his thoughts. Too much of the crap he dealt with on a daily basis was unnecessary. The ignorance of the people he dealt with, a constant issue to him.

He had woken before seven o'clock that morning and began work straight after getting dressed, keen to take advantage of being left alone while others concentrated on the 'bloody project' as he called it. Toby refused to believe that he was needed here, the small amount of data he was asked to process from the project hardly enough to pull him away from more pressing work matters. Putting his glasses back on, he opened another e-mail, the contents only adding to his workload. Undoing the top button of his shirt, Toby loosened the matching blue tie he wore until it hung low on his chest. Licking his lips, he found them dry and took a drink of water from the plastic bottle to his side before he adjusted one of his shirt sleeves.

He resented having to work within the confines of the cottage, and his shirt and tie were more to make a point of the type of place he should be working than anything else. The remaining e-mails were mostly straightforward, many that he could deal with later, and he began to work on details appertaining to ongoing projects elsewhere. Figures given on a couple of them were enough for him to be increasingly concerned.

Leaning back again in his chair, Toby picked up his mobile phone and contemplated making a few calls, but his eye was drawn to the black jacket hung over the arm of the small settee. Still holding his mobile, Toby stood and moved across the room, picking up the jacket in a gentle manner, as though it was somehow fragile. Traces of her perfume still held across the collar, strong enough for him to lift it to his face and inhale a tiny part of her. He had liked the way she had sat on the edge of his desk the previous day, the silent closeness between them helping his breath to catch in a way he didn't understand, but at the same time, enjoyed. When he had been passed a glass of wine, Toby enjoyed the way their fingers had briefly touched. Distracted from the work, he had sat with her, mildly annoyed that he had allowed her so close.

Laying the jacket back down, he spotted a small piece of paper sticking out of one of the pockets, and for a second contemplated removing it and seeing if there was anything interesting on it. Maybe it held words that would excite him or give information about her that would allow him to get even closer. No, he thought, that was too personal, too intrusive. Annoyed at his mind drifting, Toby returned to his chair and pulled it closer to the desk, and monitored figures that a while back had been concerning him. His mind, though, repeatedly filled with images.

Toby recalled part of her thigh showing below the hem of her skirt when she had crossed her legs, the skin taut and flawless. His eyes were constantly drawn to the near perfect shape of her body, unsure whether she was aware of his constant staring. Averting his eyes when she looked at him, he tried to think of an excuse, but before he could say one she moved closer to him, snaking a hand around his neck, pulling him down so their mouths almost met. When he responded to her demands, he kissed her passionately, running one hand around her perfect waist, the sensation of her body against his making him begin to lose control. As her mouth moved hard against his own, Toby recalled running his fingers through her hair, long enough for him to take hold of some and hold her tighter. Closing his eyes, he remembered how when he had felt her waist again, his fingers had moved against the coolness of her skin before they had slipped between the individual ribs. When she had pushed him back and laid across him, causing paperwork to scatter around them, he recalled the bone of one of her hips digging into him, her frame as weak as the breath that attempted to come to him.

A soft beeping noise forced Toby to snap his eyes open, the disturbing images of different women making him think that he had removed his glasses again. But as his eyes began to focus, the highlighted sections on one of the laptop screens came into view, showing the figures that had earlier been causing him concern. They were now seriously troubling him. His mouth felt so dry, the sensations of unknown hands refusing to leave him, threatening to engulf his mind. It took all of Toby's mental strength to enable him to focus his mind fully before, with trembling hands, he finally reached across for his phone.

Chapter 31

It took nearly an hour before there was a form of calm in the dining room. Page was now alone with Anthony Rowlance and the bemused Charles McAndrew who still look shocked at the force that Charlotte had used to remove Megan, who continued shouting and taunting both Sutton and Collette even when she left the room. As Charlotte took her outside, she more than once attempted to come back into the room and continue her tirade.

In spite of her behaviour, Page would have preferred Megan to have stayed. He wanted to know what she had meant by her comments, more especially about himself supposedly being lied to. While McAndrew pulled a seat closer to the table and sat, Rowlance remained standing, and after straightening out the drawings on display, waited for the response from Page that he knew was coming.

'I must apologize again for Megan,' he said, attempting to divert any questions away. As Page faced him, he continued, 'Had she not been so important for us in the last few years I would have been glad to see the back of her.' Looking across to the doorway as though she had just left he added, 'At times like these, especially.'

'What exactly did she mean when she said I was being lied to?' Page queried as he stood only inches from Rowlance.

'You should know by now that Megan likes to play childlike games with people. I've also heard that she has already been showing off to you,' Rowlance answered, making Page recall the memory game that they had played, as well as her ability to see inside his closed wallet. 'So I should take lightly any comment she makes, as most are only for show,' Rowlance added, hoping his words would be enough.

Page was less than impressed with the older man's answer and felt like pushing him more, but instead chose another angle to question the two men he was trusting less and less as the hours passed. When Collette Logan entered the room, he ignored her presence, too interested in making sense of recent events.

'What exactly did you see, Mr. Darrow?' Rowlance eventually asked, even though other questions remained unanswered around them. 'The slightest event could be more crucial than you may realise.'

Knowing that his denial wasn't going to get him anywhere, Page began to tell them of the changes that had happened. On the drawing below them, Rowlance asked him to confirm that the marking, though crude, made by Megan was accurate to his own presumed location.

'Pretty much so,' he told them, 'though as you know, I don't know the full layout of the property.'

'And you are sure that the wallpaper where you were standing was yellow?' McAndrew asked.

'Sure, it was the older type with the soft, velvety texture on raised sections.'

'Excellent,' Rowlance replied as he turned to his colleague who himself look pleased by the news. After making further entries to the page open on one of the laptops, Page noticed how a section of the house highlighted for a moment in yellow with a thick black border appeared on the screen. As quickly as it had appeared, the part of the drawing fell away, joining other coloured in differing shades.

'It would confirm the similar activity that Megan has spoken of,' McAndrew suggested as he began to look through some of the sheets of paper that had previously interested Sutton.

'What do you mean by activity?' Page asked, tiring of their half comments and unknown theories. From the pile of papers beside McAndrew, Rowlance took out a single sheet of paper and placed it down in front of them both.

'You will no doubt have seen some of these,' Rowlance stated, handing him a sheet of paper. Though the majority of symbols he looked at were too complicated in their design for him to attempt to understand, he nodded where it seemed appropriate, recalling the specific ones that Megan had shown him.

'I've seen the circle ones, and I think the triangle with one side shaded,' he answered as he returned the sheet. 'I remember Megan saying that the circle meant there had been this 'activity' thing you keep going on about. There was another circle one that had a squiggle or a line underneath.'

He looked at the two other men, hoping that his input had caught their attention. By the interested look on their faces, it had.

'Activity means that Megan saw a sighting within that particular part of the house.'

'Like Thomas,' Page said flatly as Anthony Rowlance nodded before pointing to the drawings, showing him other circles with times and dates beside them.

'All these are all the known sightings of Thomas,' Rowlance confirmed, 'where he was sighted when Megan had company, then it's marked with a line underneath. The other symbols will be explained in time.'

'And the coloured areas?'

'They, believe it or not, Mr. Darrow, they represent different years,' Rowlance advised him under McAndrew's watchful stare. 'That's all I can say on that for now.'

'So who the hell is Thomas then?' Page asked, becoming more and more confused. His mind barely acknowledged Colette as she moved silently across the room, eventually standing against the far wall with her arms folded against herself as she listened intently.

'Thomas Kenny is, or was, a former employee of ours,' Charles McAndrew told him as he stood himself, placing his hands in his trouser pockets as he began to stretch his legs by walking around the table.

'It was Thomas who first visited the house and grounds when Megan first brought the place to our attention. At the time I saw no reason why he shouldn't visit the place. We, as a company, have acquired other similar properties, mainly from an investment point of view. However, there was no obvious indication at the time of what was to follow.'

'How do mean?' Page enquired.

'We got a call from the letting agents who had been dealing with the property to say that the keys needed to be returned to their office following his visit.'

'They let him visit a place of this size by himself?' Page asked, his disbelief evident.

'It was a term of our visit. The letting agents were more than compensated for their assistance, I can assure you. Anyway, when Alex Sutton and I called at the house, we found the keys in the front door, but no trace of Thomas Kenny. We later managed to convince the agents that Thomas had indeed returned to us, even though this was clearly a fabrication, and for their part they were happy, even happier when we purchased the property soon after.'

'You bought all this because one of your employees apparently disappeared there?' Page asked incredulously.

'No,' Rowlance corrected him, 'we bought the place after Megan visited.'

'I thought you said that she had found it, surely she came to see the place.'

'You should know by now that one of Megan ability's is to locate things, this estate was one of them. When we brought her out here, she told us that Thomas Kenny was still here and being held inside due to the great power source that the main house contained.'

Page shook his head, failing to believe the nonsense that he was being told. When he closed his eyes and tried to think, images of the previous day rushed to greet him. He took a step closer to the main window and opened his eyes quickly, the brightness jolting him to his senses.

'The sightings of him that have been made have been entirely by Megan,' Rowlance now stated, 'but they are pretty sketchy, to be honest.'

Picking up a pen from the table, he used it to point at various parts of the drawing while he continued to speak. 'The clearest seemed to have been mainly downstairs, but none of them has been where the yellow coloured wallpaper predominates.'

'Well, wherever you think or don't think he is, I don't think he's going to be claiming any overtime,' Page told them.

'Meaning?' Rowlance asked.

'From what I saw of him, he was pretty much dead.'

Page saw both of the other men exchange glances as Collette, who had surprisingly remained silent through all of this, left the room.

'In what way?' Rowlance asked, unconcerned as to why Collette had decided to leave.

'Well, he had half his bloody skull missing for one thing,' Page told him. 'He was also carrying the weapon that appeared to have caused it.'

'And you can be certain of this?' Rowlance asked.

'Well, I know what I saw and heard…'

'Heard?' asked McAndrew, who looked more concerned as each moment passed. 'I thought you said he was dead?'

'Yeah, heard,' he confirmed. 'The guy that you keep calling Thomas said it was all too late and nothing mattered anymore.'

It was evident that what he had said had taken both of them by surprise, making Page enjoy the moment of taking the mystery to them.

'To be honest, I'm not sure whether what I saw was actually real or if it was a hallucination or something. Just before everything changed, Megan told me not to believe what I see. I still don't, even talking to you now,' Page added as he walked away from the table and rubbed his eyes with his hands.

'What I want to know, though, is what all this has to do with me?' he added, his mind struggling to take in everything. 'You said that Megan asked for me. Me specifically. But why? She said that the house told her to bring me here. The close protection you want is all bollocks, you and I both know that. You have more than enough of your own security team to protect her, yet you choose not to.'

Rowlance briefly looked down again at the drawing below him, as though the answer to his questions would suddenly spring out of the confusion of markings and sketches. When he turned towards him, the optimism that had shown moments before was nowhere to be seen.

'Because from what Megan has informed us, only you can protect her inside that godforsaken house, as you are the one remaining person it apparently can't harm.'

'Why?' Page asked, his disbelief more noticeable.

'Because you know what the power source is.'

'How the hell can I?' Page snapped back. 'I've never been here before!'

'On the contrary, Mr. Darrow, you have,' Rowlance told him, the tone of his voice almost unnerving. 'I know this because you were actually born in the house.'

Chapter 32

The weightlessness always made Megan feel like she was floating. Occasionally she thought that the feeling was the equivalent of flying, but without the sense of movement, the term floating seemed more appropriate. In the times when her mind sought the solitude it desired, it allowed her to take control fully. Allowing a known weakness to run through her body, she gradually let her emotions overcome her to the point where she needed, almost wished, to be cleansed. Within her place of solitude, her mind could easily expand, revelling in the freedom it was allowed. When reaching the state of mind she desired, she just allowed the places she dreamed of to come to her. All the time the cleansing continued.

The term 'cleansing tank' Megan had invented herself. Far too many times she had felt drained whenever her senses called on her, her mind and body too exhausted to answer the endless questions that Anthony Rowlance and his idiots threw at her. In need for complete silence and solitude, she came up with the idea of the tank. Too scared of the thought that they could lose her abilities, added to the fact that she knew how to play them most of the time, they had soon agreed to her outlandish plans. Even though Megan herself thought that her demands were over the top, the company had agreed to every last detail of her idea, while the benefits that she brought them continued.

The tank that Megan was now hung within, in her usual suspended state, was one of the smallest ones she used. One of three tanks that A. R. Solutions transported around for her to use, it was situated in a part of the recently restored stable block. Each unit was quick to assemble and power. A slight hum generated from the one now in use, just audible in the stillness of the area. With her arms extended, her fingertips were two feet from the edges of the glass panels. In the blue light that surrounded her, the sides of the tank were lost within the nearby shadows, giving the impression that it was actually bigger than the others.

When Charlotte had earlier helped her tuck the supports underneath her arms, she had asked, as usual, how long she had wanted to be left. Unsure even herself, Megan had suggested an hour, and smiled at Charlotte before she removed the step she had been standing on, replacing it with a frame which she rested her heels on. To an outsider looking in, it appeared as though she was suspended in air, but to Megan, she was merely floating. With no form of timekeeping, she placed the small amount of trust she possessed in Charlotte, as to attempt to lower herself down without assistance ran the risk of injury. During the first moments she had been floating, it had taken all her efforts to shake the sense of Charlotte's sadness from herself, the slightest touch from her friend drenching her in emotion. The aching within her was stronger than she had ever felt before. It drained Megan further when Charlotte had taken the weight of her body to lift her onto the arm supports, as well as to feel the aching within the older woman. Megan sensed the lack of touch that a single embrace could give Charlotte. Despite her lack of knowledge of physical contact, Megan still felt her need for close companionship, and the strained love of Charlotte's marriage, which she grasped onto so tightly, as though scared to let her grip slacken. The only comfort Megan took was in knowing the changes that were soon coming would help her one true friend.

Now though, she needed to let her mind clear. Below her feet, images formed. The water of a mighty ocean now spread out around her. An unfelt wind whipped the edges of the waves as they broke against each other, the surging mass below as endless as time itself. Above, Megan witnessed seabirds as they flew by, their bodies silhouetted against the sunlight that now broke through thinning clouds. The ocean below became transformed into a kaleidoscope of colour that made Megan's heart beat strongly. Slate grey colours became turquoise and jade, while emerald greens merged with unknown shades of blue which seemed to sparkle as the waves neared land. Silent and unseen below the surface of the water, the increasing pitch of land caused the oncoming mass of energy to rotate around itself, the weight building close to the surface to form the edges of waves that now approached the coastline.

Megan looked on as a shaft of sunlight now spread inland, highlighting a small patch of green set against russet and copper toned bracken, to where a stone cottage stood. She recalled how her first ever glance at the place had made it look like a dwelling where she could find a sense of refuge. Its white walls were almost too bright to look upon, the colour in sharp contrast to the line of rocks that lay carpeted along with the shoreline nearby. It was to touch this line of defence that a section of the waves sought, their contact a subtle mixture of incredible energy and sweet caress.

Further along the coast, the clouds had thinned, allowing the peaks of majestic mountains to free themselves of their temporary shroud, all silent witnesses to the endless lines of waves that gathered to break against the isolated stretch of coast. With her eyes fully closed, Megan stretched out her fingertips and pointed her toes downwards, keen to expose herself entirely to the place where her mind took her. Her breathing was now so light that it would have been almost impossible to detect had anyone tried to locate an individual breath. Her thoughts now as distant as the cottage upon which a doorway set inside the front wall silently opened, the simple action causing Megan's heartbeat to pulse even harder.

Chapter 33

It seemed that every passing hour now presented Page Darrow with another change of mood within the people who had come to Ravenscroft. This time, surprisingly, he found Megan in a reasonably good mood. Having not seen her since her outburst earlier in the day, he hadn't expected her to be at the dinner table when he arrived. During the afternoon, Page had taken an hour's sleep, which had done little to ease his mind following the revelation of him being born at Ravenscroft. The suggestion had seemed ridiculous at first, but the more he thought about the claim and the more he realised how sketchy accounts around his early childhood were, the more logical it was beginning to sound. The familiarity of the estate that he had felt at times was almost as though he was trying to remember something shut away in a distant memory. What concerned Page the most was the fact that all the information Anthony Rowlance knew about himself and Ravenscroft had come from Megan.

Whereas the first night most people had eaten together, now the meals people took seemed more spread out. Only he, Megan and Charlotte appeared not to have eaten so far. So much for happy families, Page mused as he pulled up a chair at the kitchen table, giving Megan a nod and smile as he sat while Charlotte finished a conversation with Charles McAndrew. From the pile of discarded plates on one of the worktops, he was the last to leave.

Megan looked incredibly young as she stared blankly at him, her eyes so innocent, as though nothing of any harm had ever graced them. When she stuck a tongue out at Page after sensing him watching her, the sudden act seemed almost childlike at first, before he noticed a touch of humour begin to spread to her eyes.

'So, you two hungry?' Charlotte asked as McAndrew said his farewells and left the room. Page did his best to act normal when McAndrew held his stare for a moment, hoping that neither Megan nor Charlotte had noticed. Page had never been much of a card player over the years, but with what he had been told earlier, he intended to keep the cards that he now had close to his chest. He did not doubt that Megan knew about the birthplace claims, and was possibly holding back more. For now, he would say nothing.

'Starving,' Megan stated almost breezily as Charlotte placed a glass of orange juice before her. The three of them ate sliced leek and bacon, topped with cheese covered potatoes. The simple meal proved to be the most appreciated thing that he had seen Megan eat, giving him the impression that Charlotte had made it for her many times before. Megan even spoke whilst they ate. Mainly in short sentences about things the two of them had done together, but as the meal came to an end, she appeared to be enjoying the attention.

'Charlotte tells me that she is teaching you to drive,' Page said as he helped Charlotte clear the table, the calm atmosphere managing to hold.

'It's too difficult,' Megan replied before draining the last of her drink, 'plus my teacher's crap.'

The laughter that came from Charlotte spoke of the bond and trust that had been carefully constructed between them. When Megan ducked away from the tea towel thrown across the kitchen at her, Page could have believed that nothing of the last few days had happened.

'Wait till you get my bill,' Charlotte told her, 'I don't come cheap, young lady.' Page even cast a smile himself before accepting Charlotte's offer of coffee. A longer, more comfortable silence fell for a few moments, where playful looks were exchanged between the two very different women before Charlotte returned to the table with the coffees. As she sat, she caught the side of the table with her hip. Her evasive action to prevent her spilling the hot drinks gave enough force to cause Megan's empty glass to tilt. Expecting the glass to break from the impact with the wooden surface, Page was stunned to see the glass suddenly become still. Even when Charlotte eventually settled in her seat, the glass remained perched at about a forty-five-degree angle, the position given its shape, impossible. It was then that Page noticed Megan was staring at it.

'Megan,' Charlotte said as the glass began to spin round, never once losing the angle that it held. When Charlotte had spoken the girl's name again, it held more edge, making her look away from the glass, resulting in it finally becoming still and upright.

'How do you do that?' Page asked as he reached for his coffee, trying to keep calm and measured. Megan simply shrugged.

'It's telekinesis, isn't it?' he asked, noting the change of look in her eye. 'The ability to move objects with your mind.'

Still, Megan remained silent, with her hands resting together in her lap as she studied him, almost impressed with his knowledge. When Charlotte attempted to make the girl open up and reply, she raised a hand as though toward her off.

'I've heard of it before,' he continued, 'even read about it once. But I've never actually believed it until the other day when you showed me how to play the memory game.'

The mention of the game caught Megan's attention further. The doubt in her eyes lessened as though there had been an understanding made between them. When he held her stare, he saw the shroud she often wore across her face lift.

'It gives me headaches,' she finally replied, 'so I don't tend to do it much.'

'Only when you want to show off,' Charlotte suggested as she tasted her drink, noticing it was cooler than she expected.

'I think I would show off if I could do it,' Page suggested as Charlotte added more hot water to her drink. When he declined on his own, he saw a look from Charlotte that urged him to continue to press her.

'Show me something else,' Page pressed, noting how she was beginning to enjoy the attention for a change. 'Promise I won't bill you,' he added. The comment made her smile weakly.

At first, Page thought that she had declined his request as the glass remained still, but when he glanced at Charlotte, he noticed a change. From beneath the top of the shirt she wore, a silver coloured necklace began to appear. The length was unknown until a small cross began to appear, the bottom of which then pointed straight towards him. It remained still whilst Megan turned her face to look at Page, even when he glanced back at Charlotte.

'Easy, peasy,' Megan told him as the cross and chain fell back against Charlotte. Page was about to make a comment when the empty glass then moved swiftly across the table, coming to rest firmly in Megan's grip.

'Any more juice?' she asked, the smile now more evident on her face.

'Not for show-offs,' Charlotte told her whilst glancing across the table at Page. After another coffee, Page changed the conversation towards the house at Ravenscroft, but the result was making Megan fall silent again. Frustrated that his change of tack had had such a negative response, he tried several other ways to get her to open up again, but each failed.

Rather than drive her away, Page told them that he was going to get some fresh air. As he stood, he saw Charlotte mouth 'thank you' to him, wondering to himself as he said goodnight to Megan whether he had done any good. When the two of them were alone, Megan contemplated chewing on a fingernail, but instead made a fist of her hand and looked across to the closed door. Charlotte couldn't help but notice what looked like disappointment on Megan's face by the time they eventually looked at each other.

Chapter 34

When Alex Sutton let the latest cigarette butt fall to the ground, he wasn't surprised to find three other similar ones lying there. He inwardly laughed as he put the last traces of burning ash out with his foot. Ever since his early twenties, he had smoked heavily in stressful stages of his life. He knew he could quit if he wanted. He had gone weeks, if not months without one, but there always seemed a time or situation which drove him back. More often, it was the reassurance that he felt when he took a moment to smoke that he knew always made his return. He wondered whether his daughters were smokers. Puzzled as to where the thought had come from or why they were on his mind more recently, he scolded himself silently before he allowed the ache within him rise to the surface once more.

He had been outside for over an hour now, and his eyes had become well-adjusted to the darkness around him. There was a clarity to the night he found appealing. A sharp definition between surfaces enabled him to move comfortably around the grounds. He had initially walked along the driveway towards the main entrance, but two birds had suddenly broken from their nesting points when he had passed close by, the suddenness of their movement unsettling him. This was enough to make him return closer to the main group of buildings. Now close to eleven o'clock, he walked beside a row of beech trees which led eventually to an area facing the front of the house. Here a low stone wall ran along the edge of the front lawn, part of which had become overgrown by unkempt sections of grass that held the sheen of the moonlight across them. To his surprise, he found Page Darrow sitting close to the end of the wall where an ornate stone vase held its height against its surroundings, making it look as though it was struggling to breathe as he was himself in the surroundings.

'Penny for them,' Sutton said as he approached, noticing that the other man remained seated, the alertness he had arrived with seemingly diminished.

'They don't make any sense to me, so I'll pass if that's okay,' Page told him as he allowed Sutton to sit beside him, adding, 'Nothing here seems to.'

'On that point I couldn't agree more,' Sutton confessed, looking up to see a section of cloud drift across, obscuring the moon momentarily. By the time he cast his eyes back to the edifice of Ravenscroft, the pale glow had reappeared across the estate. It could have been his imagination, but he could have sworn that it took the light a lot longer to illuminate the main house, even then it only caught sections around the roof and chimneys, the windows remaining almost pitch black. The atmosphere the place radiated forced him to look away.

'Have you ever been in the house?' Page asked, breaking him from his thoughts.

'I've seen the hallway,' he replied, 'but only over Megan's shoulder one time that she went in there.'

'How come you didn't go inside?'

'Wasn't allowed to,' Sutton told him as he reached into his jacket again for his cigarettes.

'And you didn't want to? Weren't curious?' Page asked as Sutton lit up, declining the one offered to him.

'In some ways, I was at the time. But I have no wish now to put myself at any further risk.'

Page was puzzled by his comments, and in ways wanted to push him further regarding the house. He wanted to know exactly what he or others knew about his past, but the feeling that the security man was as much in the dark about what was going on remained. Why not tell him what you've seen? Tell him about how Megan can make things move with just her mind. How she makes you think. How she can read your mind simply by being close. Tell him about the seemingly dead Thomas Kenny and how he's able to somehow walk around with half of his skull missing. *Shut up!* Page screamed inwardly. *She told you not to believe everything that you see, so why are you torturing yourself?* Page wiped his hand across his face, desperate to clear his mind, welcoming the darkness that concealed the anxiety that must have been showing on his face.

'And what about Megan?' Page managed to ask, trying to lift the silence that had fallen between them. 'What do you make of her?'

Sutton drew slowly on his cigarette as though the direct question had made an impact on him. He held the smoke within for a moment before blowing out a slow stream which the moonlight caught before it began swirling away.

'I'd keep clear of her as much as you can,' he finally replied.

'Meaning?'

'Meaning she's dangerous. She's a prize asset of A. R. Solutions for sure, but I find her scary. I know that might sound daft in some ways, but it's as honest a view as I can give. Her powers, if you want to call them that, are unreal.'

Page remained quiet as Sutton looked back towards the house as though recalling an earlier memory.

'A couple of years ago, possibly longer since my mind seems unclear these days, I was part of a team sent to protect Megan at a meeting in Berlin. It was meant to be a straightforward in and out business meeting that both Rowlance and McAndrew attended, but at the last moment they included Megan in their plans. We did all the usual routine that I'm sure you have done before, but towards the end of the meeting, two of our team outside the small hotel was taken out by an unknown source. I and two others then entered the building to ensure Megan was safe, but what happened then really made no sense.'

'In what way?' Page asked as a chill crept through him.

'The rest of the team were bringing Rowlance and McAndrew through the lobby area, and I watched to see that they were safely back in the waiting car, but there was no trace of Megan. I was about to check on other team members' position when the entire building seemed to pulse.'

'To pulse?'

'Again, I know that sounds odd, but that's what it did. It was as though the whole place had expanded somehow. As though you had stepped into a dream or something. I didn't know what the hell was happening. Then all the power went off and I heard the sound of gunfire and screaming all over the place. My eyes and hearing went completely haywire, and the next thing I knew, the place had fallen silent and incredibly still until two members of our team entered the building, shining torches about the place. They stopped dead in their tracks beside me when Megan slowly appeared out of the gloom.'

'And she was unharmed?' Page asked.

'She appeared so,' Sutton confirmed, 'but she looked like something out of a flaming horror film. Her hair was all over the place and she looked as pale as a bleeding ghost. When one of the guys grabbed hold of her to pull her to safety, he pulled away quickly, as though she was on fire. The next moment, she was hunched over and throwing up all over the place.'

Despite the pale light around them, Page could see a haunted look in Sutton's eye, one that he was grateful to see leave when he turned to face him.

'What had happened?' Page asked.

'I have no idea,' Sutton told him as though he sat in a confession box. 'We got her out of the place with no further incident. What happened afterwards, we have no idea. For me, the packages were safe. As you know, we move on.'

'And you think Megan caused what happened?'

'She must have. There's other stuff I have heard Rowlance talk about concerning her that sounds madder than what I've just told you.'

Page considered for a moment telling him what he had learnt that day but held back, even when the other man fell quiet. Another patch of clouds drifted across the expanse of the night sky, adding a chill across where the two of them now stood, and began walking back to the other buildings of the estate.

Chapter 35

Even though she had fallen to sleep quickly, the sleep had not been deep enough to hold Megan. Now for the third, possibly fourth time, she woke, though this time her eyes remained closed. Shifting her position again, she chose to lay on her side but failed to find the comfort needed to relax. What she needed was to clear the thoughts and images that filled her mind and attempt to focus her mind on something else. After breathing in deeply, Megan exhaled and chose the image of a field covered in snow. In the distance she could see the outline of dark conifer trees, their thick branches weighed down by the fallen snow. She wanted no disturbance in the evenness of the blanket of snow, no footsteps or animal trails, nothing but a brilliant sheet of white.

When the image began to clear her mind, Megan returned the position of her body onto her back and brought her arms out from beneath the covers. Rubbing her eyes, the tension held within them was released enough for her to relax a little before she slowly opened them. The curtain was drawn back on the single window, allowing a pale light to cast across the room. It defined the edge of her bed as well as the sole wardrobe in the far corner. In the seat close to where she lay, she could make out the shapes of the clothes laid on the back where she had discarded them before climbing into bed. Above her, the square lightshade held onto shadow, as did the angled frame of a picture on the far wall. Megan thought how different the room looked in the pale light, the contrast and heightened depth of objects holding her stare for a moment.

Feeling increasingly warm, she pushed back the covers, eventually kicking them free from her legs. One of the legs on her pyjamas had ridden up over a knee, and she raised her other foot to drag it back down just as she sensed a change in the room. Holding her body still, she looked around the room but saw no immediate change. Only when she looked back up did she notice that the ceiling was darkening, the shade of the light fitting now becoming consumed in the increasing darkness.

An unseen force suddenly lifted her from her bed. While her body remained horizontal, the sudden speed of movement made her head snap back quick enough to jar her neck. She frantically scrambled her hands out either side of her, grasping only the air around her, fearing that at any minute she would fall back as quickly as she had risen. When she came to a halt, she found herself less than a foot from the ceiling, which by now had become a pitch black layer.

Fear gripped Megan. Not from her uncontrollable position, but because the darkness that now pulsed in front of her face was familiar to her. She had not experienced it this way and certainly not outside of the main house of Ravenscroft. A deep chill now ran through her suspended body, emphasised by the beads of sweat that formed on her forehead. Her hair, which had until then hung down below her, now collected itself together as though an invisible hand was gathering it. She let out a cry as her hair was yanked upwards, the ends lost now within the blackness. Still unable to understand what was happening, Megan only responded to the voice that she had heard when her hair was pulled again. She winced in pain as she felt some tear away from her scalp.

'I did what you asked!' she finally managed to say as she attempted in vain to move her now paralysed arms.

Megan's words did little to release the pain she felt in her head as her body moved closer to the blackness until it hung like a perfectly flat cloud, inches from her face.

'I brought him,' she continued, her voice showing traces of the fear that was rising within her. Again the voice spoke to her, the words accusing and judging, but Megan again pleaded that she had done all that she had been asked. When her hair was released, she thought that her words had been accepted, but now what appeared to be an invisible hand grabbed her face.

Instead of questioning her again, she heard laughter, even though the grip upon her face remained tight. In an instant, the hold was released, only for an unseen force to be directed at her stomach, the effect so great that she was sent crashing back to her bed, her mattress struggling to cushion her fall. With her arms mobile again, Megan curled herself up into a ball, clutching at the pain in her stomach, tears forming quickly in her eyes as she begged the pain to subside.

'I did everything you asked,' she sobbed into her pillow, 'everything.'

Above her, the blackness had faded and the pale light once more spread around the light shade that swayed slightly for a few seconds, the movement unseen by the huddled, sobbing figure below.

Chapter 36

The single malt whisky burnt the edges of his throat as he slowly drained the last of the measure. Picking up the bottle again, Page Darrow contemplated pouring another, which would have been his fourth, as thoughts and images refused to let go, still bombarding his mind.

The small alarm clock on his bedside cabinet showed him it had now just passed midnight, and though his body was showing all the usual signs of needing rest, sleep would still not find him. He had contemplated taking a shower, which he thought might do him better than drinking himself into oblivion, but the pure effort of removing his clothes now felt like too much effort. More than once in the past he had used drink for comfort. For the rapid blurring of events it could bring, to help him cope.

In the short time he had spent at Ravenscroft, the sense of professionalism he applied to his work had been threatened, somehow making him drop guards which he had put into place to protect not only his body but also his mind.

Never before had Page believed there to be any truth in the existence of ghosts or anything supernatural, always assuming that those who pursued the facts had an ulterior motive behind their beliefs, usually money. But had he now actually witnessed a ghost? The figure of Thomas Kenny had seemed as real as any other person to him, even given his dishevelled appearance. The next drink that Page poured only brought back the image of the horrific wound the man had suffered, and draining the glass contents in one gulp failed to remove it. There was the possibility that what he had witnessed could have just been a hallucination brought on by god knows what, but the more Page tried to dismiss each theory that came to him, the more each seemed real. Cradling his head, he screwed his eyes up tight and shook his head, hoping to rid his mind of events. By the time he stopped, the dull ache of an oncoming headache had set in across his temple.

Don't believe everything that you see, he again heard in his mind, the image of Megan now clear even when he opened his eyes fully. *So what do you believe then?* he thought as he put down another empty glass. *And do I believe what I'm told to believe?* He had felt more than fear spreading within him when he listened to what Alex Sutton had recounted. Page still couldn't comprehend what Anthony Rowlance had told him regarding his place of birth. The details that he thought he knew of his birth were sketchy at best, but they were ones that he now hoped to cling to. Taken into care at an early age, Page had only ever known the various homes that he had been placed in, ones which he had finally grown up within, the upheaval and chaos each new place brought with it soon becoming an accepted norm. Page lay back on his bed and drew an arm across his face, hoping the shade from the overhead light would help ease his now full-blown headache, and tried to recall his earliest memory. Surely it was impossible for anyone to remember back any earlier than four, maybe three years old, so how could he prove otherwise?

A slight noise broke him from his thoughts, and despite the protests from his body, he rose with surprising speed and soon found himself listening at the doorway of his room. The sound that he thought he had heard came again, and his initial instinct seemed to be confirmed. Whoever had stepped close to his bedroom door now remained still. In his mind, he imagined that whoever was on the other side of the door had their ear pressed to the door, hoping possibly to hear sounds of movement. The glow from the overhead light no doubt showed around the base of the door, and Page more than once contemplated pulling the door open suddenly to reveal whoever was there. The handgun that still lay on the bedside cabinet made him change his mind. When he strained his hearing again, he heard the soft creak of footsteps moving away. Page closed his eyes and exhaled, the effort helping to bring a touch of tiredness to him. Flicking off the room light, he remained beside the door for several minutes until he felt sure the Coach House was again quiet. When he finally made it into bed, he lay awake for a while before his headache began to ease and sleep edged nearer.

Charlotte Wareham punched her pillow and tried in vain to make it more comfortable. She had lain awake now for nearly an hour, the remnants of her dream remaining.

In her dream she had found a slight breeze gently stirring the curtains of her bedroom within her home, though it was across the skin that she had felt it most. There was no concept of what time of day her dream held, the light around her a mixture of moonlight and twilight. Her body was hot, bathed in a sheen of perspiration that the breeze from the open window caught. Around her temples, her hair stuck to her skin. A bead of sweat ran down her top lip, the sensation pleasing, adding to her relaxed state. When she raised her head, her long hair was clutched by the hands of the body that moved against her own. As a warm mouth silenced her gasp, Charlotte responded positively, using her own hands to bring the pleasure she craved. For what seemed like hours they had laid entwined, at times their bodies almost becoming one as the love they made had bonded them deeper than anything Charlotte could ever have imagined. As the hands that had understood the needs of her now held her face, Charlotte turned her head slightly to kiss the fingers close to her mouth gently. When she had looked into the eyes of Page Darrow she smiled, appreciating his touch and understanding when she pulled him close to her again.

Charlotte sat up in bed and reached across in the darkness for her glass of water, noticing how quickly her fingers trembled against the rim before she finally managed to find it. Draining what remained, Charlotte hoped the water could wash away the guilt of her dreams, but her mind kept drifting to Page. She felt refreshed from their walk together and considered it was the fresh air that was keeping her awake at night. Maybe it was something else though. It had been some time since she had talked so openly to another person. There was a great depth to Page and a strength deep within him which was not evident at first. When they had strolled along the pathway, she had felt so comfortable that she had almost inadvertently reached for his hand.

She rested her head on her pillow, and again punched it, though this time much softer, still trying to find some comfort in it. Annoyed at her thoughts, she focused on her steady breathing. She knew deep down that it was Greg, her husband, the one who had given his commitment to her, that she should have dreamt about.

It had taken most of the afternoon and evening before Megan calmed down. Several times Charlotte had asked her to stop swearing, but the challenge to her hardly seemed to help. Refusing to talk any further, she had sulked for another hour before asking to go inside the cleansing tank. Her father was less than happy with Megan's behaviour and refusal to help with the project, even taking out his frustration and anger by shouting at his daughter. Over dinner earlier on, she had seen a strange sort of bond show between Megan and Page. Her tendency to show off had unsettled many who had come into contact with her, yet even though Page had himself been subjected to her moods and erratic behaviour, he had shown a newfound patience with her, one Charlotte felt that Megan had both appreciated and wanted. All this after he had been endured god knows what in that awful house. In the stillness and quiet, Charlotte felt more emotionally tired than anything, and hoped that some form of sleep would soon find her.

Chapter 37

Charles McAndrew was grateful to leave the spray of the M6 motorway behind him. Even the windscreen wipers seemed appreciative, giving only a single squeak as he switched them from fast mode to normal. The traffic had been heavy for most of his journey, the endless run of lorries weaving in and out of the two lanes available to them, causing enough spray to make him stick to the inside lane for the last few miles of motorway. As he reached the end of the slip road, he headed north-easterly and thought back to the events of that morning.

The time away from the gloom of the Ravenscroft Estate had done little to lighten his mood and, if anything, his visit to the Kentmere Rest Home had depressed him further.

Of course, the entrance hall, with its vivid display of plants, was always welcoming, as was the staff who never failed to greet him and other visitors with care and politeness, but they couldn't mask the emotion that awaited him in Room 23. As ever on his visits, Charles had walked with a heavy heart along the pastel coloured corridor, past a display board showing forthcoming events all the residents could soon enjoy. Day trips to local events, including a trip to the theatre, coach trips to National Trust properties, even the forthcoming visit of a guide dog called Tilly was advertised. They may as well be offering two tickets to the moon with a champagne reception for all he cared as he reached the last room on the right.

The new management, in their odd wisdom, had decided recently to remove the room numbers on each of the flats in a bid to give the home a more friendly appearance. But to Charles, no matter how they changed things and what colours or decoration they used, it would always be Room 23. He paused at the doorway before knocking slightly, running a finger over the brass plate that now graced the door, showing the name Jean McAndrew.

As normal, he found Jean seated, looking blankly out of the window. In the background, a CD player played what sounded like Dean Martin. Despite the pale light in the room, it still managed to highlight the cream blouse his wife wore, the matching slippers unworn by her feet, while her black skirt looked recently ironed. There wasn't even the slightest flicker of acknowledgement on Jean's face to welcome his arrival, and the tender kiss Charles left on her forehead went unreturned. There were the odd good days when he visited, days when her mind remembered the strangest of things that had happened between them. A film they saw years back, a holiday, the make of car she had driven, or more bizarrely, a restaurant where she somehow recalled everything that they had eaten. But others, like the one today was obviously going to be, was heart-wrenching. He'd sit and talk to her, maybe read a section of poetry that she had liked, listen to the music with her, or just hold her hand, recalling brighter days. Dean Martin was soon replaced by Frank Sinatra who sang of love during autumn in New York. Charles sat closer to Jean as the music continued, all care and worries dismissed while he gently sang along to the tune. He failed to notice when the music came to an end, any more than he saw how the shadows began to fill the room as the time passed.

Charles smiled politely at a young nurse who entered the room, switching on a table lamp before explaining that she had come to give his wife her latest medication. The caring touch and ways that the nurse gave his wife brought a lump to his throat which he did well to control.

One of the worst things that often happened on his visits was the language that Jean occasionally came out with. Quite where she had learnt such phrases he had no idea. Maybe from the television they had in the main lounge, possibly from other residents, but the vulgar words were so alien to the woman who had graced so much of his life. Another change in her he found so heart-breaking.

He stayed a further hour before the emotion became too much for him. As he stood to leave, he apologised for the time in between his visits, explaining the hectic schedule of his work, his words sounding as though they were said only to please himself and mask his guilt. He kissed and squeezed her motionless hand, and saw a member of staff appear at the door who kindly stepped back to allow him a last moment of privacy.

'I'll see you soon, Jean, I promise,' he told her gently, 'and who knows, by then things may just be different. I'm led to believe we are closer now. I know you won't understand just yet, but if what I hear is true and we are soon able to harness what we have found, I know we will then be able to use it to our advantage.'

Outside, the sound of rain falling heavier caught the panes of the window, making McAndrew look up as he turned to leave.

'And then, love, everything will change. Everything,' he added as he let the member of staff in to tend to his beloved wife.

Chapter 38

The house held a stronger sense of damp on the third visit. It was more evident on the upper floor in the two bedrooms closest to each of the bathrooms, but there was a part of the lower corridor where the air felt as though it had not been disturbed for a considerable length of time. Unlike the previous visits, Megan had appeared uneasy the moment she stepped inside Ravenscroft, choosing this time to stay much closer to Page, who was becoming increasingly concerned with her unusual behaviour.

For the fourth time now, Megan stopped and listened. Each time Page heard nothing. Before long she was moving on again, but each direction which she thought they should take seemed to contradict her earlier choice, and she appeared to be entirely disregarding the numbering system that she had first insisted on taking him by. Although he had asked her why they were checking the house out in a seemingly haphazard manner, Megan failed to answer his question. They were unable to come across Thomas Kenny or any signs or trace of any visitors to Ravenscroft. Eventually, they found themselves back in the kitchen where the air tasted so stale that Page opened all of the doorways in an attempt to clear the air. Leaning against the edge of the table, Megan looked as though she was waiting for something to happen.

'Okay, give us a clue,' Page asked her as he folded his arms and leant back against the table himself. 'Are you expecting a change to happen?'

It was late morning now and Megan had barely spoken a word since they entered the house. Page was getting used to her periods of silence, as well as her moods, but somehow felt that what he was witnessing here was something entirely different. Since a shared breakfast with him and Charlotte, Megan had spent the next two hours with Anthony Rowlance and Charles McAndrew, making Page believe that Megan's silence was an overspill from what had passed between them.

Megan moved away from him, standing close to the table where she rested a hand on the back of one of the chairs. For a moment she stroked the wood with her thin fingers before he noticed her grip tighten. For the first time in almost an hour, her face began to show concern. Running a hand through her hair, she turned quickly and moved towards the doorway which led to the hallway.

'Megan?' Page said as she backed away from the door which she had opened, chewing on one of her fingernails. When she looked across at him, he more or less knew what she was about to say.

'It's already changed,' she told him, motioning for him to come with her. 'I don't know how I didn't feel it.'

When she disappeared out of sight, Page moved quickly, fearing that he would lose her by the time he entered the hallway. Instead, he found her standing close to the bottom of the stairway where she ran her hands over her face as though she was wiping a memory away. Around him, Page saw no change in the surroundings. There was no difference in his hearing or any pressure drop that he could feel or sense like before, nothing to give any reason for the way Megan was acting. He asked whether they should take note of what markings were around them on the various doors.

'No!' she snapped at him, 'this is different. It's much stronger than before. Besides, most of the symbols don't really mean anything. They're all a load of crap.'

'What are you talking about?' he asked as he reached out to her in an attempt to make her remain still. His action made Megan back away, almost as though Page himself was the source of threat.

'You said the symbols and numbers were important, you said...'

'I said a lot,' she snapped at him. 'Most was a load of crap to mislead them.'

Before she could finish her explanation, Megan was suddenly lifted off the floor by an unseen force. Her feet dangled below her as though someone had just pulled her up by the collar of her coat and hung her on a coat hook. Her long hair splayed out around her face, hiding her features for a moment before she was thrust back right across the hallway, her body rising further until her feet were several feet off the ground. She hit the wall behind her hard, the impact causing pieces of plaster to break away, the tiny disturbed flakes falling silently around her. When Megan suddenly fell back to the ground, Page heard her gasp loudly as the air was literally forced from her. The sound of her breath was distinctive, the only sign of any change he had personally noticed. When he attempted to move towards her, to try and pull her away from whatever force had held her, he thought he sensed movement behind him. Reaching into his jacket pocket, he quickly freed the Glock 36 from the restraints of its holster and turned to find everything behind him had now changed.

There was no trace of the kitchen doorway, no hint even of the hallway or staircase that they had stood in moments before. All he faced was a corridor twice the width of the original one. There appeared to be no doorways or any form of escape, and the only light cast was coming from much smaller arched windows too high up for him to attempt to see through. With the handgun still aimed in front of him, Page spun round, his eyes frantically searching but could find no trace of Megan. All that faced him in either direction was a continuation of the shadow-filled corridors.

Chapter 39

For the third time in as many minutes, the crackling sound forced Charlotte to raise her voice.

'I said, I've been looking at the pictures from Jill's wedding!'

Pressing her mobile phone hard against her ear, she was forced to pull it away again as another short burst of static sounded, making her think the line had gone down. When Greg Wareham at last spoke, she felt her spirits lift again.

'I hope they got one of you in that dress, and none of me dancing,' she heard him say, making her laugh gently.

'The dress looks okay; even I admit that there are a couple of bad ones of you making your moves,' Charlotte replied, trying her best to imagine her husband smiling back at her.

The cost of her best friend's wedding still amazed Charlotte. The 16th-century castle had recently been converted into a prestigious hotel and had been Jill's immediate choice. The two nights that she and Greg stayed, along with eight other close friends, had all been paid for by Jill's parents. Those days and nights had been the last time that she and Greg had spent any length of time together.

They spoke for another fifteen minutes about a range of subjects, over which Greg's initial annoyance with her for disturbing him at work gradually dissipated. Each time Greg replied or commented on something, it only made Charlotte want to talk further. Eventually, she broached the subject of when he would be returning home.

'I really can't say,' he told her. 'You know how busy we are.' Another crackle made Charlotte pull her ear away from the phone once more before she heard him say, 'Besides, we've had problems here.'

You've got a problem here, she thought to herself as she closed her eyes and bit gently on her bottom lip.

'I miss you,' she told him, her voice holding an edge. 'I need to be with you,' she added before the line deteriorated further. What sounded like a farewell from him was just about heard before the line finally went dead.

'Bye,' Charlotte softly said as she pressed the stop button on her phone. Pushing a section of her hair back behind one of her ears, she turned when she sensed movement behind her and saw her father standing in the doorway.

'You okay?' he asked as he entered, offering one of two hot drinks he held. 'I thought I heard raised voices.'

'Bad line,' she told him, holding up her phone for a moment as if for an explanation of her words before slipping it into the pocket of her jeans. When she took the drink from him, Anthony Rowlance could see signs of strain showing on his daughter's face.

'You could have used the satellite phone that Charles brought with him. The reception is much stronger,' he suggested as they took their drinks and sat down on the settee in the sitting room. The grey conditions outside made the late afternoon light pour throughout the Coach House, forcing Rowlance to stand and switch on one of the table lamps close to them.

'When's Greg coming home?' his daughter asked, ignoring his suggestion.

'You know he's busy,' he told her. 'It's important work he is on.'

'More important than your daughter?'

'That's hardly fair,' Rowlance replied before taking a mouthful of his drink.

'Don't lecture me on what's fair!' Charlotte retorted, immediately standing and walking over to the window. She pulled back the blind on the window and looked out over the rear garden. Most of the garden that ran the length of the outbuildings was overgrown, with some of the branches from the nearby trees hanging close to the side of the window. Banks of grey clouds skirted across the part of sky visible, sending sheets of rain across the Ravenscroft estate. The dull thud of raindrops hitting the windowsill did little to lift her mood. Despite the poor weather outside, male and female blackbirds were busy searching the garden for traces of food, the teamwork between the couple not lost on Charlotte as she watched them.

'I'll see what I can do about getting you to see him,' Anthony Rowlance told her as he appeared behind her, resting a hand on her shoulder.

'Why's Page here?' Charlotte asked, ignoring his comment, her arms folded against herself as she continued to watch the rainfall. The sudden change of subject must have taken him by surprise as he failed to answer immediately.

'You know why he's here,' he eventually reminded her. 'He's here to protect Megan. You also know how important this work is.'

'Do I?' she asked, turning to face him. 'You tell me nothing. All I continually hear now is how important everything is to you. You bring people here that you claim are vital to your bloody project, and after a few days they've gone and everything changes. It's as though nothing here makes sense. I see nothing apart from how volatile and moody Megan is gradually becoming the longer she stays here.'

'Megan is always unpredictable,' he replied, 'in a way very much like your mother was.'

'Don't you dare bring Mum into this!' Charlotte snapped.

Anthony Rowlance stepped aside as she brushed past him, regretting his comment immediately as he noticed his daughter's breathing coming hard while snatching the book she had been reading before she decided to phone Greg. He could understand her frustration, especially when it came to her husband and the time spent apart, but when it came to Megan, there was little he felt confident enough about to tell her. As she reached the doorway, he considered taking back the comment about her mother, but instead spoke Charlotte's name, making her turn to face him.

'You know I loved your mother more than anything,' he told her.

'I know that,' Charlotte replied. 'I've never doubted that. It's just…'

'Just what?' her father asked, halting her words.

Charlotte shrugged her shoulders and held back initially on the words that she wanted to say. When she attempted to speak again, the aching loss of her mother rose again, threatening to bring the emotion to the surface. Breathing in slowly helped to settle her and she asked again the reason for Page being here.

'Darrow is here for Megan and Megan only. You would do well to remember that,' Rowlance told her before closing his eyes and shaking his head as he watched his daughter leave, slamming the door behind her.

Chapter 40

Megan's breathing came so hard that she feared she would not be able to control it. There was an aching in the small of her back that rivalled the one that she now felt across her right shoulder. Just the simple act of attempting to stand caused further pain, the effort combined with her breathing soon becoming too much for her. Placing her hands on the floor, she lowered her head, rocking it slowly until the air gradually found a way inside her. After what could have been either seconds or hours, she ended up gingerly leaning back against the wall as she tried to get her bearings. She found herself alone in a dimly lit room, the size of which she was unable to ascertain. A window stood central on the far wall though drawn, floor length curtains prevented much light entering the room. When she felt the hard surface below her, her hands ran across what appeared to be tile. The surface felt cold to her touch. A noise caught her attention, making her force herself to attempt to stand. Trying to ignore the discomfort she felt, she was forced to press herself against the wall for support, as well as an attempt at concealment. The noise, when it came again, was faint and sounded like the scraping of metal against the tile floor. Megan closed her eyes and tried to use her mind to search the room. Nothing came to her. No matter how hard she tried, she found nothing but a blankness in her mind that she failed to understand. When the noise came again, it was precise and more defined. It sounded like something being dragged across the floor.

A slight gap began to appear in the curtains, as though unseen hands were slowly pulling them backwards, allowing a shaft of light to spread slowly across the room. The improving light was enough for Megan to see that something was now visible on the wall to her side. To her surprise she found that even the walls themselves were tiled, the shape and colour matching the floor covering. The tiles were white and would have gleamed brightly had the surface not been tainted by red markings dotted around them at various points. Turning to face the wall, Megan now looked carefully at the marking closest to her and saw that it was a red handprint made of what she feared was blood. The curtains continued to open, forcing the shadows to retreat further, revealing more and more of the wall space. Wherever Megan now looked, she saw bloodied handprints of various sizes filling the walls, the impression on many so great that large drips now formed, running down the tiles, merging many of the handprints.

When the figure stepped into the shaft of light cast across the room, Megan swallowed to prevent the scream from escaping her. She shook her head frantically, disbelieving in her wildest dreams what now stood before her. By the time she discovered what had caused the dragging noise that she had first heard, the scream quickly escaped her.

Chapter 41

Page was unsure in which direction to move. It was impossible to make out which was the front of the property. For some reason, he headed to his right, keeping the windows alongside him. As his eyes became more and more accustomed to the changing light, he noticed that the position of the windows began to edge lower down. No explanation could be given as to why they had previously been so high. The size of windows remained the same though, and the light offered, though weak, soon confirmed Page's thought that he was against an outer wall. So discoloured were the windows that he failed to see any defining feature when he attempted to peer through them. Another change was that each of the windows was now set further back in the wall, and most appeared to now have window seats below them. Page felt compelled to continue to follow the direction he had chosen, even though his destination remained unknown.

Each step he took filled him with caution, his movements soon disturbing a layer of dust upon the lengths of carpet that now lined the corridor. He became aware of the dust motes slowly rising, which were now beginning to spiral around in the air where he stepped, highlighted in what little of the fading sunlight remained. Each step caused the shafts of lights to begin to diminish gradually. Keen not to lose what daylight remained, Page moved on with more urgency, and soon neared a corner which only served to raise further tension within him. Finally, he raised his handgun again, stuck for a moment between remaining close to the wall which he now flanked, and whether to move to the inner wall which would enable him to be better concealed from whatever lay ahead.

In his mind, he imagined a sudden dead end with no doorway and himself trapped with no means of escape. Glancing behind him, he found the corridor behind him remained clear though much gloomier now that the sunlight was lost. Where the hell was Megan? And how come she had not found him, regardless of how the damned place kept changing? He considered calling out her name but had an uneasy feeling that such action risked giving away his actual position.

Moving toward the corner once more, Page remained on the outer wall, pressing his back against the wall, attempting to control his breathing. The realism of his surroundings was all the more disturbing with the contact of his hand against a wall. He had hoped that everything around was merely part of his imagination and that he could glide straight through the wall and find himself back in the actual house. With the handgun firmly held, he moved swiftly down onto one knee at the same time the corridor opened out before him, hoping to make his frame a smaller target should anyone suddenly step out of the shadows. Page prepared to fire, only to breathe out deeply when he found no one challenging him. He saw no reason or explanation for the corner in the corridor which now continued much further than he could ever have imagined. About fifty feet ahead of him another corridor crossed at a point to where an unknown light source lit a large section of the crossway. Here he presumed that a skylight or possibly a chandelier type light fitting was the cause of this, which was unseen from his position. Either way, when he looked back down he found that a figure stood occupying the area directly beneath the light source.

The fact that the hooded figure stood with its back to him caused him more concern. Although the majority was bathed in light, there were areas around the folds of the brown cloth hood where the shading seemed unnaturally dark. As Page took a hesitant step forward, he noticed the shoulders of the figure had begun shaking, and the sound of gentle sobbing was now heard. Such was the grief and sorrow that filled each sob that it strained Page's already strained nerves. Too many times in the past he had listened to the sound of tears and despair used as part of the deception that he now remained vigilant as he moved within twenty feet of the figure. When the sobbing stopped, he noticed that the shoulders became less slumped, and fearing that the person may be armed, Page lowered his body back onto one knee again, his upper body pressed once more against the wall beside him.

'Help me,' the figure spoke, the voice frail yet easily heard in the stillness of the corridor. Slowly the figure began pushing back the hood it wore, revealing long black hair, the ends of which appeared to merge into the shadows of the cloak.

'Save me,' the voice now almost begged as the light in the crossway began to fade. As the figure started to turn, Page kept his aim fixed ahead of him, despite the fact that he could now see no weapon as thin, almost skeletal hands had removed the concealment of the hood. Though strands of hair masked sections of the figure's face, the look of anguish could still be seen across the face of Emma Darrow which seemed to match the horror of the punctured and scarred arms that she held out before her.

Chapter 42

Anthony Rowlance had hoped that the fresh air would help him clear his mind. The day was noticeably cooler now, making him appreciate the Gortex raincoat he wore. The slate grey cloud remained heavy, with no signs of breaking or thinning, even though the rain had now cleared. The walk over to the cottage, which he and Charles McAndrew were sharing, had seemed quite an effort, which had surprised him given that he prided himself on his fitness.

On entering the cottage, he welcomed the warmth which the building had retained, where remnants of the previous night's open fire still held. As he stirred the pile of ashes with a poker from the side of the fireplace, a stream of white smoke rose. The heat from the glowing edges of the remaining pieces of logs gave an extra touch of warmth that Rowlance savoured.

There was only one main room in the cottage, the rear of which served as a dining area with a small kitchen, an equally small bathroom, and two bedrooms finished off the single storey building. The furniture in the sitting area, a double settee with two matching chairs, was expensive as were the other pieces of occasional furniture, all adding an extra touch of comfort brought to their temporary home.

After pushing away the book that Charles McAndrew had been reading the previous evening further from the edge of the low cupboard to prevent it being knocked off, he headed into his bedroom. As ever, he kept the room tidy, with only the lighter jacket he used visible, placed upon a chair beside the single bed. For a good size room, the single window offered more than enough light for him to see well as he reached for one of two briefcases set against the room's only wardrobe. Sitting on the edge of the bed, Anthony Rowlance lifted the selected one onto the bed and lined up the correct codes on the security locks. Once found, he flicked the catches back and opened the case. Inside, he took out the sensitive documents he required, quickly checked the contents and closed the case, restoring the changed lock combination again. The two removed files only contained a dozen or so papers, and he ran his hands over them as he glanced across at the silver-framed photograph beside his bed.

The outline of the trees in Central Park showed the first signs of autumn, a touch of beauty which Rowlance had never fully appreciated at the time. He recalled questioning his wife's request to do some Christmas shopping, saying that early autumn was far too early. A smile broke across his face when he reminisced about Hannah's suggestion that they could combine the trip to New York with her mid-October birthday, saving him money in the process. During the ten-day break, he had even let work issues drift from his mind, enjoying returning to favourite places that the two of them had within the sprawling city. Although Hannah had loved the matching jewellery set he had bought her for her birthday, he had insisted on holding back her extra gift until after they had finished their dinner.

Anthony Rowlance reached across and picked up the photograph frame, finding the need to swallow to control the emotion rising inside him. There had been only two other couples in the restaurant by the time Hannah received her final gift, the staff allowing the last customers time to enjoy their private moments. The extra lines that her curious expression had etched around her eyes only added to her beauty, he had thought, the soft candlelight helping to create the perfect atmosphere. Placing the frame back down, Anthony could still hear the scream of excitement that Hannah had let out, and recalled the grasp of her hand when he told her that Greg Wareham had come to him to request permission to ask for his blessing to marry their daughter. Hannah had adored Greg since the first time Charlotte had brought him to their family home, and had always hoped that their lengthy relationship was leading somewhere. The happiness which his wife had felt over the next few months had not seemed that special to Rowlance at the time, but now they were as precious as anything he could recall.

A simple stumble the following February had seemed nothing at the time, but he now knew that it was the first sign of the troubles ahead for them. Dismissing herself as being clumsy, even the third time, it was only when Hannah blacked out at a charity fundraising event that Anthony suspected something was wrong. The following tests and scans failed to stay in his mind, as did other incidents, but the day the two of them sat opposite the neurosurgeon and one of his nurses who had remained to help break the news did. The memory remained as clear as though it had happened yesterday.

The scent of recently polished wood still held around the desk that Hannah's test results lay on. One of the three framed pictures on the wall behind the sombre faced man opposite them had been slightly askew, making Anthony want to interrupt his tenderly chosen words so he could straighten the frame, as if to make it help to stabilise the collapsing world around him. He recalled the exact clothes he had worn that day, the aftershave chosen that morning, the texture of the fabric upon the arm of the chair that his hand had brushed against as he had reached for Hannah's hand. But many, if not most of the surgeon's words had made no sense, just one of them hanging in the air, one with as much hurt and anguish that neither he nor Hannah could take in. Inoperable.

The memory stayed with Rowlance as he left the bedroom, closing the door firmly behind him. Tucking the files under his arm, he stood beside one of the chairs facing the fireplace and closed his eyes, stretching out a hand to steady himself against the back of the chair.

With Charlotte's wedding only two months away, Hannah had insisted on not telling their daughter the extent of her illness. Her attacks were mostly hidden, and when she came down with a heavy cold during the March of that year, it helped to give a reason for her poor health during the wedding preparations.

Of all places, Charlotte and Greg chose New York for their honeymoon, making them both absent when Hannah had one of her most severe attacks. How Rowlance had hated the brain tumour as though it had been an actual person. By the time his wife slipped away one evening into a permanent state of peace, he and Charlotte embraced at her bedside as though to gain support from each other, only a month after they had all seemed so happy.

With the warmth of the fire now gone, the cottage felt chilly as Anthony brought himself back to the here and now. He pulled the collar up on his coat as he left, closing the door firmly behind him before locking it. Work had been his solace, his place of escape, and he knew no reason to change that now. As he made his way back along the pathway to the main concentration of buildings, he hoped that work could now be the answer for his thoughts and possibly his prayers. An increasing breeze caught the side of his face. As it did, the tops of the trees close to the approaching buildings caused the trees to sway slightly as though touched by the chilled air. Several crows circled high above them, each one calling out loudly at the figure below who clutched the files he held tightly as he increased his pace.

Chapter 43

Megan had only briefly glimpsed Henry Talbot once before, but that glimpse alone had been enough for her. Then she had been in the main hallway and saw him pass at the top of the stairs. A simple glance from him had caused unease and fear to sweep over her, making her retreat as quickly as she could for the doorway. Now, with the grinning figure of Henry Talbot standing less than ten feet in front of her, her initial thoughts and fears about him were soon confirmed.

Henry was overweight, though in an odd and rather strange way he carried the weight well. There was no overhang around the trousers he wore and no misshaped areas in his legs or stomach, just a fullness of his frame which made Henry appear almost overbearing. The thin, wired glasses he wore were perched on a small, upturned nose, his closely cropped hair and thick neck making his head seem far too round for his body somehow. Thin lips pulled back further to produce a smile that at first offered warmth, but soon held something which Megan believed to be a display of the cruelty hidden within him. While Thomas Kenny had seemed in horror at his surroundings, Henry appeared to be revelling in them. His watery eyes scrutinised Megan, one of them occasionally twitching as he attempted to hold his smile. There were several sweat stains under each of his arms that gave an impression of heat, but the source was unfelt by Megan. Her mind was drawn to what Henry held in one of his hands.

Henry Talbot clutched the lifeless body of a young girl no more than eight or nine by her hair. The yellow coloured dress she wore was heavily bloodstained, some of it looking quite fresh. Most of the blood appeared to be coming from the wound across her lower body where a long spike of metal still hung, the length long enough to reach the ground. As Henry now stood still, the metal spike no longer made the chilling scrapping sound across the floor. Megan felt fear engulfing her, not just from Henry, but from the doll-like girl whose golden hair thankfully covered whatever horror her eyes must have witnessed.

'You're not real…' Megan managed to blubber as her mouth struggled to form the words, 'none of this is real.'

'You think not?' Henry asked in a surprisingly soft voice before he released his grasp on the young girl's hair. The small figure fell clumsily to the ground while Megan's legs scrambled beneath her as she tried in vain to back away from him.

'Does this feel real, my dear?' Henry shouted, all softness having left his booming voice. Almost deafened within the confines of the room, Megan attempted to shield her ears as Henry grasped at her hair. Tears formed in her eyes as he screamed words at her again, pulling her hair harder. Spittle from his accusing words mixed with tears that etched down her cheeks.

'I've been alone for a quite a while now,' he told her, his voice soft again, but far from reassuring. 'I wasn't allowed to get close to the others, so it's nice to have some company finally.'

A long knife now appeared from Henry's other hand, which he slowly moved close to Megan's face. The tensing of her body pleased him. After tracing it down one her arms, he used the tip to cut through one of the cloth bracelets on Megan's wrist.

Again, he yanked Megan hard by her hair, but this time she managed to strike out at him, catching the side of Henry's face. The surprise movement was enough for him to lose his grip on the knife, which clattered noisily against the tiled floor. Even though the connection was brief, the touch against his cheek felt cold and clammy, repulsing her; the contact was also enough for him to let go of her hair suddenly.

'Bitch!' Henry screamed as Megan broke free, attempting to move away from him quickly. She closed her eyes tightly and tried to concentrate on the wall ahead of her as she moved forward. Close behind she heard the scraping noise of the metal spike and knew that Henry had retrieved it. The stench of his sweat now hung heavily in the cold air around her, and she could feel his breath on the back of her neck and hair as she tried desperately to concentrate on something, anything to free her mind from the nightmare around her as she fought to escape with her mind.

As Megan felt fingers entwining her hair once more, the light began flashing before her, jolting her senses even though her eyes remained closed. She continued to inch forward, how she didn't know, all the time blinded by light. The far end of the room failed to come to her, even though she moved forward much quicker than before. Her legs were weakening under her, each step feeling as though she was moving in slow motion. Her flaying hands were becoming so heavy that she felt as though she was sinking into deep water. When she tried to scream, Megan felt herself falling, and soon the pure white light was gone and only the darkness she fell into seemed to exist.

Chapter 44

Page closed his eyes as he felt tears begin to fill them. He raised his right hand which still held the weapon, and banged his wrist against his forehead, attempting to wake himself from the surrounding nightmare. When he opened them, the figure of Emma still stood before him, but now her features had changed and she reminded him of the picture he had concealed in his wallet. She looked puzzled, a slight frown the only blemish on her flawless face. Her expression now seemed as though she appeared not to understand what was happening. When Emma offered a smile to reassure her father, its warmth overwhelmed Page, making him lower the weapon and move towards her. Biting down on his bottom lip, the pressure helped him confirm that he was indeed awake and that this wasn't some mad dream that he was experiencing.

'I've been so lost without you,' Emma told him, her words as gentle as falling snow, reminding him of days when they were both younger and life made more sense. When her smile began fading, it became replaced by a look of need that implored him to reassure her by being held.

'How can I tell that it's you?' Page asked, his words sounding weak to himself as he walked within several feet of her.

'What do you mean?' Emma asked incredulously. 'Can you not tell it's me?' Her eyes still asked the question as she moved forward, embracing him before he could begin to answer. Page felt as though his heart was going to explode. Every scar ever etched on his mind and body seemed to disappear in an instant as his daughter clutched him tightly. With the side of her head pressed against his chest, Page could smell the clean scent of her hair, the perfume whose name he could never pronounce: the one that he was always telling her to not wear too much of.

Page recalled a school trip she had taken to Europe where he and Jayne had met her at the airport and both laughed out loud as they saw her smiling face come bounding towards them. An evening in a restaurant came to his mind, where to onlookers they would have appeared like any young family. It was one of the first times that Emma wore an evening dress and makeup, a first glimpse of the woman she would never become. All these thoughts appeared in what could only have been seconds, yet to Page, the time could not be told. Without seeming to move, Emma gently stepped onto Page's feet and lifted herself up slightly, a personal thing that she did with him when she was younger to show him how much she was growing. Page held onto her so tightly that he feared she would suffocate against his chest. How long they stood there, he had no idea, as all time seemed lost. He cared nothing now for his surroundings and the situation he was in; all that mattered now was that Emma was here.

When he looked over her shoulder, the corridor remained the same with the poor light still struggling to hold back the shadows. Above him, the source of light that had first illuminated his daughter could now be seen. Strands of cobwebs attempted to mask the illumination from a decorative chandelier that continued to shine down as Emma began to break away from him. Still holding onto one of her father's hands, Page realised that her eyes were being drawn further down the corridor as though she had been distracted by something. He felt her move close against him when the figure of a woman appeared.

There were no doorways close to where the figure now stood, making Page wonder where she could have possibly come from. Dressed in what looked like a black shawl, the woman was perhaps younger than she first appeared. She was barely over five foot in height, her frame slight, unkempt, brown hair had been unevenly pulled back off her shoulders, revealing a worn face which showed clear evidence of the hard life that she lived or had lived. The little light that cast upon her showed deep lines which helped to age her face.

'You shouldn't have come here,' the woman said as she began wringing her hands together while shaking her head slowly, 'you really shouldn't have come.'

When the woman began to turn away, Page called out, fearing something that his mind tried to tell him had nothing to do with the retreating woman.

'Please don't leave,' he called out, his words this time holding enough strength to make her pause. As the woman turned to face him once more, Page felt the young hand on his own begin to tighten. When he looked down, he found that Emma's soft skin was changing, the skin withdrawing to expose the bones and joints in her fingers. Her knuckles began to bulge, almost protruding from her skin, making them look as though they would burst through the skin at any second. Her grip tightened further as she raised her arm higher, allowing the sleeve of her cloak to fall back, revealing once more scars and puncture marks etched upon her skin. Page tried to release her hand but

Emma's grip remained too tight. Moving now to face him, he found that the features of her face had also changed. The skin had been pulled tight, making her eyes appear to sink back into her skull. Dark rings had formed under her eyes and across her cheekbones, where the thin skin became spotted and pitted. When she attempted to smile, the once simple action caused her lips to break in places, a clear liquid weeping from the cracks that appeared upon them.

'You failed her,' the mystery woman called out, her words holding both menace and accusation.

Horrified at what he now looked upon, Page managed to scream somehow and break free of Emma's grip. He recoiled back against the side of the corridor, the grotesque sight of his drug-ravaged daughter still looking at him.

'You said you'd help me,' Emma said as a clear liquid began to run from the side of her mouth. 'You said that you could make it right again, but it's too late now Daddy… it's all too late…'

The image of Emma Darrow began to sway as most of the control in her body seemed to desert her, making her collapse to her knees. The only strength she now held was enough to make her hold out a pathetic hand towards him. The palm was upturned, the needles that failed to stay in her grasp now spilling from her hand.

Page felt anger rising within him; he wanted to scream out loud until the madness around him disappeared. Remembering what Megan had told him about not believing what he saw within Ravenscroft, he closed his eyes and fled down the corridor. He cared little where he ran to, each step hopefully taking him further away from what he prayed in his wildest imagination wasn't real. As he began to feel brave enough to open his eyes, he found himself running past rows of windows, each of them showing only weak daylight. Now he feared not finding a way out of the endless corridor. He pleaded for an opening or a doorway from which he could escape, but none came. On and on he ran with nothing but blurred windows flashing by him as his heart threatened to overload within him, every muscle and sinew in his arms and legs crying out for him to stop. When the corridor finally ended, he found himself facing a doorway. It was one he recalled seeing before, though now the locks that had once secured it lay on the floor on either side, each still covered with traces of disturbed dust.

For the first time since he had fled the images that he had seen, Page looked behind him only to find the corridor empty and quiet as a tomb. Somewhere deep inside him, a feeling was growing, one which he in some ways welcomed, yet also feared. The urge or maybe a need to open the doorway was suddenly so strong, as though an answer or an explanation lay within. Page reached for the door handle. He held his breath as he slowly opened the door.

Chapter 45

The sensation of nails being pulled slowly down his back caused Toby Connor to remove his glasses, throwing them clumsily onto the bedside cabinet behind him.

Opening his eyes, he struggled to take in the wondrous sight before him, the smile and contentment more than evident on his face. Although they had previously worked together when the company's I.T. system was updated, it had been only since they had come to Ravenscroft that Toby had begun to notice Collette Logan. Maybe that was because she was working away with Megan and Charlotte, and, in truth, on the few times their paths had crossed, she had seemed too inaccessible and too 'out of his league' for him to even consider his chances. *So much for that theory,* he thought to himself as Collette's fingers now reached the top of his spine. Toby rotated his head slowly in time to Collette's experienced touch as she began massaging the muscles at the base of his neck.

Toby was sitting on the edge of his bed with Collette across his lap, her unbuttoned blouse allowing her body heat to warm his bare chest. Where her skirt had ridden up, it allowed his hands to feel the smooth firmness of her thighs, the sensation of his touch against her body making his mouth go dry. When Collette moved closer to him, raking her fingers through his hair, Toby cared little about the beeping coming from the other room where two of his computers were calling for immediate attention.

When Collette took his head in her hands and began to kiss him passionately, he knew he would have collapsed in disbelief had she let go.

Toby had been surprised when she had knocked at his door nearly an hour ago. Initially annoyed at being interrupted at his work, he had forcibly pulled the front door of the cottage open, half expecting it to be either Sutton or Rowlance. He was even more surprised to find the perfectly made up P.A. holding a couple of bottles of champagne. The first bottle, which he had opened while Collette made herself more comfortable, had now been consumed, mostly by himself. As he had taken another drink from the second bottle to steady his nerves, his mind was too elsewhere for him to consider offering Collette another glass. The increase in his body temperature being put down to the situation he found himself within.

He had thought the couple of evenings that she had spent talking with him had merely been for company. Now, as his hands pushed her blouse free of her shoulders, Toby reckoned he more than knew her intentions. Kissing her on one of her exposed shoulders, he felt the excitement rising within him as she arched her back and gasped gently. But Toby Conner had little experience in deception and even less knowledge of the ways that people used each other to gain the information they badly needed or craved. The sweetness of the champagne had masked the liquid that Collette had added to a couple of his drinks when he had excused himself to go to the bathroom.

As Collette stood, she smiled knowingly at him as she began to loosen the zip at the rear of her skirt, provocatively allowing it to linger on her thighs before stepping out of it. Toby ran his tongue over his bottom lip, noticing the dryness his mouth felt. When he ran the back of his hand across his forehead, the perspiration was heavy, some of it running into his eyes. God, he felt hot. When he felt his eyes closing, he adjusted his position, feeling annoyed at the sudden tiredness that seemed to be creeping over him. Through increasingly blurred vision, he thought he saw Collette raise her arms as though doing some strange sort of dance before the room began to spin and he felt himself falling slowly backwards.

Collette wiped her mouth with the back of her hand and spat onto the carpet, disgusted at the remnants of the cheap champagne that had lingered in Toby's mouth. As she stood, she composed herself while looking down on Toby's thin frame. *How dumb could some people be?* she thought as she stepped across to retrieve her jacket draped over the nearby chair. As she picked it up, she paused, noticing something on the floor partially lost in the shadow of the chair.

It was one of Megan's stupid bracelets, one of the coloured ones that she usually wore. As Collette ran it between her fingers, she failed to recall the last time she had seen the girl wearing it. *What the hell is Toby doing with it?* she wondered as she removed a small handbook from her jacket. She tucked the bracelet in another pocket and concentrated on the contents of the manual as she walked hastily to where the two computers continued to beep. When she sat at the desk, the faint glow of the screen caused her eyes to sparkle as a mixture of annoyance and excitement caused her heartbeat to increase. Still dressed only in her underwear, Collette soon silenced the beeping sound as she began to type on one of the keyboards hastily.

Chapter 46

The falling sensation for Megan ended with a resounding crash at the top of the stairway. Winded from the impact, she rolled over on her side, clutching at the carpet beneath her as much for confirmation of where she was as it was to ease the aching from the impact.

In the area around where she had fallen, Megan could see dust particles spiralling around, agitated by her impact. Focusing her eyes away from the silent spectacle, she rolled over again, attempting to rise only to pull back suddenly when she found herself close to the top step looking directly down an angled stairway. Still feeling disorientated, her breath caught when she imagined herself falling again. Slowly she pushed herself back until she managed to stand, not sure whether she was now back in what she could perceive as standard conditions. Megan pushed her unkempt hair back and at the same time, arched her back to try and remove the ache that had already set in there. As she wiped her nose with one of her hands, she saw traces of blood left upon it. When she attempted to swallow, her throat struggled with more blood that now ran back down her throat. Trying to ignore this, she managed to stand, and moved beneath the stairway window where she looked down the upper corridor in both directions. Even though everything around her appeared to be normal, she took tentative steps forward in one direction before stopping when her instincts told her that her choice was wrong. Each time she tried to visualise any part of the house, her mind found no traces of movement, and the only doors that her mind would allow her to see remained firmly closed.

Megan knew she needed to find Page fast. If she failed to find him and he ran into the likes of Henry Talbot or others, God knows what could happen. Just how she had managed to get free of Henry she still hadn't worked out. For the moment, her biggest fear was what games the house would try to play with Page, if indeed it wasn't already doing so.

Outside the second of the bedrooms she passed there came a sound of movement from within, making Megan pause outside. When she tentatively put an ear against the door, the sound came again, making her quickly reach for the handle, hoping that the sounds of movement within had been caused by Page.

Instead, when the door opened, she found an empty room facing her, the light from the window highlighting the faded pattern on the oval rug that lay upon the wooden floor. Something about the room, which she couldn't quite place, seemed to lure her in, making her feel that an answer or explanation lay within. The further she stepped into the room, the more her gaze was drawn to the window itself, where a mixture of light and shade appeared to be distorting the glass. When she got within a couple of feet of the window, the glass panes seemed to be normal again, making her wonder what she had seen or if she had imagined it. Across the edge of her face, she felt a sudden chill and turned to face the doorway just as someone rushed towards her.

Anthony Rowlance welcomed the interruption from Alex Sutton. The papers that he had brought from the cottage had been making very little sense to him, and he had stepped away from the dining room table to try and clear his mind as the security man had entered the doorway.

Now, as he followed the younger man, the sound of their footsteps crunching on the gravel pathway sounded almost intrusive to his thoughts. Rowlance saw that the cloud cover was finally breaking, though any brightness that was attempting to show remained weak. He stepped aside a few puddles, one of which Sutton walked through, seemingly oblivious to how the water soaked the bottom of one of his trouser legs. Whatever was important enough to disturb him now seemed all the more urgent by the man's eagerness to reach the main house. A stream of smoke circled in front of Sutton as he stopped and turned to face Rowlance, the security man drawing heavily on his latest cigarette. It had been over two hours since Megan and Page had entered the main house of Ravenscroft, and the stillness around the place seemed almost overpowering. Only the occasional cries from crows in the high nests in nearby trees broke the silence.

'So, what did you want to show me?' Rowlance asked when they reached the front of the main house of Ravenscroft, hoping that there was no trace of the unease that he felt in his voice

'I noticed it a few weeks back,' Sutton told him, 'on one of the times when you were all away. I and two others had arranged to meet more or less where we are standing, after a security sweep, when I sensed something.'

'Sensed what?'

'At first, I wasn't sure. I thought it was simply my mind playing tricks.'

'Alex, for god's sake, get to the bloody point,' Rowlance suggested, the chill in the air more noticeable now. It had been ten years since Anthony Rowlance had managed to quit smoking, but the temptation of a moment of calm that a cigarette could now give him was increasingly tempting.

'It's the atmosphere around the place. The stillness.' Pointing towards the main house, Sutton took a couple of steps to his side before he continued. 'Look up towards the eaves, close to the far corner, where the windows with the cracked panes are.'

Rowlance did as instructed but saw nothing untoward. Nothing about the windows in the area where he looked seemed any different. With the breeze that he had earlier felt having now fallen, even the ivy close to where he looked remained unmoving. He was about to turn away and ask Sutton to explain further when something appeared to disturb the area above one of the windows. Traces of leaves and dirt fell down the side of the building, making Rowlance believe that a small bird had disturbed the area, but nothing showed to confirm his theory. 'Look at the glass below and the brickwork nearby,' Sutton told him, though he needn't have bothered as Rowlance could now see for himself. The panes of one of the windows were somehow bulging out, reminding Rowlance of how the material moved when being blown into shape. There seemed a fluidity to the glass that now matched the movement happening in the brickwork alongside, as though they had become part of a sheet-like image now being disturbed. As quickly as the effect started, it returned to normal.

'What the hell was that?' Rowlance asked, his eyes not leaving the building.

Sutton gave a short, nervous laugh before stubbing his cigarette out on the gravel below them.

'I have no idea,' Sutton confessed. 'At first I thought it was my eyes messing with me, but I've seen it a few times now.'

'You should have told me,' Rowlance told him, his eyes still scanning the building for other sounds of movement.

'And tell you what?' Sutton retorted. 'That the building is somehow moving.' *Or pulsing?* he thought to himself.

Rowlance didn't reply, as words seemed inappropriate. He looked across the full face of the building, trying to concentrate on various sections, unsure whether he wanted to see any change. But his mind was sent reeling by a crashing sound that broke the stillness around them. The splintering of wood set against the shattering of glass was nothing compared to the sight of the figure that suddenly came crashing through one of the upstairs windows.

Although the noise was sudden, the next few seconds seemed to happen almost in slow motion. Taken by surprise, Sutton had little time to make sense of what he had seen before the figure began descending quickly to the ground. Moving instinctively in front of his employer, Sutton glanced up at the opening in the window only to find that there was no trace of any damage to any of the windows other than the cracked and broken panes that had been there before. When he approached the figure laying on the gravel area in front of the house, it was surrounded by fragments of wood and pieces of shattered glass.

Rowlance knew it was Megan the moment she had started to fall. Her long hair wildly dancing around her, her pale skin stood out sharply against her black coat. He had prepared himself for the impact of her thin frame against the hard ground, fearing that if she wasn't already dead, the fall would be enough to take her away, yet her landing seemed almost cushioned. His eyes attempted to deceive him once more by showing him a form of black mist that quickly evaporated from around her as she finally became still.

Chapter 47

The light only illuminated the top of the wooden staircase. Across the edges of the bannister, thick cobwebs hung, the density of many showing their age. Others that hung down in front of him were yet to be completed, the silent and unseen makers having scurried away into the darkness as Page cleared them with his free hand, the firm grip on his handgun seemed to be his only touch with reality. The lower steps faded away into the gloom below, making Page reluctant to venture further down the stairs, yet when he descended another five steps and peered into the darkness, he could make out the form of a wall opposite the staircase as his eyes adjusted slightly to the light. Tiny beads of sweat were forming on his upper lip, making him wipe them away, hoping the simple action would help calm him. Page felt his heart rate increasing with each step he took until he eventually reached the bottom of the staircase.

He was surprised now to find that the light from above enabled him to see a couple of old-fashioned switches fixed to the wall facing him. Page moved as quickly as the light would allow to flick them both on, where, to his relief, the remainder of the cellar now became illuminated.

The area in which he stood was small compared with the rest of the rooms now revealed. After stepping through an archway, Page found himself in a room over thirty feet long. The width of the room was hard to determine with other rooms leading off it, the sizes appearing to all vary. The brick walls had been lined at some time, but dampness had penetrated sections, causing parts of the coating to have broken away in places, the pieces lying on the concrete floor. Bare light bulbs hung down on various lengths of aged cords of cable, the glare from the lowest lights causing Page to lower his frame to prevent him from squinting. Moving across the main cellar room, he held his arms out in front of him with the handgun aimed in readiness for anything untoward. Nothing came. Nothing filled any of the eight rooms that he checked, making him convinced that, at least in this part of the house, he was alone.

Lowering the weapon did little to ease his heart rate, making him use his free hand to run his fingers through his hair while breathing out.

At the far end of what appeared to be the main room, a small metal grate was fixed to the top of the wall. With no additional light cast from it, nor any trace of a draught perceptible, its purpose was unknown. Close to this, his eye became drawn to markings on the right-hand side wall. They ran for about a six-foot section and, on closer inspection, he could see that something had at one time been fixed to the wall. He ran a hand over the fixing holes, and as he turned away from the wall, he felt a curious familiarity about the view he now had. Page had no idea why he thought he had seen this view before. There was nothing untoward about the position, but when he stepped across the room and stood in other spots, he no longer felt the sensation.

It's your mind playing ticks, fool, he told himself and attempted a wry smile. The noise he then heard removed the smile in an instant. It was the childlike sound of a musical box. A slight pause between each note eerily played. The smell of wax upon a wooden floor came to him, causing his mind to reel. From the corner of his eye, he saw movement pass one of the openings, making him quickly turn, raising the weapon once more. A blur of a vision passed before him, the action blocking his view of the entrance and too quick for him to pick out anything other than candlelight. Even in the briefest of seconds, there was an unerring familiarity which made him quickly retreat across the cellar room until his back caught against the edge of the arched entrance that he had first stepped through.

If Page had been surprised by what he thought he had seen or heard, what faced him when he stepped through the archway caused knots to tie in his stomach, the perspiration that had initially only coated his upper lip now spreading to the rest of his face, the chill that spread throughout his body cutting deep.

There was now no trace of the staircase he had descended, or anything else for that matter. Where light from the upper floor had partially lit the stairway on his descent, now a wall of complete darkness faced him. There was no change in the light conditions, just an increasing density of the blackness that filled the main cellar room from floor to ceiling. The surface was so perfectly flat, as though he was looking at a glass surface. Fearing what could now be concealed in the blackness, Page instinctively raised the Glock 36 again, the muscles around his mouth tensing as he thought to keep his composure. A slight gasp escaped him when a voice came out of the black wall.

'Daddy, is that you?'

The voice of Emma Darrow was unmistakable to those who had known her. Even though they had lived in various parts of the country in her short life, the slight southern accent had always been noticeable. To Page, there was no mistake.

'I need your help,' the voice continued, but was now laced with fear. 'I need you to help me find my way home... please, Daddy, help me.'

This is impossible, Page thought, refusing to hear what his mind was telling him. He closed his eyes tightly and turned his face away as if in denial, all the time his index finger tightened around the trigger of the weapon as he desperately wanted to turn away.

'You couldn't save her then, so why would you now?'

The much deeper voice startled Page and made him open his eyes fully. When the voice which he believed to be Emma's spoke again, the new voice cut her short. The deeper male voice carried a menace that made the chill within Page seep deeper as though his very soul was under scrutiny.

'Emma!' Page cried out, 'I'm here, honey. Where are you?'

'Over here,' she replied, yet the words now appeared to come from behind him. Page spun round to find himself alone, and when he heard the words spoken again, they were so close that they almost made him jump. Now falling into a state of shock, Page spun round frantically in search of Emma, only for the deeper voice to say the same words over to his right.

'Over here, over here, over here,' the two voices now continually instructed him as he finally stood still, having almost lost all sense of his direction until the voices began to slow, the final words sounding as though the two voices had combined into just one.

'I don't know who the hell you are!' Page shouted, 'but I swear I'll start shooting if you don't show yourself.'

Only the black wall stood in front of him, the voices having fallen silent. Page tried desperately to think, to try and gain some control, but images forced their way to the front of his mind. Images that he would have scarcely have considered moments before.

A businessman he had given close protection to in Tehran stretched a hand out for him to shake, while white linen curtains were pulled silently back to reveal an Egyptian woman he had got too emotionally close to. A small child, too scruffy and unkempt to determine age or sex, ran across a roadway as the sound of explosions tore through the air around him.

'Which one should I choose?' the deep voice asked as a figure stepped out of the blackness. The whiteness of the headscarf tied around the figure's head almost glared at Page against the dark background. The words spoken by the stranger were unheard, though the agitation across his face showed the anger and irritation the words no doubt held. From beneath the blue robe the man wore, Page saw him sway slightly as he began to raise the semi-automatic weapon he had been concealing. The movement, though slight, was enough for Page to react in an instance. The figure stood almost ten feet from him and stood no chance as Page fired several times. Page expected to hear the impact of each shot, but heard nothing. His ears still rang to the sound of the fired weapon, the confined space more than emphasising the power of the Glock 36. However, no figure now stood before him. Instead, to his amazement, the four bullets that he had fired now hung suspended in the air, each spinning slowly several inches apart from each other.

Page now heard laughter coming from the deep voice, laughter that almost sound mocking.

'Come, Page, you didn't think it would be that easy did you?' the voice now deadly serious, any warmth the laughter had held now distant.

Staring as though trapped in the most surreal nightmare he could never have imagined, Page stepped forward to examine the bullets that still spun silently in the air. The revolutions of the nearest one had almost come to a complete stop now, enabling him to see at close hand the marking upon it. In an instant, all four bullets shot forward as though just fired, silently being engulfed in the blackness before him.

Chapter 48

In her mind, Megan was still falling, even though no sense of movement came to her. Nor did any sense of sound, and not the slightest trace of light was found whichever way she tried to look. When her hands grasped frantically at the air around her, there was no sensation against her hands or fingers, just an all and consuming darkness into which she continued to fall.

For a moment she contemplated whether she had died. The darkness would seem to confirm this, but it was the fact that there was now no sense of feeling or touch around her, as though she had fallen into a complete state of nothingness. Then something seemed to pulse through her mind, the sensation bringing back one of Megan's earliest memories.

As a small child she had known that her mother was dead, but inside, she felt nothing towards her. It was so strange, she thought, that everyone around her spoke of someone who had given her life, yet there was no connection with the woman that she could feel. Her father said that he had merely taken on board the love of the woman that he had shown to her in photographs and old films, where the picture jumped too much and the images never seemed to stay still enough for her to see them. As time had passed, people started to speak less of her, and Megan's life became centred on her father and his increasing need for her to help him. What only seemed like normality to her, was then called an ability. A talent. Something that had been a gift to her. Despite all the things that she had ever found, ever traced, ever struggled to retain her control over, her father had never asked her to find the one person who had been the reason for her being alive.

That sense of nothingness had remained with her. It lay wrapped in the bedclothes that she slept in, in the pocket of coats and clothes that she took shelter within. It lingered behind her in shadows, even on sunny days when she told herself she should have little or no cares. Always waiting for some reason, waiting for what, she had no idea. Until one day when she found herself within the midst of a raging ocean that fought a seemingly endless battle with the howling wind that carved and whipped at the enormous waves around her. The metal ground beneath her feet had actually shaken as if the sensation was an announcement of its arrival. And then it had come, uninvited and unwanted. Swamping her with a feeling that if she closed her eyes for long enough, she would find only nothing.

The brightness that greeted Megan held no welcome. The light had been weak at first, at times fading away again, but the more she became aware of those around her, the more it had strengthened, bringing with it voices that both jolted at her mind and senses. When her eyes eventually opened, blurred figures looked down at her. She felt something placed upon her forehead which, if anything, only added to her discomfort. Megan felt something take hold of one of her hands and tried to move to shake it off, but her weakness was no match for the strength next to her. Turning away from the other figures, she concentrated on the one closest to her and felt a familiar sensation begin to run through her body. It helped to calm her, while at the same time bring some form of clarity to her vision. The sight of Charlotte

Wareham smiling back at her was more reassuring than anything Megan could ever remember.

'Hey, you,' Charlotte said, struggling to hold strength in her voice. 'I thought I'd lost you.'

Megan tried to move as she returned the smile, but the discomfort in her back and shoulders remained. After a couple of further attempts, she managed to sit up, finding herself on the settee in the sitting room of the Coach House. Under the blanket that lay across her, she discovered that she was still clothed, apart from her coat which had been removed and put on the back of one of the chairs close to where Anthony Rowlance and Charles McAndrew stood to look on.

'Welcome back, Megan,' Rowlance told her, though she detected little compassion in his voice.

'What happened?' Megan managed to ask as she saw Collette Logan enter the room.

'You fell from one of the windows,' Charlotte told her, squeezing on one of her hands. 'One of the upstairs windows. I can't believe you survived the fall.' Megan looked away as she recalled the memory of hurtling backwards in the bedroom, the uncontrollable force pushing her back, sapping all her strength until a moment of sudden impact, then the falling sensation that went on and on.

'Quite how you survived the fall is indeed a complete mystery,' Charles McAndrew agreed before he was interrupted by Rowlance.

'Where's Darrow?' he asked directly, making her try to recall scenes inside the house.

'He's gone,' she told him, adjusting her position.

'What do you mean, gone?'

'Gone. One minute he was beside me, then something happened and he was gone. I have no idea where.'

As her temperature began to rise again, her vision became distorted once more. When Charlotte held the cloth to her forehead once more, it eased slightly, but she could feel the dampness of her hair plastered against the sides of her forehead which began to spread down her body, making her want to free herself of the constraints of the blanket.

Megan started to feel weakness overcoming her, her vision beginning to fade. Words came to her, yet she felt they came from elsewhere and were spoken by another.

'They're all dead. Every one of them. Everyone you ever brought here.'

Now the room itself appeared to be slipping away from her as she felt herself pulled more upright, the force too great to be that of Charlotte. Megan drew on all the strength that she could find within herself to enable her to see the face of the figure holding her. The strain showing on Anthony Rowlance's face brought a curious sense of pleasure to her.

'You promised!' he snarled at her. 'You said you could contain it!'

'It's too great… too much.'

'No!'

'It's going to spread, Anthony… it's going to spread oh… so… much.'

The more she spoke, the more Megan's voice began to alter. The words seemed to come from deep within her throat, and although they could see her lips continue to move, the words felt far too distant.

'You have no idea what it's capable of, what it knows and feels. You can never dream of having it as it won't let you,' her voice was fading, forcing Rowlance to lift the girl's body close to his ear simply to enable him to hear her words. Behind him he ignored his daughter's attempts to pull him away. 'It knows what you want,' Megan managed to say, her eyes beginning to glaze over, 'knows what you want to do, but it won't let you.'

'Why not?' Rowlance demanded.

'Because…'

There was no whiteness to Megan's eyes now; her pupils had dilated so much that Rowlance now stared into two black orbs. He felt the young girl's body becoming limp, and although her words were barely audible now, each one seemed to echo around his mind, 'because you wanted to change time, everyone's going to die.'

A weak laugh managed to escape her before she lost her vision completely and found herself beginning to fall once more. Too weak to attempt to grab onto those around her, Megan let the darkness take her, not knowing what it held for her this time. She knew that her childhood thoughts had been wrong, that what the dark held deep within it was simply waiting for the chance to be used, and it was more frightening than anything she could ever have imagined.

Chapter 49

Although he knew he had no means of escape, Page retreated into the main cellar area, the confined space he had stepped into now almost too claustrophobic to bear. No sooner had he stepped through the archway than it faded away as the wall of blackness spread out before him once more. The blackness appeared to remain impenetrable. To his left, it appeared to soften somehow along the edge, giving Page the impression that the change was meant for some reason. There was no way of knowing what depth the blackness had, whether it filled the cellar stairway and the changing corridors of Ravenscroft, or whether the wall was just the thickness of a screen or veil.

'Hello, Page.'

The voice startled him, not just because it had spoken his name, but because the clarity it held was unnerving. 'It's been too long, far too long.'

'Who the hell are you?' Page asked, knowing his words sounded all too insufficient.

'Who or what I am is unimportant,' the voice replied, now so clear it was as though the voice was coming entirely from the wall of darkness before him.

'Where's Emma? At least tell me that.'

'Emma has gone, Page. You know that more than anyone. What you saw was mostly what we wanted you to see. True to say, some people find it hard to move on, and we make use of them as we so wish. You yourself were just shown old memories. Ghosts of the past, you could say.'

'No!' Page retorted 'I saw her here, she was right before me, and I felt her against me when I held her.'

For what seemed seconds yet could easily have been hours, there was no reply to Page's comment. In that time, the sensation of his daughter's body against his own remained strong enough to cause tears to well in his eyes. Swallowing, he tensed his jaw and raised his weapon directly at the darkness.

'Your anger is of no more use here than your weapon,' the voice then told him. 'You should be concentrating on trying to protect the person who is most important to you now.'

How can anyone be more important than Emma? he thought as he lowered the weapon once more. When was anyone? Jayne maybe, when they were both so young and naive, but the time that they'd had by themselves had been so brief. When he ran a hand through his hair, he held it still as his hand reached the base of his neck, lost for words. The voice then stated what he guessed he had been trying to say.

'You failed to save Emma, yet you may be able to save Megan.'

Shaking his head, Page stated that he cared little about saving anyone now.

'Oh, but you do. It's how you must repay.'

'Repay?' he asked, almost laughing at the suggestion, 'Repay what?'

'Your guilt, of course,' he was reminded. 'The one thing those who have failed always carry with them, the part of you that you have been running away from ever since. That was, until Megan found you.'

'How could you even begin to know about that?' Page asked, struggling to keep a sense of the exchanges of words between them.

'Ha!' The voice laughed, 'I've talked to Megan long before she found you amongst the chaos of sand and heat.'

'What the hell are you talking about?'

'Surely you remember Tikrit, Page? So much tension and hate in the air that day, most of which remains as we speak. Surely you remember a flash of blue amongst the chaos and madness, in the moments before the sky rained glass…'

Tikrit? Christ, how long ago was that? Three, four years, maybe longer? He had no idea when he tried to place the date, even though the images and memories held strong in his mind. As he stood almost disbelieving what he was hearing, figures of a distant, almost forgotten crowd began to appear around him. When his mind took him back to a day which had begun to merge with so many chaotic ones of recent years, the intense heat of that day began to smother him as unknown faces passed by, their movements slow and laboured. Each mouthing the words, 'You need to save her, Page. You need to save her now more than you know…'

As the words faded in his ears, Page sensed movement next to him and looked to see his former colleague Burnett turning to face him. From the confines of a constricted cellar, Page now found himself standing alongside a sand-blown road where crowds of people swarmed all around him. Further voices began to fill the air, though their words and meanings remained unknown. The tension in the air was so tangible that it forced him to follow his colleague Burnett to where the agitated crowd parted to reveal more of the road along which a white Mercedes approached. The movement of the vehicle began to force the figures to move quicker, the surge causing a weak old lady to stumble and fall to the ground. Page took a step forward when he noticed a small child come forward and begin to help the frail woman who mouthed words which Page again failed to understand. Raising a hand to shield his face from the bright sunlight, he saw that both of the figures had now turned their attention to the vehicle close by. Slowly, the sounds around Page faded, the words of Burnett and the shouting crowd around him lost.

The Mercedes was almost alongside him now, enabling him to catch first sight of one of the figures within the rear of the car. As it turned to face him, it was almost as though he were watching a film rather than a memory, as he saw the decorative scarf fall away to reveal the face beneath. The shadows within the vehicle only seemed to emphasise the thin features of the person he had recently come to know.

The shaking of Megan's head seemed almost in time to the ticking sound that began surrounding him. The slow and forceful jolt of his body felt the full force of the explosion's aftershock, failing to prevent him from continuing to look upon the vivid blue colour that filled the girl's eyes as a cry came from her silent mouth.

Chapter 50

There were times when Megan often failed to differentiate between where her dreams began and ended, and the point where the confusion of the start of each new day for her began. As she drifted out of consciousness in the early part of the night, her dreams had come to the fore. She recalled a previous visit to the house, one where the contents were unknown to her. But none of the scenes would hold for more than a few seconds, and what glimpses she saw of figures and faces were too distant or blurred for her to recognise. Her senses felt weakened, her inbuilt defence slowly being lowered. When she attempted to concentrate on any single image or feeling, she felt herself drifting away into a sea of chaos. Somehow though, she finally fell into the deepest sleep that she had ever known.

When Megan finally awoke, her entrance into the day was free of the usual chaos of senses and colours that generally greeted her. There were no flashes, no rush of whispers, and no pulses or tremors. Megan simply woke up. That alone was enough for her to realise that something was different. The air within her room felt stale when she breathed in. Freeing her arms from the constraints of the duvet cover, she cleared away the strands of hair that obscured her vision before finally looking around her. The chair that faced the bottom of the bed was free from the pile of clothes that it usually held. Her coat could no longer be seen hanging from the hook on the back of the bedroom door, and when she glanced across at the wardrobe, the light within the room was strong enough to show her that the contents had all gone. Pushing back the cover with her legs, Megan was forced to stop suddenly when the aching of her body hit her. The left-hand side of her back protested at the sudden movement, as well as her right elbow and knee. Surprised to find herself dressed in a t-shirt and shorts, she looked down at red marks across one of her thighs. Matching ones were on her right arm. Although her touch appeared gentle when she touched the area around her elbow, the contact caused her to winch at the broken skin, bruising already beginning to show. In the confusion of her thoughts, Megan then recalled hitting the ground hard from a fall.

When she pulled back on the wardrobe door, her thoughts about her clothes being gone were confirmed. Even the drawers were empty. Megan spun around when she heard the sound of voices coming from outside. When she rushed to the window, she noticed some of her clothes folded on a chair. A pair of jeans, along with socks and underwear, were placed on top of her dull, pink sweater.

Ignoring the pain she felt in her body, Megan looked out of the window and caught sight of three security men passing below, as well as the edge of two cars parked close to the archway. More worrying for her was the blankness of her mind. Whenever she tried to find any image other than her surrounding thoughts, she drew a blank, as though something was blocking her mind. Reaching down for the pile of clothes, she quickly pulled on the jeans and socks before running her hands through her unkempt hair in an attempt to place some order to it. Pulling the sweater on, she was still putting an arm through one of the sleeves as she bounded down the stairway, noticing that even the light around her felt wrong.

Charlotte Wareham stood beside the middle of three cars parked close to the archway, her folded arms remained as rigid as her expression. The sight of the security men loading items into the boot of the leading Mercedes held her stare for a moment before raised voices pulled it away.

'Anthony, listen to me, please,' Charlotte heard Charles McAndrew plead to her father who held a hand out to him as though to halt his words.

'We've come so far.' McAndrew continued, 'We can't leave now.'

Before he could continue, he was disturbed by the arrival of Megan, who was being held back by two of A. R. Solutions' security team. Seeing her distraught expression, Charlotte hurried across to her, casting a disapproving look at her father as she passed.

The fears that Megan had had about the light were now confirmed as she struggled to free herself. The breaks in the clouds allowed only a paling sun to break through, the stretched shadows confirming her opinion that it was late afternoon. *How long have I slept,* she wondered, *and what is happening around here?* Freeing an arm from her temporary constraint, she struck out, catching the security guard across one of his temples. Before he could regain his grasp, she heard Anthony Rowlance call for her to be allowed to pass. She went from constraining arms to the shelter of Charlotte's arms in the briefest of seconds.

'What's happening?' she pleaded as Charlotte brushed back her hair, seeing how pale her face still looked.

'We're leaving,' Rowlance interjected before his daughter could speak.

'But we can't, not yet,' Megan protested as McAndrew joined in.

Anthony Rowlance had dealt with people in various ways over his lifetime, making tough decisions, always trusting his judgement, but now he was failing to keep hold of the situation around him. *It is too close,* he thought. Too close to those he cared about most, and too close to the pain of loss he had struggled to control over the last few years. As Megan pulled away from Charlotte's hold, she faced Rowlance, her face full of anger.

'Anthony, listen to her,' Charles McAndrew implored as the onlooking security men awaited further orders.

'I have,' Rowlance snapped at his colleague. 'You heard her words yourself. They're all gone, all of them,' he added as he cast a glance at the edifice of Ravenscroft. *Has this place ever looked so foreboding?* he wondered as he turned his eye away from his daughter's stare.

Turning to Megan, he glared at her with what looked like contempt. 'You were the one who said it couldn't be contained,' he snapped at Megan. 'You said we had no chance now as everyone had gone.'

'Where's Page?' Megan asked, ignoring the older man's accusations.

'You tell me – you're the one who's supposed to know where things are.'

When she glanced across at the main house, Megan felt weak, unable to understand why she was failing to gain any form of control. Each time she tried to use her mind to access the inside of the house, to find a single item within that she could recall, all she saw was a blackness which made her feel queasy the more she tried.

She looked on as Charlotte tried to get her father to change his mind, demanding to know what had been going on in the house, but her words drifted over him. The security men began leading her back to the Coach House as the loading of the cars resumed. What brightness remained in the day was starting to be lost as the cloud began to thicken once more, casting further shadows across the Ravenscroft estate.

Chapter 51

Page found himself lying face down on the cellar floor, his hands grasping feebly at the dust-covered concrete floor beneath him. When he rolled over, the images and heat were gone. It took him a moment to compose himself, and even when he managed to sit up, his shoulders remained hunched.

'But that couldn't have been her,' he said almost silently, with his head still bowed.

'Why not, Page? the voice asked. 'They tracked you there through her. You recall the sensations you felt, don't you? The clarity of it all.'

Parts of that day in Tikrit filled his mind once more, but Page forced his mind to clear them.

'Some,' he admitted, 'but I had no idea what was happening. There were sensations that…'

'The sensations, all the feelings and fears you felt, were caused by Megan,' Page was then told, 'but in the end, it was her actions that saved you.'

The scenes of Iraq that had attempted to fill his mind now changed to a military hospital bed where he had laid for several days, recovering from surgery to remove pieces of shrapnel. Raising a hand up to his chest, Page felt as though each of the scars his body still bore surged with sudden heat. His chest tightened, and he recalled drifting in and out of consciousness, grasping at the bedclothes he had laid within whenever his dreams had failed to leave him. There were always so many doors to choose from, so many corridors in which he never seemed to find the end to. In the only time that his dream allowed him to leave the endless corridors, Page found himself descending steps to a floor which only seemed to contain darkness. Whenever he awoke, Page recalled several figures standing at his bedside, though his vision had been too poor for him to see them enough. Believing them to be members of the medical staff, he had let them move and tend to his body as they seemed fit. But it was one figure in particular that he now recalled. The silhouette of a figure had come during the night and stood at the bottom of his bed, as though cautious of approaching. Page closed his eyes and brought the vision to the front of his mind, allowing his memory to return a greater form of clarity to the image and allowing him to see the paleness of the skin and shadows around the eyes of perfect blue.

His body appeared to sway slightly when his eyes snapped open, making Page use one of the sleeves of his jacket to wipe the perspiration off his face, the coarseness of the material enough to break his mind from the images. The darkness continued to face him as he attempted to make sense of what he was both feeling and experiencing.

'What has any of that day got to do with here and now?' he eventually asked.

'It's the same thing in many ways,' the voice told him as though trying to reassure him.

'How can it be?'

'The similarity about that day, that time, is no different. There was a presence there long before the two of you met. So much land saturated with what I guess you may call evil. Mixing and merging in the sweat of those that walk, live and fight there, passed on through countless generations, as well as in those who have recently fallen upon the polluted sand. Oh, it's been there for centuries, Page, maybe longer, and will linger on there until the time comes for it to move on. Here in this house, it is just the same, on a smaller scale maybe, but there is still the need.'

'The need?' Page asked.

'Oh, you could never understand fully what the need is for us to be in places like that.'

'But the conflicts there are all to do with land, beliefs and occupation,' Page protested.

'Wars mask issues,' he was told. 'Armies fight armies with little thought or care on either side. If only two of your kind are left standing after all the others have fallen, do they not then continue? Blind to logic or reason, until eventually only one stands and claims control. Control of what? What hangs in the air around them and within the very earth they walk upon will always win. Its needs having been sated. Strength has been gained to enable it to move on.'

'This is madness!' Page shouted, raising his hands to his head and pulling on his hair, clutching the weapon tighter than he had before.

'If you say so, Page, but we could talk for hours about madness. Time makes sense of all the madness and butchery which people create, as they feed on what is in the very air around them. In time your historians will revel in the greatness of those people and their actions. So it's all just another moment in time, as I told you. But this time, here and now, is all about you, Page. So feel honoured; you have been brought here to be part of the final act.'

'An act of what?' the coldness spreading through him.

'An act of closure. The decay that you have seen and sensed since coming here is because our time here is fading. For this, you and others needed to be brought here.'

'And you used Megan for this?'

'Oh no,' the voice denied, 'not to begin with. Chance or ill fortune brought the first two close to here. Megan was simply used as a form of energy to bring the others like yourself.'

'But why bring us here?' Page asked.

'A birthplace for you all. I, we, us, whichever way you wish to look at it, we have to move on. As I have already said, our time here is fading. Soon the place will collapse and crumble in on itself, and the people and events will get lost to what you would call time.'

Words failed Page. He was unable to believe what he was hearing. He slumped against one of the walls, his head bowed as he struggled against the tide of his emotions. When he found what to him seemed the courage to speak, his words were barely audible.

'But why kill them?'

'To feed,' the voice told him, 'that's what the need is. The need to gain enough strength to enable us to move on and make the next journey.'

'But to kill innocent people?' Page questioned.

'No!' the voice then boomed, 'They chose to take what life they led. They used part of the energy installed in them at the moment of birth from this place to perform their so-called 'ways'. The pathetic lives you are attempting to protect were not as innocent as you might think.'

Still slumped against the cellar walls, Page lowered his head and closed his eyes as the voice continued, listing the events of the lives of the others born in the same place as himself.

'Thomas Kenny has murdered more people in his line of work than you could ever imagine. From his last foster parents and unknown strangers, to several homeless people who he came into contact with and duly despised. He contracted himself out over most years of his life to kill all sorts of people, simply in return for payment. Henry Talbot, who you have not had the pleasure of meeting, lived the majority of his life as a paedophile. Some of his actions have even sickened me at times. Evelyn Muscroft, who you encountered with Emma, turned a blind and sick eye to the actions against endless children, of those in positions of power within the religions you people bow down to. But the most curious one brought back here, aside from yourself, is Matthew Jarvis. He was the last one that Megan brought here. While the previous ones we soon fed on, Matthew entertained us.'

'In what way?' Page asked, still not believing why he wanted to continue talking.

'Matthew Jarvis was always repentant for his actions. He also wrapped himself in clothes of religion, preaching about the way people should live their lives, while all the time he had tastes which regularly needed sating. When he came back here, he immediately sensed the power within the place and used it to recreate the feelings and sensation he had experienced.'

'What became of him?' Page asked as he somehow found the strength to stand once more.

'Over time we tired of him and let Henry Talbot loose on him. Strange how he didn't find the acts so appealing when forced upon himself. Oh, you should have heard the screams, Page.'

'You murdering bastard,' Page said as he wiped away more sweat from his face. His body ached all over now, and despite the warmth his face felt, there was a deep chill spreading through him as laughter filled the air.

'Oh, that's so rich coming from you, Page. They all lied and deceived. They all took lives and gorged on cruelty installed within them from the fabric of this very place. But each of them abused and took parts of the power that was not theirs to use.'

'So you took it back?' Page said mockingly.

'We only took back what was ours in the first place. What was given to all of you was always going to have to be repaid someday.'

'Enlighten me,' Page retorted. 'What the hell did I get given that could connect me with those people?'

'What you and the others took was the power of protection.'

'Protection?'

'Yes. The power here protected you all. You have all taken scars and bore wounds, but only others around died. Did they not?'

Page had no answer. Had he wanted to, he could easily have recalled numerous days when he had survived life-threatening situations, days where he had put his survival down to a mixture of training, judgement and luck. Now all his beliefs around those times seemed to have been shrouded in deceit.

'And what of me and what of Megan?' he wondered aloud.

'Megan is what we call a finder,' the voice told him, 'a finder of threads that sway around the edges of what you people refer to as power, often led by us to bring people to feed upon. Does another find of your precious oil not bring with it the threat or the hostility of war? How long do you think you could survive if the supply was to suddenly stop? You people preach about democracy and helping your fellow man, but in the end, greed and self-interest prevent you from sharing what could be evenly spread out amongst each of you.'

'But I thought Megan could find only obscure things,' Page suggested, wondering when the subject would switch to himself.

'She simply pulled on threads left by other people. I agree she chooses to use it for odd reasons, so sad really, as she is so strong. The depth of her real abilities is unknown even to her. Soon though, she is to be challenged. Some of those steps are already being taken, and when that time comes, oh, we will feed.'

'And will I go?' Page queried, having resigned himself for inevitable bad news.

'Initially, I would have said yes. That was to be the final part. But now a change is taking place, something that will soon affect you. Strangely, it was unexpected to even myself, but isn't that the beauty of both life and death?'

Laughter again filled the confines of the cellar as the voice within the darkness thought about the irony of its own words. 'Aren't they divine?' the voice asked Page. 'All those delicious surprises that your life brings up.'

Page looked down at the weapon he still held in his hand and thought of Thomas Kenny. Was this the situation which he had been put in, when it was too late to repent for the actions of his life? Returning the weapon inside the holster within his jacket, Page exhaled, defiant that he would take no such course of action. Still, doubt threatened to surface, demanding to at least be heard. His mind drifted back to Iraq, back to the day when he was led to believe Megan had first found him.

'Just a place in time, Page,' the voice told him, even though the thought was locked in his mind, 'a place like hundreds, maybe thousands more. Over there it's encased within the heat and sand, with others it's within floods, drought and famine. We are not choosy. We simply go where the work is, as you often say.'

Again, laughter filled the cellar though Page could feel no humour. His body ached as badly as his mind now. All sense and reason seemed to have deserted him as he rested a hand on the cellar wall and looked down at the floor.

'And what now?' Page asked as he faced the wall of darkness again, 'Do you decide?'

'Oh come now, Page, sometimes we need intervention to add to the pleasure. But note this; we will soon leave here, and the house will feel the full force of our departure. Others are coming, others who want to change and interfere with our plans. We could easily stop them, but instead, we will give Megan all the help she needs to provide the entertainment!'

When the laughter returned to him, even Page found a sense of humour, for what reason he had no idea.

'Stand by, Page; it's going to be quite a show!'

Chapter 52

'And you're quite sure?'

'Look at the figures again for yourself,' Toby Connor suggested as he removed his glasses and blew away a small fly that had landed on them. He felt beads of perspiration across his top lip, and wiped them away with the back of his hand before replacing his glasses. Before him, Anthony Rowlance turned over another sheet of paper from the pile the younger man had handed him, the concern on his face mirroring the unease which Toby felt.

When he attempted to rotate his neck to lose the stiffness that he felt there, the movement only caused his headache to increase. Despite the heat his body still held, Toby had woken from the deepest sleep he had ever known to find himself half-naked, huddled up and shivering uncontrollably. He had little recollection of what had happened with Collette, and after he had focused back on the two computers that had been asking for his attention, he paid it even less attention as he tried to control the programs running on the screen before him. He usually hated anything to upset or unsettle Anthony Rowlance, but now the concern on the elder man's face made him confident enough to speak on.

'They've lost pressure on at least five rigs. You can see the latest readouts speak for themselves. At seven of the main oil sites in the North Atlantic, drilling teams are reporting all kinds of chaos going on. There have been anomalies being recorded for several days now in our system, ones which I couldn't trace as I'd have liked to on the crappy system we are using here. I've spoken with Draker and Copeland on Alpha 5; they've been experiencing unseasonal storms. O'Neil lost two drilling units in as many days. I can't make contact with at least a dozen of our other lines. Our system here it isn't strong enough. We simply don't have the capacity here to do hardly anything at the moment. All this I told you weeks ago!'

There were times, especially recently, when Anthony Rowlance could have throttled Toby Connor. His skills and ability he rarely questioned, but lately it was the tone of his voice at times that made his anger rise. Now, as he looked through the figures that he had been handed and on the laptop screens below him, he had the urge to shove them so far down his throat that the best surgeons around couldn't retrieve them. Rowlance closed his eyes and breathed deeply before he turned to Charles McAndrew, who had been silent during most of the conversation around the dining room table. The late afternoon shadows were beginning to spread across the room, their arrival as unwelcome as the expression McAndrew wore. The disappointment etched upon his face cut deep into Rowlance's heart, mirroring his thoughts and emotion.

'Make some further calls,' he said as he returned the paperwork to Toby. 'We need to know what the hell is going on.' The younger man gave a weak nod, as if he understood that they were now definitely leaving.

'I'll get the rest of our gear packed up,' he told Rowlance as he pushed his glasses back up his nose before turning to leave, his smile broadening as he closed the door firmly behind him.

'Charles, I have no choice,' Anthony Rowlance solemnly said as he slumped into one of the seats close to the window. With the two of them now alone, the moment seemed all the more poignant. How many times had he sat beside the windows of his home, viewing a world that had changed in an instant? The continued expansion and success of his company since he had lost his beloved wife had never been enough to fill the void within him. A vacuum he had planned to fill.

'Anthony?' the voice seemed as distant as his thoughts which were now distracted as a small bird hovered close to one of the window panes, its wings working frantically to keep it in flight. How Hannah had loved the birds that both lived in and travelled to their garden, with each season adding variety. When McAndrew spoke again, Rowlance rose from the seat and reached for his jacket laid across the table. After slipping his arms inside, he adjusted the collar as McAndrew faced him.

'I'm sorry,' was all Rowlance could think to say as he gathered the last of his own paperwork on the table, his hands resting on the briefcase that now held them. 'If I thought otherwise, we would stay.'

He could almost feel Charles McAndrew's heart break further as he headed towards the doorway.

Chapter 53

How long Page sat with his head in his hands he had no idea. His body and mind felt so emotionally and physically drained that he doubted he could take in any more. Part of him, what he days ago had called his professional side, was screaming at him to find Megan and continue his assignment. The job had always been everything. Always. But now all concept of time and reality seemed lost to him.

As his mind began to reel again, he pressed his back against the wall where he sat, feeling the searing heat of places, as well as the freezing temperatures that had accompanied his work. His body rocked as the memories stirred up, the amount of impact his body had taken over the years. The two bullets that his arm and shoulder had taken in Israel now burnt in his body which made him keel over, saliva running freely from his mouth as he attempted to stifle the cries and pains which his memories brought back. When he looked at what had been a brightly lit cellar, he saw a line of figures walking past. In his ear, he could hear the crackle of commands that had filled that moment, seconds before the roadside bomb had blown away the four men patrolling in front of him. Cracked ribs and cuts and bruises were all he had suffered that day. Many had called it luck at the time, a view he had believed and held onto in so many ways. But had it all been to someone else's plan? Had it all just been a stage play, a series of events of incredible coincidences that would lead him here, a place that had given him protection? The price of his fortune being that an unknown voice out of the darkness would have the final say.

Somehow he knew he had to at least attempt to leave this place. Managing to stand only increased the number of images, all now fighting for his attention. Both Jayne and Emma now held out hands for him to take, promising to lead him back to a safer, more peaceful place. He could smell the scent of each of them, the perfume on the nape of Jayne's neck, the moisturiser that she loved, as well as the clean, wholesome scent that Emma had had since being a child. At that moment he would have surrendered to them had their eyes not been filled with a darkness that, even through their unique beauty, mocked and taunted him?

'No!' he screamed as he made for the cellar steps. If he failed to make the short distance, he would let the darkness he had witnessed take him, and hopefully bring an end to what was happening. The impact of his foot on the first step seemed to jolt his mind clearer, enough strength returning to his body to enable him to climb back into the house he wished he had never seen. The darkness had allowed him to leave, for it had now spread elsewhere within the house. It had separated into much smaller parts that would soon all link together and seek the vengeance that it so desired and craved.

Chapter 54

The scratch on his shoulder was over six inches in length and thick enough to cause Toby Connor concern. Twisting his body round further enabled him to see two similar ones underneath. These, though, were thankfully smaller and lighter, but still sensitive to his touch. As it caused more discomfort now, he regretted using antiseptic to wipe over the main scratch. Tossing the used wipe in the small waste bin, he gave a shake of his head before pulling his shirt back on. Toby studied his reflection in the bathroom mirror as he fastened the last of the buttons, thinking he looked tired and gaunter than usual. Thankfully his headache was weakening now, though he still contemplated trying to find some painkillers to ensure that it would leave. After running the cold water tap for a few seconds, Toby scooped up handfuls of water and tried to wake himself further by cooling his face. The hand towel he used to dry his hands and face brushed against his bottom lip, making him recall thoughts of Collette Logan.

With no recollection of quite how far their intimacy had gone, Toby had gone to find her to try and get some clarity to his thoughts. There was, however, no tenderness in her voice when she had spoken to him, nothing he felt he could or would relate to with her. He returned to the small kitchen of the cottage and poured himself a glass of water. As he drank, he recalled a weekend away he had taken years ago with Abby Lawrence. God, what made him think of her now? He drank a further two glasses, remembering the hotel that they had chosen for their stay in London. It was more expensive than either of them could have afforded at the time, and they had been so unsure of the etiquette in the hotel's restaurant that they had ordered room service throughout their stay. Toby smiled, finding the feeling almost alien to him as he thought about Abby's carefree ways, her warmth and sensitivity, and how she liked to be held until she fell asleep. Why did he ever…? *Get a grip,* he told himself as he returned to the table where he had been working for the past half hour. Rubbing the bridge of his nose with his fingers, he rested his elbows on the table and stared at the various files he had currently open on his laptop.

Toby was sure that he was coming down with something now. His glands felt swollen, and there was the beginning of a sore throat whenever he swallowed. Toby's energy levels had never been able to break any records, his frame as slight as his mood most of the time, but he felt like the longer he stayed at Ravenscroft, the more he believed he was gradually becoming weaker. What he was now looking at on the computer screen before him was hardly helping with his current state of mind.

Before checking on his shoulder in the bathroom, Toby had taken full advantage of being free from Anthony Rowlance and his clowns. He'd been busy copying files and making 'slight' adjustments to some before transferring files to a safer place only he had access to. Now, when he tried to open the remaining files, they failed to appear. He cursed under his breath as he tried several more times, the same result coming no matter what system he went on. There was no plausible reason that he should suddenly be unable to open the one he now chose. He had opened it many times recently, but now each time he tried to access the files that he had been working on with Collette, all that came up was an odd symbol of a laughing horse set against a coloured background. The symbol was about two inches high and looked like something out of a child's game. Clicking the nearby icon again, hoping he had made the simplest of mistakes, Toby felt his mouth go dry as the laughing cartoon horse continued to mock him.

The sound of someone disturbing the catch on the front door made him click out of the file, returning to one of the few that he could access. He caught a trace of Collette's scent moments before she rested a hand on his shoulder, hoping that it would remain there.

'Everything okay?' she asked, leaning down so her words sounded soft in his ear.

'Fine,' he lied, closing down another file, pulling forward slightly to avoid any further touches from her. If she detected this, Collette kept it to herself, now letting her fingers stray across the two other computers sealed within their carrying cases.

'Within an hour, we'll be out of here,' she told him, a sly looking smile now filling her chiselled features, 'so close everything down for now and try to look a little bit more enthusiastic for god's sake.'

'And this is the only way?' Toby asked as he closed down the laptop. He turned to find little warmth showing on Collette's face. At first, he even thought that she was about to strike him when she approached, a trace of a twitch showing on the side of her mouth. Instead, she raised her hands and cupped his face, the smile returning.

'It is. Trust me,' Collette told him before kissing him hard on the mouth. When she pulled away, she bit his bottom lip gently, the action making him pull away. 'Oh come now, Toby,' she teased him, 'don't get all coy now, you weren't complaining before, and don't forget, you need me. Without me, you wouldn't have all that I've already let you have access to.'

'Let's get going, can we?' Toby asked while placing the laptop into the last empty carrier. The hairs on his neck were raising at the sound of Collette's taunting laughter that began to fill the room.

Chapter 55

The air within the Mercedes felt stale and oppressive, making Charles McAndrew loosened the knot on his tie, as much for some air as comfort.

Lowering the window helped, yet the still air outside felt lifeless. The branches of the trees close to the main house were visible from where he sat, so still they could have been frozen in time. McAndrew had felt something unusual the first time he visited the estate, and until the last day or so, he failed to put a finger on what it was. Now, as he waited to leave this place for the final time, hopefully, it seemed so clear to him. The estate felt corrupted by the presence of the main house of Ravenscroft. How he hated the place. Hated the way he had allowed it to give him hope, which had been found to be false.

Charles regretted the anger that he had earlier shown to Anthony Rowlance. The claims and accusations that he had thrown had threatened to put a divide between them. Their friendship was too strong for the allegations which he had made.

In the seat in front of him, one of the company's security men sat impassively, focused on three of his work colleagues assembled close to the two vehicles. McAndrew could see Charlotte Wareham had stood to talk to her father, her arms crossed almost in defiance in front of him. She kicked loosely at a stone or something on the ground, her head slightly bowed, causing her to push strands of her hair back behind one of her ears. Charlotte deserved better. He had often thought that the life the company now provided her was almost unfair. He had always been fond of her, finding her ways and manners graceful. Take her away from here, Anthony. Take her away and let her live the life she wants. Hannah would have wanted that more than anything.

Despite the warmth the late afternoon still offered, and the relative warmth inside the Mercedes, Charles McAndrew felt a deep shiver run through him.

Anthony Rowlance felt his daughter's pain as he hugged her. The painful need against him the same as it had been when she was a small girl. When one of the security guards came closer, he glared at him, making the man check his step, keen to hold onto the moment for some reason. When he eventually released her, he nodded in the man's direction, as though to confirm the thoughts of the security man and others, which were that they should be making a move.

'I want us all free from this place,' he told her as he watched her smile weakly at him. 'Too much has happened here, more than I should have allowed to happen. I can't keep you and Megan here any longer.'

'I know,' Charlotte agreed, 'but I want to know that Page is safe.'

Her father held back his resentment at her comment and began walking her over to the car in which Charles McAndrew waited. He assured her that he would have the house searched before they left, which did little to ease the tension showing on her face.

'You could always come with Charles and me,' her father suggested. 'I can leave Collette and Sutton to see to Megan.'

'No,' she replied shaking her head. 'I'll see to her; you know what she is like.'

They spoke for a few moments longer before Collette Logan came over and took further instructions from him. With a kiss on her father's cheek, Charlotte returned to the Coach House, keen to check on how Megan was.

Charles McAndrew looked on as Collette helped one of the security team load the last of the assortments of cases into the car boot. Collette's vehicle, parked near the cottages, would take her and Toby with the remaining laptops and items she was keen to keep close to her. When Alex Sutton walked over to join Rowlance, his expression did little to lighten the way Rowlance was feeling.

'I want you out of here within the hour, along with Charlotte and Megan, all the way back, okay?' Rowlance ordered as they walked over to the cars, 'Clear what equipment can't be left and then get yourselves out as soon as possible.'

'And Darrow?'

'Give the downstairs of the house a quick search,' he ordered, 'and I mean a quick one. Make it look genuine, if only to please my daughter.'

Sutton stepped back as another security man climbed aboard the Mercedes with Rowlance and McAndrew. Sutton reached into his jacket pocket for his cigarettes as the support security Mercedes that had been patiently waiting started its engine, soon following the matching vehicle as it pulled away. He clicked his lighter several times before the small flame began to show, unnerved by the slight tremble in his fingers before smoke began swirling around him.

Chapter 56

There were two security men standing outside of the sitting room entrance by the time Charlotte made it back inside the Coach House. Both dressed in the usual black uniform, one of the two spoke briefly into a mouthpiece he wore when he saw Charlotte approach. Charlotte knew that the taller of the two had been working at Ravenscroft since she had first come herself, but couldn't recall his name, always feeling that the sombre expression he usually wore more than matched the surroundings at times.

Keen now to leave herself, she wanted to make sure Megan was okay and at least in a calm enough state to leave. Just what her views were going to be, she couldn't imagine. When she went to pass in between the two guards, one of them held out a hand, halting her in her tracks.

'Sorry, Mrs. Wareham,' the tall guard told her, 'but we've been asked to keep you two separate.'

'I beg your pardon?' Charlotte exclaimed, at the same time pushing his arm away and reaching for the door herself. When the other guard stepped across to block, Charlotte attempted to dodge him, but soon felt one of her arms being pulled back, preventing her from entering.

'No one is allowed to see her now,' the guard who had spoken into the earpiece informed her before suggesting she took the matter up with her father.

The vibrating of the doorway behind the two guards made them both turn inquisitively. Making use of the distraction, Charlotte waited for what she knew was about to happen as she had seen it before and knew of Megan's intentions. The vibration now centred on one of the doors and intensified to the point where it appeared the door clasp would no longer hold. Then, as quickly as it had started, the sensation stopped, making both guards look at each other for answers. Charlotte moved swiftly when the door that had remained relatively still suddenly flew open, her movement unexpected and took both of the security team by surprise. Once through the doorway, she stopped and urgently pushed the door back, placing her foot on it.

'If you've got any problems,' she snapped, 'you take it up with my father.'

Charlotte was surprised to find her breathing coming heavy as she closed the door behind her, and was even more surprised when the security men failed to follow her. Had she not been concerned about Megan, she would have liked to argue her point stronger with the security members, both of whom she felt appeared overly agitated for some reason.

The light had remained poor in the sitting room for most of the day, the hours drawing on making shadows edge closer towards Megan who sat cross-legged in a chair placed close to the window. Her head was bowed, the sleeves of her jumper pulled down over his wrists, and her black coat was discarded at her feet as though she had only recently removed it. Charlotte was surprised when Megan eventually looked up at her to see that the young girl's eyes were red and swollen, still holding onto remnants of fresh tears.

'Megan, what's wrong?' Charlotte asked gently, cautious over what mood she would be in as she knelt down beside her.

'Everything,' Megan replied sullenly before sniffing loudly, the concerned look on her face now becoming more serious. Lifting her legs, she curled herself up in the chair and wiped a hand across her nose before she began chewing on one of her fingernails. When Charlotte reached out to hold her hands, Megan attempted to pull them away, but Charlotte had anticipated her actions and moved quicker than expected, taking a firm grip on them. She gave Megan a short shake as though to get her to her senses as she looked her straight in the eye. A tingling sensation appeared to emit from Megan's hand, which she tried to ignore.

'Listen,' she told her firmly, 'we have to leave here. My father tells me that we have problems elsewhere, work problems that need our help. So whatever is wrong, we can sort out on the way, okay?' Charlotte pushed back strands of Megan's hair that attempted to hide her less than impressed face. 'More or less everything's packed, so we just need to get ourselves moving. What I do need to know from you is where Page is.'

'He's gone,' she told her flatly before looking blankly out of the window.

'Gone? Where?'

'Doesn't matter. The house has him now,' Megan said as she began to chew on one of her fingernails. When Charlotte gently pulled the girl's hand away, she felt a trembling across it.

'Megan, what do you mean?' Charlotte asked. 'You're not making any sense.'

'Page has gone with the others. And there are no problems,' she replied. 'That's what's wrong.'

Shaking her head, Charlotte again asked her to explain.

'All the data that everyone's been looking at and getting worked up about, all that they're jumping up and down over, it's all bollocks,' Megan went on to say, 'all false programs that I have set up.'

A sense of unease that had been creeping through Charlotte now spread like wildfire, making her stand to attempt to calm herself. Running her tongue over her bottom lip, Charlotte wasn't surprised at the dryness she found there.

'What have you done, Megan?' Charlotte asked just as Collette Logan and Alex Sutton entered the room. Collette wore a slate grey top which more than matched her expression, the matching jacket, skirt and boots giving her a sense of height that for some reason made her look more dominant to Charlotte. Turning to face the two of them, Charlotte saw that the two security men who had tried to prevent her entrance were now carrying automatic weapons. Both remained stationary in the doorway, both watching her intently.

'What she's done,' Collette announced, 'is set a course of actions that were supposed to make us all panic. Panic enough to leave here urgently.' A smile was beginning to show on her face, in complete contrast to Alex Sutton, who looked as bemused as Charlotte felt.

'Quite the computer expert on the quiet is our little freak show,' Collette informed her, throwing a glare in the younger woman's direction. 'The trouble is, Megan, that I found what you were doing a long time ago and simply played along with it. The fact that your actions have caused Anthony and Charles to have already left is more convenient than you could ever imagine.'

Now totally confused, Charlotte asked Megan what on earth Collette was talking about, but Megan's face remained impassive, as though she was being held by what the other woman was saying. Now standing leaning against the wall beside the window, Megan folded her arms and looked as though she was struggling to control her breathing.

'Collette, what the hell are you talking about?' Charlotte asked, her patience now all but gone. Turning slightly, she reached out a hand towards Megan's, hoping to help reassure her, but saw an almost glazed look now held the young girl's face. The only movement was a slight twitch on the edge of her left eye, as though something had surprised her. In the background, Charlotte could hear Alex Sutton becoming more and more agitated, but she was transfixed by the change she was witnessing in Megan's face. Charlotte failed to hear the words being spoken to her correctly. Only when she stood and turned did she see what had caused this.

Collette Logan held a silver coloured handgun firmly underneath Alex Sutton's chin. The end of the weapon seemed out of proportion with the part she held. On a recent work assignment, she had seen others using a similar thing to silence the use of such weapons. Before she could speak, Sutton was pushed forward by Collette so that he now stood on the opposite side of the room to her. As if to grab some sense of reality to what was happening, he pressed a hand against the wall he now stood beside. Sutton's expression did little to put Charlotte or Megan's mind at ease.

'Sit down!' Collette ordered as she used the handgun to motion Charlotte back toward the settee. When she failed to move, taken with shock over Collette actions, her order repeated, this time her voice carried more menace.

'What the hell do you think you are doing?' Sutton finally asked, the tone of his voice sounding grave as the security guards stepped across, blocking his way with their raised weapons, his superiority over the two men now lost.

'I need Megan,' Collette told him, a smile firmly held upon her face, 'or rather, the people I know need her.' Glancing across, Collette could see how the backlight of the window highlighted the girls' thin frame, the image repulsing Collette. On the settee, the now sitting Charlotte held out her arm towards Megan, as though for reassurance to herself as for anything else.

'Come here,' Charlotte said weakly, wondering why the two security men hadn't challenged the other woman.

'Shut up, bitch!' Collette screamed at her, her voice echoing around the room. 'I'm sick and tired of hearing your bloody whining voice.'

Collette ran her fingers through her short hair, the weapon looking more significant than ever against her head as she exhaled deeply, lowering her hands slowly as if to emphasise she had regained control.

'Megan, you're going to come with me. No questions. No games, tricks or pissing about, okay?'

When she looked away from her, Collette saw that Sutton had taken a tentative step forward. The movement was enough for her to raise the handgun and point it directly at him. 'If you don't want to be reliant on a wheelchair for the rest of your life, Alex, I suggest you stay perfectly still from now on.'

'Why would you shoot to injure me?' Sutton asked. 'If you were to get out of here, you must realise that we would raise the alarm long before you reached the entrance gates.'

Collette gave off a suppressed laugh, which added a chill to the coldness that Sutton was already feeling. As Collette continued to talk, he glanced at Megan whose expression oddly failed to show even the faintest of reactions since the two of them had entered the room. A dryness filled Alex Sutton's mouth brought by the change he saw in Megan, her manner causing him more concern than the weapon pointed at him. Over the last few years, he had been witness to frightening scenes brought on by her actions. Most had been unseen by the majority of the security team, even those closest to her at the time, while others had caused such terror in him that some of her actions still filled some of his nights. He knew Collette herself knew of the girl's capabilities, so her actions seemed bizarre, to say the least.

'You'd never even get her out of the Coach House,' he informed her, hoping to keep talking to divert her mind, 'let alone get her to move under your instructions.' Finally, Megan did look up, a flicker in her eyes as though Sutton's words had mirrored her thoughts. Still, though, the pontificating Collette held the stage.

'Do you think that I've not thought about that? Have you not noticed how nobody is coming to help? It may surprise you to know that these two here will do exactly what I tell them to do. As will others,' Collette sneered, motioning to the guards behind her. 'Everyone has their price.'

When Charlotte tried to intervene, it only raised Collette's anger more.

'Oh please,' she told her audience while circling the gun around as if trying to calm herself again. When she brought it to a halt, it was directed straight at Megan. 'Name one thing about this freak show that I should be concerned about.'

Her comment released some emotion on Megan's face. Far from being annoyed at her choice of words, she merely smiled, pushing her hair back behind her ears.

'Her power,' Sutton told her solemnly.

'Bingo! Bullseye!' Collette shouted. 'First time, Alex, I'm impressed. If you weren't such an annoying bastard, I'd applaud you.'

Collette licked her bottom lip as she was forced to suppress laughter within her, her enjoyment at the bizarre conversation evident.

'And how do you propose to contain this power?' Charlotte asked, her annoyance overriding her fear as she abruptly stood, her words matching that which Sutton not only thought but was about to say.

'By simply shutting that power source down,' Collette told her as she firmly squeezed her index finger against the trigger, increasing the pressure that she had been holding for the past few minutes. Charlotte Wareham had no time at all to register even the tiniest of thoughts before the bullet struck her in the centre of her chest. It effortlessly shattered her breastbone, tearing away a large section of one of her lungs as it quickly passed through her body, leaving a large exit wound behind her. The second bullet hit her directly in the throat, instantly rupturing her air supply, the force causing her head to flick upwards as her body fell back against the settee beside the onlooking Megan.

The suppressed noise of the fired weapon barely sounded across the room, yet the scream that erupted from Megan pierced everyone's ears. When silent sobbing replaced her initial cry, Megan's mouth remained agape as she ran towards her friend, clawing at her now lifeless body. She implored her to wake up, as though somehow she had just fallen into a deep sleep. Megan heard, but never saw, the third and final shot that hit Alex Sutton just above his right eye. The swiftness of Collette's actions holding the look of shock on his face as his body recoiled against the wall, traces of blood staining the area behind where he had stood. For a second his body held still before slumping down like the strings on a life-size puppet that had suddenly been cut.

'Removing the focus of her trust,' Collette continued even though Megan and the two security men under her control were now her only audience. 'Removing her only source of refuge will shut her down as though simply flicking a bloody switch.'

Collette laughed loudly whilst the dumbstruck Megan still clutched Charlotte's unresponsive body. Blood had already stained her clothing where she had held her friend tightly against her, some of the blood caused strands of her hair to stick against the side of her face. The other woman's words were distant, almost muffled, as if the words of a passing stranger. Megan desperately wanted to shout out, to scream so loudly that something would register in the blank eyes that continued to look back at her. When she pawed at her friend's face, the action caused her eyes to close, making Megan sob louder and want to hold on tighter. Someone then grabbed hold of her tightly, causing her to become unsteady on her feet before one of her sleeves was then suddenly pulled back, allowing a needle to be hastily stuck into her arm by Collette. As Megan felt herself pulled backwards, her body was too numb to notice that it was her long hair that was being used to separate her and Charlotte. By the time she was forced to attempt to stand, she had failed to register the arms under one of her own as the two guards began to drag her out of the room. Tears ran down her cheeks from increasingly tired eyes, her bottom lip suddenly uncontrollable. No familiar tremors came to her. No change in atmosphere. No sensation or change in colour. Nothing to suggest that there was any purpose or need to what was happening. Megan even failed to hear the droning noise that was now becoming louder and gradually descending nearby.

Chapter 57

The downdraught of the rotor blades caused the long grass below the landing Blackhawk UH-60 helicopter to swirl around itself as though caught in a storm filled sea. Highlighted by two lights cast down from the underneath of the fuselage, dead leaves that had gathered across the bases of the nearby hedges and bushes were scattered, whipped up in the temporary gale along with small pieces of gravel and stone. Even before the landing gear had made contact with the ground, figures began to emerge from the drawn back fuselage doors of the helicopter. Although capable of carrying up to a dozen troops, only six disembarked, each dressed in black combat gear with no part of their faces recognisable under the headgear and visors each wore. Each armed with 9mm Mp5 automatic weapons, they began to disperse in pairs quickly, each following instructions relayed to them by their leader. One of the leading two figures that rapidly approached the Coach House spoke further instructions into a small mouthpiece. The weapons were raised to eye level and pointed directly at the people that emerged from the doorway.

Even by the doorway, the noise and downdraught of the helicopter couldn't be heard by the drowsy Megan, who stumbled again on weakened legs as Collette motioned for the security guards to pull her forward. Megan could barely hear the words directed at her, let alone the ones Collette shouted at the two blurred figures she saw approach against the darkening background. Megan could feel her head beginning to droop forward, her mouth failing to hold back the drooling saliva, her legs barely strong enough to support her. Every movement she now made seemed to bring more discomfort to her body.

'Search the whole place,' Collette said to the head of the armed figures, referring to the Coach House and outbuildings as she relieved the two security guards of the burden of Megan's uneven weight. 'There should be no-one else, but check anyway. No-one leaves.'

As the two armed figures headed inside the Coach House, two more came forward under Collette's signals and swiftly fired two shots, striking each of the two A. R. Solutions guards with shots to the head, their startled bodies dropping quickly to the ground. There were to be no witnesses to the plan now unfolding. After checking over the two bodies, they took charge of Megan who had slumped to her knees, bewildered by what was going on. As they began to move her towards the waiting helicopter, one of them noticed that Megan's right leg was dragging along the ground, her already scuffed shoe scoring a line across the gravel beneath them.

Finally free of Megan, Collette backed away against the side of the building and took out her mobile phone. In an attempt to drown out some of the noise of the engine and still spinning rotor blades, she pressed a hand against one of her ears as she began searching for Toby's number on her phone.

Megan had already felt the sensation coming upon her. It pulsed through her body at an increasing rate which she struggled to keep deep within her. Unseen by others, lost in an array of chaos filled shadows, the darkness found her, easily overriding the sedative injected into her. Across her chest, the familiar tightness spread. Her body temperature rose swiftly, with her shoulders beginning to pull back as darkness spread throughout her, making her strength and senses quickly return. The pulsing had now reached both of her temples, the heat more noticeable now across her face and neck.

'If they take you, they'll abuse your power and drain the energy and life from you.'

The voice was so clear to Megan that she was surprised that the two figures still moving her forward appeared to have failed to hear it.

'When they've used you for what they want, they will discard you as a freak. A sideshow. Someone to be both feared and loathed.'

Megan closed her eyes and tried again to focus on the images of snowfields, where the pureness of white offered to ease her mind. But the voice held both warnings and hate within its words, making her fail to focus enough for her to be confident in her abilities. The one thing that was clear was that if they got her aboard the helicopter and pumped more drugs into her, she was going to struggle to cope. The pain that she felt over losing Charlotte surged again, the dull sound of each shot printed in her mind, making her want to cover her ears and imagine it all away. When she glanced down at the blood stains upon her clothing, the sight was enough for her to regain control. Though the full use of her legs had returned, she exaggerated the limpness of her body, making one of the figures pause slightly in an attempt to strengthen his grip. Through the night vision goggles he wore, the man looked down at the young girl and saw her head was beginning to rise on her twisted frame. Inside him, a gut feeling told him that something was wrong, but it was not until the girl's face became more visible in the light cast by the helicopter that he began to react. The armed man attempted to stop, but his colleague continued his speed, causing Megan to slip from his grasp. When the other figure turned quickly in an attempt to retake hold of Megan, he was transfixed by what he saw.

Megan's eyes had turned a vivid blue, the colour even showing through the light-sensitive lenses of each man's goggles. The blueness was unreal somehow and appeared strong enough to illuminate the clothing of the men holding her. Around her eyes the shading increased, making her eyes look almost sunken by the time her face became perfectly still.

A piercing noise erupted from her. So intense that it momentarily deafened the two men, forcing them to retreat, each grabbing at their ears in an attempt to kill the excruciating pain. One of them managed to pull the small earpiece free of his ear just before his eardrum exploded under the intense pressure. Blood was already seeping from them both as he fell to his knees, clutching at his ears as the pain reached unbearable levels. Megan looked away now and saw that the other armed figure had dropped to the ground, his body twisted, screaming as blood pumped freely from his nose and one ear, the force pushing free the shattered earpiece.

Through the cockpit window of the helicopter, the pilot looked on, mesmerised as he watched the two figures fall. Immediately he asked for confirmation of what was going on from the other deployed troops. Only loud static greeted him on the radio. He repeated his request while continuing to monitor the controls on the central column, as well as in front of him, as the figure of a young woman turned to face him. The two lights on top of the helicopter then seemed to illuminate her, highlighting the length of pink clothing underneath her long coat. Her hair blew wildly around her face, which he could understand given the downdraught emitted from the aircraft, but the intense blue of her eyes seemed both unreal and unnatural.

Again, he asked for confirmation on his radio headset, the edginess of his voice now unsettling even himself. All this time, the static around him increased. He could now both feel and hear the pitch of the engine changing. Looking down at his instrument panel, he saw an array of warning lights flashing across in front of him. He reached out to attempt to correct what was going wrong before him just as the entire frame of the helicopter began to vibrate. Reaching instinctively for the controls, he managed to say, 'What the…?' just as sparks began erupting from many of the controls. Unable to tell if it was intense vibration or an actual electric shock, the pilot watched on in horror as the blue seemed to intensify in the woman's eyes. On either side of her, the two disabled, armed men still grasped their ears, their movement seeming to weaken. The vibration had become so intense across the helicopter that the pilot was failing to control it. The left side wheel of the undercarriage began to rise, and he would have sworn that he could see a strip of blue light flashing around him as the heat inside the cockpit rose incredibly.

Having initially turned her back on the scene, the high pitched noise of the helicopter engines caused Collette to turn quickly, dropping her mobile phone in the process. She cursed under her breath even though no one around her could have heard anything above the incessant noise. In the fading light, Collette's hand grasped blindly for her phone as she knelt, failing to understand why Megan now stood alone and erect, her arms extended on either side of her.

With her back to Collette, Megan's features were unseen, so she failed to see the broad grin that now filled the young girl's face. Almost blinded by the brightness of light that now pulsated around the helicopter, Collette fell to her knees, the impact on the stone gravel jarring her body. Just as she attempted to shout across to Megan, the light intensified further, and the force of the exploding helicopter threw her back towards the Coach House. The boom and rush of the explosion were strong enough to implode several of the windows in the front of the main house, Ravenscroft, shattering what silence remained within. The heat soared all around Megan, singeing the edges of her hair. The force of the second explosion from which she would later presume to be a separate fuel supply, forced her to take a step backwards to enable her to stay standing. All this time her arms remained extended on either side of her. Only when the edges of her coat began smoking in places, as small sections of burning fabric and metal had brushed past her, did she finally lower her arms. As the intense heat that had blown over her began to dissipate, Megan clutched her arms around herself as she now gasped for air.

Collette still shielded her face from the flames and smoke. Luckily the position she had sheltered in enabled her to find her missing mobile phone. Grasping it up quickly, she managed a slight smile when she saw that it still appeared to be working. What content there had been for her in her smile faded when she looked back across the still burning wreckage of the helicopter. One of the two soldiers had managed to stand again, though he still held a hand to one of his wounded ears. His weapon hung down beside him, his shape silhouetted against the yellow and gold of the flames. Collette screamed more out of annoyance than injury when she saw that the only other figure she could find a trace of was the soldier's accomplice. Of Megan, there was no sign.

Chapter 58

Three times she dialled before he finally answered. Had she not known that only Toby Connor had access to the particular mobile phone number she had rung, Collette would have sworn it was somebody else speaking.

'It's all gone,' he told her again, his voice as weak as it had when he had first spoken.

'What the hell are you talking about?' Collette demanded, pacing back and forth.

Little daylight remained now, the shadows spreading rapidly around the main house. The blazing wreckage of the helicopter added a surreal light across parts of the building. Many of the windows across the front which had been shattered by the explosion appeared to be darkening now, as welcome as freshly dug graves. All around where Collette stood, sections of wreckage burnt and smouldered, the piece closest to her was kicked hard as her annoyance and frustration mounted.

She could have continued asking him to explain himself clearer, but deep within her, the words he had spoken would always remain there to twist and turn her stomach in knots, sucking the very air out of her.

'It's all gone,' Toby repeated. 'Everything we had in our system is gone. All the data, all the codes. Everything has been wiped, Collette. Everything.'

Collette closed her eyes and clenched her free hand tight enough to cause one of her nails to pierce the palm of her right hand. Ignoring the discomfort, she tried to regain composure over the implications of Toby's words. Delivering the detailed information of A. R. Solution's business activities; access codes, passwords, and the unique data relating to Megan's specialist work, had been a core part of the exchange that Collette had promised to deliver, the fact that Megan herself had been orchestrating what appeared to Collette as her own escape had only helped.

Toby had soon located where she had hacked the company's computer system, and allowed her to continue, believing her actions had not been discovered, which had helped to remove Rowlance and McAndrew, along with the majority of the security team.

The leader of the assault team, Briggs, who had returned from the search of the Coach House, now tried to get her attention. Collette glared at him, holding out a flat hand to stop him, interrupting him.

'You're still there?' Toby asked, continuing when he heard a grunted response. 'You're finished, Collette. That freak has wrecked everything.'

'We're in this together, if you remember!' she screamed at him, her anger rising further when she heard him laugh nervously. 'Listen, you bastard, get what's left and make your way around here now,' she told him, not caring if her words caused suspicion amongst any of the assault team.

'What's left?' Toby enquired. 'You mean the extra money you've been filtering away? The amounts that you failed to inform me about? Oh, don't worry yourself about that part. I moved that a while back and have it all safe and sound.'

Collette could feel perspiration forming on her face even though her body temperature was falling rapidly. Anger somehow managed to hold onto her tongue as she felt compelled to hear what else Toby apparently wanted to tell her. As it was, his comment was brief, yet nearly caused her legs to buckle from under her.

'Goodbye, Collette,' Toby added before hanging up.

It was ironic that the gateway that Toby Connor drove through unhindered was the one that Collette Logan herself had ordered him to leave unmanned to enable them both to go unseen. Toby even paused at the rear entrance to the estate and looked back, though little could now be seen in the fading daylight, only a glow of what looked like a fire showing close to the main house. No one approached; he didn't expect them to as something had obviously gone wrong on the estate, the anger and frustration he had heard in Collette's voice confirming his thoughts. On leaving the cottage, he had taken Collette's Audi A3, a nervous smile filling his face as he adjusted the driver's seat and mirror. Now the seat beside him held only the laptop and files of Collette, including all that she needed now that she had changed sides, so to say. It was to have been so much more, the two of them leaving together, but now he didn't care. Distance was the only thing he needed between them now.

Confident that he hadn't been noticed, Toby turned the headlights on and picked up the mobile phone given to him by Collette. He looked at the screen and smiled, his face partially illuminated by the bright screen. The number calling him had no name listed on it because it didn't need one. Collette was the only person who had access to the phone. Toby swallowed hard, gripping the steering wheel firmly before tossing the still ringing mobile out of the window. Woodland soon skirted the road, the increasing shadows of the overhanging trees helping to conceal the vehicle that drove hurriedly away.

Chapter 59

Like others visitors before, both of the first armed figures to enter the main hallway of Ravenscroft were surprised by the interior of the property. A firm kick had been enough to make the door lock give way. The ornate hallway light reflected on the millions of glass fragments scattered around the floor, many tiny pieces crunching under the weight of the two figures that moved purposely, scanning the hallway, ensuring the entrance was clear before motioning for others of the team to follow.

The only threat known to all of the assault team was the lone security man that had been brought in to protect the girl, and while his whereabouts were reportedly still unknown, they more than outnumbered her apparent bodyguard. The thought of this helped the team leader, Briggs, and his sideman, Doyle, to focus on the operation that was still in progress, even though they had all witnessed the destruction of their main form of escape. Briggs had seen at least two vehicles parked in the courtyard and knew that they could utilise these once the girl was secure. The team used only surnames to communicate, each of them knowing most, if not all, were false. Doyle took a position to the left of the hallway, glancing briefly up at the overpowering staircase as his leader signalled for Davis and Keene to follow inside.

Briggs really would have preferred to have more personnel to search a house of this scale. Surprised to find the condition of the house belied the exterior, only the broken glass scattered around the floor close to the entrance gave any indication of the events that had recently happened. Another thing that concerned him was that the majority of the rooms of the building were now lit, the brightness failing to lift the gloom he and his team felt. Briggs knew that if they could isolate the electric supply, their night vision equipment would give his team an advantage. Content that the hallway was secure, he planned to leave the additional two members of the group, O'Connell and Walters, who had now entered, while the four of them began the search of the house.

Briggs noticed that an amount of blood still appeared to be flowing from one of O'Connell's ears and neither he nor Walters seemed to be able to hear properly. When Briggs attempted to assist one of them, his gesture was halted by Collette Logan who then entered, pushing him away, the level of her anger now more evident.

Jesus, what the hell is happening? Collette thought to herself as Briggs again attempted to help one of the injured men, and what was she herself doing in here? There was something churning inside her stomach that made her want to double up. It had hit her the moment she had stepped inside the doorway, as hard as though someone had stepped straight through her. Ignoring her discomfort, Collette tried to reassure herself with the fact that she had six highly trained, highly armed men with her who were surely more than capable of finding the freak show that she could now so easily bloody strangle. Everything else had gone wrong so far, and now she was playing a stupid cat and mouse chase inside a house of which she had heard bizarre tales about.

'Leave them,' she snapped at Briggs, hoping to regain the control she so craved. 'Our only concern is getting hold of Megan. I want that bitch back here, unharmed, now!'

Chapter 60

The third bedroom door that Davis kicked at remained unmoved. The jarring against his leg caused him to curse out loudly before kicking even harder against the area above the door handle, wondering why it had resisted more than the others. This time the extra effort was enough to send the door flying backwards only to reveal, as the two previous rooms had, that it was empty. Behind him, Keene called out, 'Clear,' making Davis head onto the last remaining door. Keene had already checked the bathroom at the end of the left-hand corridor, making this the only place on this side of the house that the girl could be hiding. With the same force, Davis kicked back the door and burst through the entrance with the Mp5 aimed ahead of him.

The scale of the room now facing him was greater than anything he or Keene had seen so far. It was at least fifty feet long, if not more, with the width almost half of that. Completely out of proportion with the rest of the house that they had seen, Davis wondered where on earth they were. A large bed, with what appeared to be fresh bedding, lay to the right-hand side of the room, with low cupboards on either side upon which two lit table lamp stood. Opposite, an enormous carved stone fireplace, the frame of which almost reached the ceiling, contained a recently prepared fire. Even though flames had yet to warm the room around where Davis stood, the scent of freshly cut logs hung heavy in the air. Cautious of his guard dropping, Davis moved forward, skirting past the bed towards a doorway that stood at the far end of the room. The closer he got to it, the more the light began to show around the edge of the door frame, showing on closer inspection that it was slightly ajar. He gave hand signals across the room to Keene, who quickly responded, silently taking a position on the opposite side of the room as Davis moved within a few feet of the doorway.

Over the last few years, Davis had been part of numerous similar situations like this, in far more dangerous conditions, but the increasing unease he felt within him was beginning to cause him great concern. *It's a teenage girl for god's sake!* he told himself silently, *not some brain washed bloody terrorist.* Yet when the doorway opened, the figure which then appeared made his mouth go dry as sandpaper, his heart thumping against his rib cage.

'Down on the floor!' Davis shouted, his order booming loudly around the room. He had no idea who the man could be or why he appeared to be bare-chested. The wounds that lined his torso bled heavily in places, but it wasn't this or the large handgun that the man held down by his side, it was the maniacal expression upon Thomas Kenny's face that forced him to repeat his demand.

'Drop the weapon!' Davies again ordered as his heart threatened to burst through his rib cage. Thomas obliged, the dull thud of the weapon against the wooden floor doing nothing to ease Davis's anguish.

'It's too late… too late,' the bare-chested man muttered as he turned to reveal the large head wound that freely pumped blood down his scarred shoulders and back. Davis fired instinctively, the sound of the discharged weapon oddly sounding muffled to him. Even so, a scream of anguish left him as a series of bullets racked the back of Thomas Kenny. Under the massive impact, the figure was thrust backwards, the body spinning around wildly before falling out of sight behind the frame of the door. Davis raced forward, not trusting that the man was no longer armed, even though no other weapons were visible. In the brief seconds that he took to step into what he could now see was a bathroom, Davis wondered why the man could even have been alive before he had repeatedly shot him given the extent of the injury he saw across his head. The sight that greeted Davis when he stepped into the room made his eyes bulge as big as his rapidly beating heart, whilst bile rose quickly in his throat as he took in the sight around him.

The room was around twenty feet square and contained nothing more than a bath, set against the far wall, filled with a dark liquid that appeared to be blood. So full was the bath that it ran freely over the edges, spreading around part of the now twisted frame of Thomas Kenny below. On the white tiles that lined the windowless room, more blood streaked down them, appearing to form words in places. Most of them spelt out the words 'too late' or 'much too late'. Struggling now to keep control of his mind, Davis felt his eyes being drawn away from the sight before him to the wall to his left, wherein two foot-high letters, again made with blood, was written the message.

'It's too late, Shaun.'

The sight of his actual name amid the carnage was too much for Davis, who now failed to hold onto the bile within him. Collapsing onto one knee, he pulled his face visor clear, retching to the side of the figure below him. Needing to focus, he called out to Keene, wondering where the hell his colleague could be, at the same time reaching out to turn the figure below him over. The blank eyes of his partner, Keene, looked back at him, the entry wounds of Davis's shots lined across the front of his body. For some unknown reason, no protective body armour now covered his colleague, the horrific injuries making Davis cry out and recoil backwards, his unmeasured movement helping to slam the door behind him. He held a hand across his gaping mouth as from the blood filled bath a figure began to slowly rise, the movement causing a further spillage of blood around the tiled floor. The figure wore the distinctive Kevlar body armour, yet the night vision goggles were pushed back on top of the head of the blood-soaked features of Thomas Kenny who smiled weakly before saying, 'Too late, I'm afraid. Far, far too late…'

Davis screamed and frantically attempted to climb to his feet, but he slipped, banging his elbow hard against the tiled floor. The doorway seemed to have now been replaced by what looked like a black wall, the density of which somehow held a curiosity for him. Now, almost impossibly, the black form moved forward and Davis chose to embrace the blackness rather than face the madness behind him. By the time he was fully consumed, the screaming really began.

Chapter 61

Traces of dust and cobwebs remained on the shoulders of Megan's coat even after she had attempted to brush them away. As she stepped back into the lower corridor, she left the section of wooden panelling that she had removed to conceal herself when she had heard the others approaching. Within the narrow confine, her mind kept drifting back to Charlotte. Moving a hand inside her coat, she could still feel the damp section of her clothing where blood had soaked into it. Closing her eyes, she tried to clear her mind and shut out the pain she was feeling. When she heard one of the assault team approaching, she clenched her fists and attempted to hold her breath, fearing that the slightest sound would give her away. The louder of the two voices she could hear stood right alongside where she was, making Megan fear the panelling would be ripped off the wall and hands would reach in to grab her. But after speaking to another of the team members, the corridor had fallen silent. Too silent. The change in atmosphere and pressure told her that the house had changed once more.

Megan was surprised when she finally looked out to find the corridor partly filled with furniture. Of the men searching for her, there was no trace.

A tall display cabinet was closest to her, with shelves of old books were visible through the leaded glass doors. The spines of many were cracked with time and use; the titles faint and discoloured. As if to confirm that what she was seeing wasn't just an illusion, Megan ran a hand across the cabinet, the smoothness of the wood soothing her mind for some reason. Underneath two of the windows she passed, ornate wooden chairs sat empty, as were the open drawers on a small bureau where stacks of papers stood, held in place by polished stone paperweights. Megan paused by the bureau and looked at the top document, studying the writing. The faded ink masked the words she attempted to read, and the sense of intrusion was making her move on. When she did, she approached more doorways.

A noise ahead of her drew her attention away, making her continue along the corridor which angled slightly before coming to an abrupt end. Megan found herself facing another doorway which, when she opened and stepped through, brought her back to what looked like the main kitchen of the house.

Most of the fittings in the room were of similar design to those she recalled seeing on previous visits, but before, where many of the cupboard doors were either open or missing, most were now closed. Moving close to one of them, she pulled on the small handle, revealing shelves full of provisions inside. She repeated the same action on other cupboards, as well as drawers next to the sink. On the table were neatly stacked, clean plates and bowls, which gave an impression that they awaited someone to store them away in their relevant home. What had caused the noise which she was sure she had heard was unknown. She moved across the kitchen to where another closed doorway stood, Megan remaining unsure whether to stay in the kitchen as the feeling that she was somehow intruding was growing stronger within her. After checking behind her to ensure she wasn't being followed, she returned to the doorway through which she had entered, failing to see the shape that waited in the shadows. The figure moved quickly, pressing a hand against her mouth to silence her as she looked unsuspectingly backwards.

Page felt as though his hand had received a form of electric shock. He had found himself suddenly walking into yet another corridor, this one entirely different to others he had seen. It contained several items of furniture set against both walls. The decoration spoke of a bygone era, as did the style of furniture he viewed. Small framed paintings filled the spaces between the windows, many showing scenes of unknown places. The stale air seemed almost overpowering, making Page want to stop and open a window to allow some fresh air to penetrate. Like many of the other corridors, the house seemed capable of showing him the length was uncertain. When he heard the sound of an approaching doorway opening, Page had reached instinctively inside his jacket pocket, using both his hands to aim the Glock 36 ahead of him in an instant. Unsure of who was approaching and fearing what the house was now about to present to him, Page had taken the only cover he could find – in the shadows of a tall wardrobe close to the open doorway.

Of all the people he wanted to appear, it was Megan. She still had to be his main reason for even being there. Unsure of whether she was alone or if she was being followed, he had switched hands with the handgun, reaching out to pull her into the shadows.

Moments before he had come across the dark corridor, his body had been calling for him to rest, to find a place of peace where he could begin to take in all that he had learnt. But when he had pressed his hand over Megan's mouth and chin, all his senses seemed to explode. It had only been a couple of seconds at the most, but his hand had felt almost stuck to the young girl, as though an immense heat had been directed at him. When the sensation forced him to release her, nausea had swept over him and he was forced to hold a hand out to the wardrobe to prevent his legs from collapsing under him.

When Megan backed away, her appearance startled Page. Her wide eyes underneath a sea of unruly hair, were filled with fear. The reduced light around them caused the area around her eyes to appear almost bruised. Under her black coat, there seemed to be bloodstains across the pink jumper she wore. On the shoulders of her coat, traces of cobwebs could be seen, hanging mostly from sections of dirt still held upon it.

'I thought I'd lost you,' Megan said weakly while slowly running a hand through one side of her hair.

Page felt unable to answer, his body weakened from the contact with her, and he gave into the demands of his legs and slumped down with his back against the wall behind him. Raising one of his knees, he placed the handgun on the floor beside him and clenched his fingers, attempting to lose the sensation as he looked across at her.

'What happened?' he finally managed to ask, the amount of unease in her expression unsettling. 'And where the hell are we now?'

'Somewhere we shouldn't be,' she replied, ignoring his first question whilst looking down the corridor each way.

'We need to go,' she continued, motioning with one hand for him to stand. When her words failed to move him, Megan leant forward until her face was barely inches from his own. 'We really do need to go.'

'Or what?' he asked.

'Or we'll never get out of here.'

'We're not going anywhere until you tell me what has happened. I thought I heard gunfire.'

In the increasing gloom at the end of the corridor, Megan recounted only the details of her fall from the window. Only occasionally did her eyes meet his while she spoke, all the time the discomfort she felt at recalling the events making her resume biting on one of her fingernails. All the time she spoke, Page believed she was holding back from telling him something.

'What caused the fall?' he asked her, but his words failed to register with her, making him raise himself on one knee and snap his fingers in front of her face. The simple action made her look at him as though she had only just woken.

'Megan, how did you fall from the window? What were you doing?'

'The house pushed me out, alright!' she told him, clenching one of her hands so tight that one of her finger nails pierced her skin.

Compared with what he had experienced in the cellar, her words actually made some form of sense. He felt that there was nothing the house could now show him or make him believe he was seeing. When he managed to stand, Page straightened one of the sleeves of his jacket that had ridden up his arm, ignoring the discomfort his body felt.

'We must go,' she told him, unsure herself of which direction, the thought disappearing within her as the faint sound of music could be heard in the distance.

Chapter 62

The commotion on the left-hand side of the upper floor drew Briggs back along the corridor. Preferring to use the night goggles upon his headgear, he used his weapon to strike out at the overhead lights he passed, the glass pieces scattering to the floor around him. Now concealed within the partial darkness, he smirked at his increased confidence as he glanced briefly into each of the rooms he passed, finding each empty. The screams and gunfire that he had heard must have come from one of the last two rooms he neared. With the Mp5 raised before him, he edged forward to find the last doorways, like previous ones, open. Again, each room was empty, as was the bathroom at the end. Briggs turned quickly, checking behind him, confused and puzzled by what was happening. He was in doubt that the noises had come from where he now stood, but only empty rooms surrounded him. Maybe he had missed something. Something concealed. Yet hadn't all the rooms been empty? *Check them again,* he thought, at the same time wondering where the hell Doyle was. Moving quickly, he scanned the bathroom at the far end, only darkness showing in his eyepieces. When he repeated his searches of the four other rooms, he found them all as before – empty. The final room he searched was nearest to the open landing space, yet when he stepped back out into the corridor he found he was much further down than expected, with dozens of doors stretching out as far as he could see. He was beginning to worry what was happening and why no sound or answers came in his ear as response to his requests for progress from the rest of the team. Briggs retreated the way he believed he had come, his footsteps now sounding loud against the hardwood floor.

Doyle had discarded his night vision goggles, preferring to use the natural light around him. Since being a child, he was confident of finding his way around in poor light. Throughout his military training, he had used this natural ability to his benefit, surprising all around him by his keen vision in poor lighting conditions. *Too many bleeding carrots that my grandmother had forced me to eat as a child,* he had often mused to himself as he began moving cautiously from room to room. More than once his mind asked what was so special about the young woman they had come to collect. There was supposed to have been no resistance, and in fairness, he and Briggs had seen none, having both been out of sight when the helicopter exploded. The explosion had ripped through the air, the sound echoing around the sides of the large house where they had both taken position near the entrance as instructed. While Briggs had remained in place, Doyle raced around the side of the large house. In the glare of the fireball ahead of him, his colleague had recounted how he had seen the figure of what looked like a woman with both her arms extended, emitting what appeared to him to be a blue light all around her. A second, smaller explosion had forced him to take cover and in doing so lose sight of her just as she moved away. Doyle, though, had seen the figure run towards the main entrance to the house and had confirmed that it was a young woman, her hair wild around her gaunt looking features and frame which the flames highlighted.

At that point, he had been unsure as to who she was and what risk, if any, she posed to the mission. To gain an advantage, Doyle had sunk back into the shadows at the side of the entrance. Though the girl had been in a hurry to reach the property, she had briefly paused as though she had possibly seen or sensed him. *Unlikely,* he had thought, as he considered himself something of an expert when it came to blending himself with the natural surroundings. Content that he had been wrong, Doyle smiled as she moved on, opening the door, and moving urgently inside. Having kept his position until he knew he was safe to appear, he had then come across Briggs, to whom he had recounted the details. Doyle had no idea who the short haired woman his team leader had shown up with was, but she had attracted his attention immediately. Whilst instantly attractive, it had soon been lost by her agitated and more than pissed off manner. She had then begun giving instructions about how the girl was to be brought back unharmed.

We'll see about that, he thought as he began his search of the upstairs corridor, finding to his disappointment, that the next room he came to was also empty.

To his right, he now saw the shape of a figure moving alongside the outer wall. Presuming that it was his partner, he moved silently forward, becoming aware of an increasing chill in the corridor.

Chapter 63

The vast silhouetted shape of the airliner appeared to be motionless in the air as it made its steady descent towards Manchester Airport. Charles McAndrew had been watching it on and off for the last two miles, and by the height, he judged it was close to landing. McAndrew had always thought how graceful aircraft looked as they were coming in, and just how on earth they managed to get the damn thing airborne in the first place puzzled him. In the seat alongside him, Anthony Rowlance began filing away the paperwork that he had been working on for most of the journey. A couple of times they had struck up a conversation, but each time it had been interrupted by phone calls. Only a small percentage of phone lines which Rowlance tried seemed to be contactable for some reason, the desperate need to regain some form of order and control showing on his friend's face. The tension between the two of them remained even though a fair distance was now between the two travelling Mercedes and the Ravenscroft estate. The near silence though was almost welcomed by McAndrew, who had preferred to gaze over the passing countryside in an attempt to take his mind off how he was going to face Jean next. How graceful she always was to him. He had promised her things would change for the better, but had he really expected that or had he been swept along on the false hope of others? He glanced at Anthony Rowlance when he attracted the attention of the security man in the front passenger seat.

'Make a detour,' Rowlance ordered, holding his mobile phone to his chest, making the security man in the passenger seat turn and face him. 'Go straight to the Arlington Hotel.'

When the guard nodded to confirm his request, Rowlance added, 'And go by the southern entrance.' Behind, once the message was relayed, the following Mercedes moved closer.

Charles McAndrew was about to query what had brought about the change in direction when Rowlance shot out a hand to silence him.

'That's ridiculous!' Rowlance shouted into the mobile phone, having resumed his conversation. Clutching the phone harder, he ordered, 'Get me Rowling, now!'

Concern grew rapidly in Charles McAndrew, strong enough even to take away the thought of both Jean and Room 23. Darren Rowling was head of the main drilling project that Toby Connor had been supplying information for the last few days, information that had attributed to their hasty return to Manchester. Rowling was a trusted member of staff and if his actions were alarming his employee, it was something to be concerned over.

'But I've seen the readouts,' Rowlance then claimed, drawing McAndrew's attention back to the conversation. 'What you are saying makes no sense with what I've seen with my own eyes.'

After more heated exchanges over the phone, Rowlance hung up. When he pressed the stop button firmly, he spent several moments staring at the blank screen as though answers for his thoughts would appear.

The greasiness of Kelly Goodwin's fingertips caused her to press the wrong contact number on her mobile accidently. She cursed loudly, though the latest guitar solo from Guns N' Roses muffled her words as it continued to blast out from the speakers around her. Glancing up, she checked on her position with the surrounding traffic before flicking down the list of contacts until she found Nadine's name again. Kelly found it hard to believe that Nadine was now twenty-eight. Although she was three years younger than her best friend, she had always considered them to be the same age, almost like twins, as their ways were so similar. The excitement of the birthday party that the two of them, along with others, would soon be enjoying made Kelly press her right foot down harder. The engine of her Renault Cleo responded instantly.

The traffic on the M6 had been heavy for most of her journey from the Midlands, using up quality time with the girls, she joked to herself as she glanced in the side view mirror beside her. *They should get all Lorries off the bleeding road,* she thought as she pulled out to overtake the latest one that attempted to delay her. Safely past, she pulled in again and took another handful of salt and vinegar crisps and filled her mouth, this time wiping her fingers on the side of her seat before she reached again for her mobile. Kelly needed to let Nadine know that she was running late and would go straight to Deansgate Locks, close to the city centre. *Better to go there first,* she thought, *instead of checking into the hotel we are all booked into.*

'Hey girl,' she shouted into her phone when the connection was made, at the same reaching over to turn her CD player down. Managing to hold the driver's wheel using one of her thighs, she adjusted the position of her mobile against her ear when she struggled to hear her friend's reply.

Another couple of crisps reached her mouth by the time she managed to hear Nadine's repeated words, 'It's gonna be a riot!' she told her, struggling to suppress her growing excitement. 'So long as we all got together. We should…' The silence that cut off her friend's words, made Kelly glance at the screen of her phone. To her annoyance, she had lost the signal.

'Shit!' she said looking down to flick through her contact list again. Kelly had no idea where the black Mercedes had come from and even less idea why it now cut straight across in front of her. The brake lights took Kelly's eyes off the approaching junction and made her pull the wheel to her left to prevent her driving into the back of it. But her judgement was wrong, and her greasy fingers failed to hold the steering wheel safely. When she tried to correct her position, her speed was too fast, making her front wing connect with the rear of the Mercedes.

Anthony Rowlance had been trying to keep his voice measured as he related the information that his three phone calls had made. How on earth could all of Toby's data been so wrong? More worryingly, how could he have accepted what he had been told without checking himself? *Jesus, what is happening?* he thought as he felt the swift movement of the vehicle as the driver made his manoeuvre at a speed to reach the rapidly approaching junction. He saw the worry in Charles McAndrew's eyes just as something hit the rear of the Mercedes.

Kelly screamed at the impact with the Mercedes, her braking strong enough to cause the rear end of her Renault Cleo to begin to come round. Her hands were now too greasy and unsteady to take control of the vehicle, and she had no idea that the following black car was also moving across to take the motorway exit. On the passenger seat, her mobile began to ring the moment the second Mercedes slammed into the side of her car. The impact shattered the window beside her, the blast of air blowing part of her hair across her face as the continuing rock music and the blasting of car horns sounded around her. She closed her eyes as the Cleo was spun completely around, the view of oncoming traffic appearing on her windscreen. The further jolting of her car colliding with two other vehicles made her scream again.

The security driver of the lead Mercedes needed all his experience to regain control. Having counteracted the force of the impact against the rear, the driver used the gearbox to rapidly slow the vehicle, skilfully handling the movement enough to guide the vehicle down the slip road. He was able to pull onto the verge of the roadway where the following three vehicles came to a halt beside them.

Anthony Rowlance and Charles McAndrew found themselves holding an arm against each other to steady themselves, even though the driver of the vehicle had at least regained control. As McAndrew looked back, the following group of vehicles, including an HGV he recalled passing moments before, ploughed into the back of the support Mercedes. For what could only have been seconds but felt to have taken much longer, there was a screeching sound of metal colliding as the mass of vehicles moved forward for another hundred yards or so before coming to a sudden halt.

Charles McAndrew could see the bewildered Anthony Rowlance mouthing words to the driver of their vehicle, but he failed to hear them. He closed his eyes from the chaos around him and thought of Jean. For so many years his wife had been all that he really ever wanted. He smiled as she appeared to him and took his hand in hers. Her touch was strong and graceful like he remembered, as a single tear ran slowly down his face.

Chapter 64

Briggs had repeatedly tried to get any form of response from his team through his earpiece as he crept through the changing corridors of Ravenscroft, but each time found it completely dead. Even so, he kept it in place, hoping that it was just the section of the house that he was in that was causing it. Without contact with the rest of the team, he knew, like the others, he was going in near blind in their search for the young woman. His night vision goggles gave him an edge though, he told himself as he approached a doorway ahead of him. The rooms he had previously searched had been entirely bare, so he was surprised to see that within the one he now scanned, there was furniture. No traces of heat showed in his eyesight, only the edge of a large bed and accompanying wardrobes filled the room. With his weapon raised continuously in front of him, he opened both of the room's wardrobes, finding them like the rest of the room – empty. With his back against one of the walls, he prepared to exit the room just as a small figure hurried past the doorway.

It was the old-fashioned clothing of the young boy that Briggs had noticed in the briefest of glances, the whiteness of his shirt and socks appearing a faded grey against the darkness of his crumpled trousers. When he stepped back into the corridor, he found the boy stood about twenty feet away from him, looking into another room. Before Briggs could move closer, the boy began clapping his hands, laughing loudly as a young girl no more than seven or eight joined him.

The boy hugged the girl as though he had missed her badly before the two of them turned to face Briggs, who felt his skin become as cold as ice when he saw that the eyes of both of the children were missing.

Doyle could not see why the form of his leader failed to show in his now worn goggles. He was close to him now, less than twelve feet, yet his increased movement failed to show any trace of his body in his lenses. Discarding them by lifting them onto his forehead didn't help; it was only then that doubt began to tell him that it possibly wasn't Briggs at all. Patches of light started highlighting the figure who appeared to be much smaller than he had initially thought. Leaning more on his heels to conceal the sound of his movement, he moved with increasing caution as the corridor began to veer to the left. There the light improved dramatically, fully illuminating the figure he had been following.

Doyle pulled the Mp5 tighter against his shoulder as he moved silently across the corridor, revealing a sight that surprised him.

A young girl skipped along the corridor, her auburn hair bouncing up and down at the movement. Where her feet touched the floor, millions of particles of dust erupted into the air as though she was leaving a trail of magic sand behind her. When she suddenly stopped, the girl looked back at him as though only now aware of his presence and smiled widely, showing a slight gap between her uneven teeth. The line of freckles across her small nose added a cuteness which matched her large eyes. She used a hand to encourage him forward before resuming her skipping once more. When the angle of the corridor increased, she disappeared out of sight, making Doyle move quickly forward as though drawn on by the girls' actions.

Doyle himself then abruptly stopped when he saw light streaming from one of the bedrooms. There was no sign of the girl now, but traces of her footsteps still showed in the dust upon the threadbare carpet. The light from the doorway was now bright enough to cause Doyle to lower his head slightly, forcing him to have to squint to enable him to see clearly.

'We should join the others,' a voice said behind him, making him react instinctively by striking out. He felt the side of the weapon make contact with who had spoken. Doyle was horrified to look down on a small boy, no more than ten, lying face down with blood seeping from the wound across his forehead. Still aiming his weapon, he used one of his feet to gently tap the small, unmoving figure.

A piercing scream broke his eyes away from the boy, to where a series of shadows flickered around the doorway ahead of him. Making a swift decision to move, Doyle burst through the doorway, firing his weapon as he did so. The line of bullets raked the far wall, some of them shattering the few remaining intact windows while others only found the soft plaster upon the wall. When the sound of gunfire diminished, Doyle was amazed to see himself standing in an empty room.

The sensation that suddenly hit him brought with it a mixture of both confusion and wonder. He had sensed movement behind him, yet he showed or felt no urgency to see what had caused it. Even the sight of the silver-haired man who now faced him failed to add to his surprise. The sight of the grinning girl beside him, the one who he had followed in the corridor, was enough for him to attempt to raise his weapon again. Doyle found his hands empty.

'There is no need to panic,' Mathew Jarvis told him softly, 'no need at all really.'

Doyle frantically tried to find another weapon upon him, unaware how fortunate he was to catch sight of the new arrival. Only Megan herself had ever seen the thin, sombre features of Jarvis, his skin even paler than it had been whilst alive. His words, like his body movements, were slow, almost intentional, as though a more devious side to him was just below the surface. Sections of his religious robes were stained in what appeared to be blood.

Doyle again grasped at his body armour, looking for any form of weapon. He found his hands repeatedly slipped off his body due to a red substance they were now covered in. When he looked down, Doyle saw a figure lay below him, the body armour heavily stained with the same substance. Even though the face of the unknown figure remained concealed, Doyle felt his mouth instantly dry as he tried to make sense of what he was seeing. The white line of a scar he had worn for the last ten years seemed more evident than he recalled, the deep crimson blood around his throat only looking to emphasise this more. Doyle clutched at his throat and felt a warmth upon his hands that bizarrely appeared welcoming. He took a few steps back into the room, away from the replica image of himself on the floor, just as other small figures began to appear around Mathew Jarvis. Several of these, ones in which eyes remained, began to grin as he backed into something, causing him to fall backwards. He had expected the figure he fell over to be another child, one perhaps to have knelt behind him to help him fall, but the lifeless expression of Briggs failed to show any humour. Doyle attempted to scream, but his action only caused more blood to ooze from his open wound.

'Once you get past the shock, it's almost manageable,' Jarvis told him. 'Being dead has its downsides; the pain remains, as does the guilt and anguish, but over time, they become unbearable.' Then, almost laughing, he added, 'At moments there can be so much fun.'

The laughter of the children became engulfed by a black form which surged into the room, more than matching the darkness which Doyle found when he closed his eyes. The simple action was only delaying the terror which followed.

Chapter 65

Initially, the music had been less defined, almost making Page think that he had misheard or even imagined it, but now that they were closer to the source, each individual note could be heard. The tune was unknown to Page, but it reminded Megan of a jewellery box which Charlotte had shown her when they had first started to get close, the thought making emotions rise within her.

They were surprised when a stairway began to appear through the gloom before them. As the items of furniture had diminished, so had the numbers of windows, reducing the quality of the light around them. They believed that they had reached what appeared to be the end of the corridor, but beyond the stairway a much narrower passage continued. How far, it was impossible to tell.

Initially grateful that it only descended, Page's unease remained when he stood at the top of the stairway peering downwards, seeing that after a long section it appeared to turn back on itself. It had been too much, he guessed, to hope for it to have been the central stairway of the house, and he felt annoyed at himself for building his hopes up for a quick exit. He shook his head at Megan's suggestion that they take the stairway, insisting on moving on, possibly taking the passage instead. Page was about to tell her to follow him when he saw Megan suddenly stop and turn her head as though she had heard something. She was about to say something when a voice spoke, a deep voice which sapped at the energy and will of Page.

'You need to show him,' the deep voice said. 'You need to show him the truth, or you'll never leave.'

Megan moved quickly towards him, but her steps quickly became laboured and heavy. She could see him reach an arm out to her whilst mouthing words that she failed to hear, as beneath her feet the stairway appeared to widen.

The sudden change almost caused Page to pass out. Nausea was again sweeping over him. As he felt himself begin to overbalance, he feared that he would fall down the stairway and lose sight of Megan once again. His attempts to call out to her had all but failed as the pressure against his face and chest increased. His lungs protested at the lack of breath they could find and fearing a fall would now follow, Page pulled his elbows close to his sides, cradling his head as the floor appeared to fall away from beneath him. As if woken suddenly from a nightmarish sleep, his eyes snapped wide open. As he lifted his hands slightly away from his head, the slight gap enabled him to see through his fingers to see where he now was. To his dismay, Page found himself alone, standing at the top of a narrow wooden staircase.

The change in air pressure was soon noticeable, as was the dip in temperature, as perspiration began to cover his body. Page felt his shirt sticking to his back as he reached inside his jacket to feel for his weapon. Panic gripped him when his hand touched only the empty holster. There was some reassurance, but just a small amount, when he noticed the weight in his jacket pocket and found to his relief that he must have put it in there earlier.

The handgun was still fully loaded when he checked, but he had no other ammunition with him and knew there was nothing to waste if he needed to use it. A sound caught his attention, making him quickly take hold of the weapon, only to point it directly at Megan who stepped out of nearby shadows.

'Jesus, stop frigging well appearing like that,' he told her, lowering his arms. 'You'll end up scaring me more than the bloody house itself.'

Megan ignored his remark, failing to see his attempt at injecting a touch of humour, and began to descend the staircase. At first, Page thought that they had found another entrance to the cellar, but when he followed her, the stairs only ran down a few steps before emerging into a chamber, off which led three matching doors.

A curious odour filled what little air that he felt he could breathe. Not overpowering, but subtle enough to hold an interest in him. It was one which Page thought he should know, but at that moment failed to recognise.

The stone floor of the chamber was clean and bare, the walls surprisingly as dry as the main cellar area which he had earlier been in. As Page walked into the centre of the chamber, the low ceiling caused him to raise a hand against the glare of the crude light fitting hanging from the ceiling.

'What is this place?' Page asked, his mind filling with questions all the time.

'It's what I needed to show you,' she answered, moving forward and holding out her hands to him. The skin upon her face looked as pale as bleached bone, the lack of colour only highlighting the dark rings that had taken refuge around her eyes.

When she came closer to him, her eyes appeared more profound than he could recall.

'You need to see,' he heard Megan say even though her lips remained unmoving as she stared intently at him, 'you need to see where it all began. The place of your birth.'

Taking her hands in his, Page felt as though his body had suddenly hurtled through an opening in the floor. When he looked down, the stone floor remained the same below him. The shadows around them began moving at increasing speed, causing the doorways which he had seen to sway violently around him. He attempted to close his eyes, to lose the madness he was witnessing around him, but found that he was unable to do so. Just when he feared he would lose hold of Megan's grip, a series of jolts caused him to adjust his footing to prevent himself from overbalancing. His face felt as if it had been plunged in a bucket of ice. When he tried to break free of the girl's grasp, he only felt it tighten. Within a few moments the swirling sensation stopped and he found himself alone in a small room which appeared no more than ten feet across. Only a single bed, a small bedside table, and a wooden chair occupied the place, the crumpled bedding suggesting it had recently been slept in. Light from the bedside lamp cast shadows across several items of clothing laid on the back of the chair, with what looked like stains of blood on some of them. A sound caught his ear, making Page glance across to his left where he could see another doorway slightly ajar. A line of much brighter light edged the door, his curiosity making him move closer. He strained his ear against the wooden door in an attempt to hear any sounds within. The sound of running water could now be heard. Pushing the door slowly open, Page called out as the doorway revealed a figure who stood with its back to him. The figure failed to respond to his arrival.

'She can't hear or see you,' he heard Megan say even though when he looked around him there was no trace of her.

'Who is she?' he asked as he moved alongside the woman who he could now see was rinsing her hands in a deep stone sink. The black hooded shawl which the woman wore showed only traces of the grey hair beneath, the edges lining her aged face. Her hands showed her age stronger as she rubbed them together vigorously, and after reaching across to turn the running water tap off, she patted her hands together on one of a series of towels stacked beside the sink. Page noted several of the towels in a pile close to the woman's feet. Several of these were heavily stained and damp, as though the woman had attempted to clean them at the sink.

The woman sighed heavily and rested her hands on the edge of the sink as though her body was too weak for her to continue to stand. There seemed a great kindness in her lined eyes, like they held an amount of wisdom that Page would never know.

'Who is she?' he asked again as he watched her turn to leave the room.

'Her name is unknown, but she came here to offer help to those that needed it at the time.'

Page followed her into the room that he had previously stood in, but this time he found the bed occupied. The old woman leant over a figure lying on the bed which now turned slowly, allowing the older woman to brush back the damp hair around her face. The young woman's features were sharp, though a weakness showed in her eyes. She seemed grateful for the help she was receiving, the traces of a smile beginning to show at the edges of her mouth and eyes.

When Page stepped closer, he could see what looked like another bundle of towels laid next to the woman, unseen from where he had been looking before. The young woman's eyes were drawn down now, showing concern as signs of movement came from within the bundle. A mixture of curiosity and fear ran through Page's body and mind, his presence to the scene feeling almost intrusive in some ways. When the edge of what Page could now see was a towel moved, a small limb protruded to reveal the tiny fingers of a hand unfolding, reaching out towards him. Lifting the bundle slightly higher now, the woman smiled weakly as the face of her child became visible, the small mouth giving out another cry as though it had come from Page's very own. Around him, within the stifling heat of the small room, Page became aware of what the smell he had earlier sensed was. It was the scent of a birth.

Where there had been warmth in the young woman's face moments before, there was now concern as the old woman continued to stroke the side of the mother's face.

'You must take the child away from here as soon as you can,' the old woman almost croaked, 'far, far away. I have done all that I can for you; this place holds nothing good for him. Nothing but evil here. You must take him away and keep the child safe.'

On the small table alongside the bedside lamp, a small musical box slowly played its delicate and soothing tune.

A sudden jolt took Page away from the room. A thousand questions fought for attention as shadows arched across the small room, many hiding the figures around the bedside. Desperate now to keep hold of them, Page struggled to move as he sought to get a better view. He felt not only his body but his mind being grabbed at, the pressure within the confined room engulfing him. The sensation of falling released him, though a new sense of panic set in, only to be taken away in an instant when he found himself face down on a wooden floor.

The coldness of the surface made him attempt to stand, but his body protested too much at the sudden movement. He needed to return to the scene that he had been witnessing, to see what he could scarcely believe. The hand that grabbed the collar of his jacket brought him quickly to his senses, the tips of Megan's hair brushing gently against his face as she leant over him again to pull once more on his form.

'Get up!' she cried at him. 'We have to get out of here now.'

Before he could answer, the sound of gunfire filled the air close by, masked only slightly by the screams that soon accompanied them.

Chapter 66

There was no limit to the pain that Collette Logan wanted to exert on Toby Connor. The useless bastard had help ruin everything. All the planning she had done, and all the crap that she had put up with Rowlance and his company over the last few years. But Collette realised that Toby was now the least of her worries. She had made guarantees to certain people, and promised people who she dared not disappoint. It was hard to believe that all the work that they had done together was somehow gone. Everything was within those files; all her contacts, all the points of access to the money that she had redirected, everything. More annoying, Toby had kept all the backup files they had both made. Collette swallowed hard, forcing herself to focus. It was vital that she put what had happened to the back of her mind and concentrate on the here and now.

Beside her, O'Donnell stood more or less alert, even though traces of blood still showed against parts of his pale features. He looked eagerly around the hallway where the three of them stood, his actions understandably unsettled.

O'Donnell's left ear was still incredibly painful, to the point that it occasionally caused his balance to be affected, but at least the bleeding had stopped. Trying not to think about what long-term damage had been done to his hearing, he looked across to where Walters continued to hold a white cloth to one of his injured ears. Unsure of how long they had been waiting for the others to search the house, O'Donnell took another circuit of the hallway, keeping the automatic weapon ready to use. He felt vulnerable with Walters looking too weak to assist him.

Should the situation arise where he needed help, he began doubting whether he could cope by himself. Inside, he prayed that they could leave this godforsaken place as soon as possible, and that Briggs or the woman had a clue as to just how they were going to get away from the estate. It wasn't as though they were in hostile territory or that they had any resistance to concern themselves, but there was something about the house that was unsettling him. They were looking for a teenage girl in an empty house. Nothing more than that. The rest of the team, like himself, were fully armed, yet an increasing feeling was growing in him that it wasn't going to be of any use.

Collette had now given up trying to contact Toby Connor on her mobile. All she had gotten on her previous attempts was a constant ringing, the repetitive sound only annoying her further. Pocketing the mobile, she pursed her lips as she checked the time on her watch. Jesus, they should have been away from here by now. The freak show, Megan, should have been close to being delivered, and Collette should be away from this place and taking the first steps to shaping her life the way she wanted, and more importantly, needed.

Ahead of where she stood in the hallway of Ravenscroft, O'Donnell paced back and forth, waiting like she was for contact with the rest of the team. The other remaining member of the assault team occasionally glanced at Collette, his expression full of concern, as though expecting further instructions from her.

When he reached the bottom of the staircase, O'Donnell lowered his weapon slightly, using his free hand to touch the more painful of his ears. The ringing sound had subsided, but the pain and discomfort remained. He also feared permanent damage had been done to the right ear as he couldn't hear anything at all from it. The times that Collette had spoken to him, he had been forced to angle his head to enable him to hear properly. If the events of the last hour had not been enough for him, the house that he now found himself in was unsettling him. Aside from the hallway, both he and Walters had only been in the sitting room and kitchen, yet that was more than he wanted to see of the place. Everywhere he stood, he felt as though he was being watched, almost scrutinised. He took a couple of tentative steps up the staircase, craning his neck to look further up. *Stop spooking yourself,* he thought as he tightened his grip on the automatic weapon's handle. Retracing his steps, he felt his mouth go dry when he looked across to where Collette Logan stood.

As though she had sensed his scrutiny, Collette asked what had alerted O'Donnell.

'What the hell is wrong with you?' she asked as Walters himself began taking an interest.

O'Donnell felt unable to answer as his eyes were held by the stare of the woman who stood behind Collette. Quite why she hadn't reacted to the woman's arrival herself he was unsure of. The changing situation made him readjust his aim as he stepped towards them. O'Donnell guessed that the woman was in her late sixties, with a swept-back hairstyle and black clothing only adding to her stern appearance. For what reason the woman was wringing her hands O'Donnell had no idea, but her actions were alarming him.

'Step away,' O'Donnell ordered, the weapon now aimed directly at the woman as he repeated his words.

Collette had no idea what had gotten into the man's mind or what the hell he was looking at. She was about to speak again when Walters also stepped forward, also aiming his weapon. Following the other man's gaze, Collette looked across to the doorway which led to the kitchen but saw nothing untoward. Walters himself wondered why only his partner seemed to be concerned by the woman who was advancing quickly towards the short haired woman. Walters felt movement in his left ear, then felt a pulsating pain sweep over him as the trickle of blood started to flow down the side of his neck. He had to stop this. He had to stop the awful feeling that was rising in him. Not wanting to wait for instructions and seemingly oblivious to the concerns of O'Donnell, he pushed Collette aside and began firing, raking bullets across the figure of the elderly woman.

Chapter 67

There was a trembling which refused to leave Page Darrow's hand. He had been holding out his hands for over a minute now, watching how an area around the wrist and the tip of his index finger refused to stay still. Unable to decide whether it was nerve damage or evidence of his crumbling mind, he lowered his hands, forming a fist before he banged it against the carpet beside him. Sitting hunched with his back against the wall of another corridor he failed to understand, he watched the dust that rose from the impact of his fist, wondering how something which he believed didn't exist could look so real. As if to prove a point, he blew out and watched the tiny particles separate and spiral silently away.

'Page, we have to keep moving,' Megan said as she knelt beside him. When she went to reach for his hand he pulled it away, fearing what her touch could show him. 'Do you want to sit here and let the house consume you?' she asked as she stood looking down at him, 'because that's what will happen if we stay.'

'You sure?' he asked her, surprised that words could still come. Before collapsing where he now sat, he had been bombarding her with question after question about what he had been shown. Many of his issues remained unanswered, hanging in the air between them like the strands of glass from a broken window.

'You have misled me over most things,' he continued, 'and yet I fail to understand why you came back for me. You could have simply said that you couldn't find me.'

A nervous laugh escaped Megan as she turned away from him, folding her arms tightly around herself. Megan contemplated biting on one of her nails, such was her need for comfort, but pulled it away as it reached her mouth, biting down on her bottom lip as she faced him again.

'I had no choice,' she told him, her words sounding as honest as anything she had ever said, 'When I started to discover what the house held, I had to make up something for people to believe.'

'To believe?' he queried.

'The numbers and symbols I showed you and others. They were made up to keep Rowlance and his team happy.'

'They must have had some form of order,' Page suggested.

'To begin with, they did,' she agreed, 'but you've seen some of the ways that this place changes. I really could have told them any shit and they would have taken it in.'

'But the different eras that the house has shown, was that not true?' he asked.

'That much is true.' Megan confessed.

'So why have these times been so important to Rowlance and McAndrew?'

Megan knew that she had too much to explain to him. Too much that she couldn't tell him. Her main concern was to get out of the house, sensing that something terrible was about to happen.

If she began to say what had happened outside, the pain of losing Charlotte would race to the surface, threatening to make her lose control. *Tell him what he needs to know and work the rest out later,* she thought.

'Those instances showed the house in previous years,' she finally told him. 'Some of them, like the corridor with the yellow wallpaper, was the house thirty years ago.'

'But that's impossible,' Page retorted, soon realising how impossible his own words were.

'Rowlance wants to harness the energy of the house to enable him to go back to that period.'

Standing, Page wiped his face slowly with his hands, not wanting to begin to understand her explanation.

'Why?' he asked, his voice barely a whisper.

'To help change his and McAndrew's lives,' Megan said as she chewed on a fingernail, more out of habit than need. 'McAndrew's wife is ill, like really ga - ga. Lives in a loony bin or something similar. Rowlance's wife died recently, and they think they can go back and change everything, make them well again.'

Page didn't know what to feel, or what to think. Her words sounded like those of a delusional psychotic, but he knew in the short time he had been with her, even though she had misled him so much, that she was the one voice to listen to, and above all trust. He wanted to push her for more answers. He wanted to know whether Charlotte knew of this madness. A strong tremor then ran through where they stood, the force enough for him to adjust his footing. Before he could say anything else, the air seemed to change, a change which even Page sensed.

The dim corridor held a musty smell that matched the older pieces of furniture that stood between doorways which neither of them wished to enter. Page stood and walked closer to Megan when he thought the wall alongside him had moved.

The expression on Megan's face confirmed his initial thoughts. Even in the poor light, her face looked as pale as ever, her eyes showing too much unwelcome knowledge. Another tremor ran under them, causing particles of dust to fall from the ceiling. When two successive ones followed, the force was much more significant, forcing them to take hold of pieces of furniture to prevent them from losing their footing. In a glass-fronted wardrobe next to Page, some of the contents were disturbed, the sound of movement within caused him to take a firmer grip on the Glock 36.

'Something's coming,' Megan said as Page felt a slight breeze disturb the stale air before catching the side of his face.

'Come on,' he told her as he took hold of her coat by one of the shoulders, pulling her back along the corridor. When she resisted, she held a hand and raised her palm towards him, needing to gain his attention.

'You need to know something,' she told him as the tremors intensified. 'Things changed before I found you again,'

'With the house?' he asked.

'No. There are others here now. Soldiers or something. All of them are looking for me. All…'

Megan never finished her words as an invisible force suddenly pulled her away from him. Page tried in vain to reach her, but the distance was too wide. Megan had sensed the blackness seconds before it enveloped her arms, pushing them outwards, slamming her back against the wall before seeming to dissipate. Even though neither Page nor Megan could see anything around her, whatever force still held her increased, raising her off the floor, pushing her slowly up the wall. The back of her hands were pushed back flat against the wall, the bent wrists already aching under pressure. Her small feet flayed beneath her as she tried desperately to retain a form of hold.

Something struck Page hard against the shoulder, the force spinning him around before he was then hit hard across the face, the force great enough to split his bottom lip. He fell back hard, his breath knocked from him. Luckily he had managed to keep hold of the handgun, even when he was hit again as he attempted to stand. Before him, Megan was now held firmly against the top of the wall, her chin raised as though showing the force that now held her.

The words, 'You could have been the last one!' boomed around them.

Page felt his stomach turn at the sound of the deep voice and knew that if he ever got out of the house, he would pray never to hear it again. He was forced to look on as thin strands of what appeared to be black smoke began to circle in front of Megan.

'Oh, what delights we could have had with you,' the voice suggested as two of the black strands began pushing back the sides of her coat. Tears were forming in Megan's eyes as one strand of black caressed the side of her face. When it brushed against her mouth and probed within, she gagged while attempting to turn her head away.

'Such delights,' the voice now almost whispered as one of the strands began to travel underneath her sweater, exposing a section of her thin waist before concentrating on the area of her breasts. Mocking laughter filled the corridor as the number of strands of black smoke increased, each kneading at parts of the young girl's body. Inside, Megan begged to just black out, to find release from what was happening. She longed to be floating over waves of an ocean, swooping low over them as her mind sought the place of solitude that her dreams held. But nothing came to her, just the thought and feeling of total corruption as she felt her body violated.

'Leave her!' Page finally managed to scream. 'Leave her alone, you bastard!'

Again, laughter was heard before Page felt himself seized, the pressure upon him forcing his heart to beat heavily against his ribs. When it reached a point where he felt his body could take no more, Page found himself hurtling backwards, colliding with a small chair. The weight and force was enough to break its back before collapsing as its pieces helped to halt his movement.

'You have brought us much in our time here, enough for us to be almost sated. Yet even now as we feed, there is something more here, someone which we wish to make use of. This place will be lost soon and you should get out before we get too greedy and change our minds.'

As the voice drifted into fading laughter, the force against Megan weakened. She fell suddenly, landing on one of her arms, the impact making her cry out in pain.

'Leave the one we want alone,' the voice whispered into Megan's ear as her hair was pulled severely upwards. Her aching body hung motionless, all energy drained from her before a final blow struck her across the eye, splitting the skin beneath her eyebrow. The side of Megan's head hit the floor hard as she was finally released, the falling pressure sucking air from her as the corridor around them began to spin violently.

Chapter 68

Collette Logan failed to understand what had happened. She looked incredulously at where the gunfire from Walters had cut across the wall and doorway behind her. The wood was splintered around the large entrance holes in the door panels, and large chunks of plaster lay upon the narrow passage beside the staircase. Walters stood staring at the doorway while one of his hands wiped away the perspiration that covered his face.

'But you must have seen her!' he shouted as O'Donnell helped lower the weapon that Walters still aimed at the doorway. He said nothing to him or Collette as he still failed to understand where the woman he had been looking at had gone. The description that Walters had given them as to what the woman had looked like chilled him as he could have been giving a witness statement to his own account. Quite how the woman could have been laughing as the bullets had raked her body was beyond him, as was the fact that the gunfire had failed to attract anyone's attention was not lost on him either. Only silence surrounded them now, the stillness like a tomb.

'There's no one there, you idiot,' Collette snapped, storming into the centre of the hallway.

'I saw someone,' O'Donnell protested, instantly regretting his words when he saw her reaction. With her fists clenched by her sides, Collette leant forward slightly and stamped one of her feet as she screamed out loudly. Her petulant, childlike display was making O'Donnell want to floor her there and then. Tiring of this whole pathetic charade, he turned away from Collette just as the hallway lights flickered slightly. It was only a brief interruption, possibly less than a second, but when the light settled, it appeared paler to Collette. She felt disturbed by something that she couldn't quite put her finger on. Her unease had already been rising enough before Walters started shooting at imaginary people, but now the feeling reached a point when her eyes began to scan frantically across the hallway. Despite the relative warmth the house entrance still held, Collette had noticed a chill descending. She ordered the two men to pay attention at the same time something appeared to pass by in her peripheral vision. Turning quickly, Collette found there was nothing there when she looked, and she thought she had been mistaken, but another flicker of the lights made her look across to the doorway opposite her which was slowly opening.

As Walters reacted himself, he moved gingerly forward, expecting someone to step through at any moment. No one came. When the door reached its opening limit, O'Donnell had already positioned himself on the opposing side to Walters, ready to kick the door and clear an opening for his colleague.

Collette regretted not having kept the weapon she had used earlier, and gestured for the small handgun fitted in the shoulder holster of O'Donnell's bodysuit. When he handed it to her, the weight, though slight, gave reassurance and a more content feeling as Walters stepped into the open doorway, scanning the room, prepared to fire his weapon again at the smallest form of movement. But he found the room empty, as did O'Donnell when he followed.

'All clear,' Walters told Collette moments later when he stepped back into the hallway. Switching on the room's lights as he left, his words failed to placate Collette as she was stunned to see how accurate his words were. The room had been one of only a couple that Collette had looked inside. Then it had looked like any other sitting room of a house of such stature, only the many sheets that had shrouded pieces of furniture looking unusual. Now as Collette stepped towards the doorway, she couldn't take in the sight which she now saw. The room was entirely bare. There was not a trace of any single item. There wasn't even a sight of the large fireplace she recalled seeing. Even the carpet was missing, the room now only holding a layer of dust gathered over time. Resting a hand out to steady herself against the doorframe, she took no notice of Walters who then entered the room, watching as the woman began looking around her as though trying to get her bearings. There had to be some mistake, she thought as she looked back, but the plate beside the door showing numbers and symbols remained the same. Collette recalled Megan talking about the numbering system that she had given the place, proving that she had not been mistaken.

A sound elsewhere made Collette race back into the hallway where she looked up as something else caught her eye, something at the top of the stairway. A mixture of relief and anguish filled her when she looked upon Megan who stood at the top of the stairs looking down at her.

Chapter 69

A smile finally fell across Collette Logan's face at the sight of Megan. This was partly due to her own calm reaction to seeing her. She needed to put an end to this whole pantomime, to regain what she craved most – control.

'Hello, Collette,' Megan said slowly from beneath a mass of unruly hair. A large section covered one of her eyes, making the visible one appear larger than usual. Megan wondered whether Collette had noticed how different her voice sounded when she spoke, as well as how her words were almost a second behind her lip movement. She suppressed a slight giggle inside herself as she stretched out her fingers, surprised at the heat she now felt across her skin. When she blew out gently to try and help remove the hair that obscured part of her vision, her lips felt parched, the dryness in her throat as evident as the swelling she felt across her glands.

Megan had little recollection of what had happened to Page as she walked toward the top of the stairway. There was also no recollection of how long it had taken her to journey through the house to arrive at the spot where she now stood. With each step taken, the house seemed to change constantly. Corridors narrowed and shortened, doorways that she approached either opened by themselves or just faded away as the way ahead for her was revealed in a kaleidoscope of images.

At one point Henry Talbot had come close to her, but she had ignored his jibes and abuse just as she had ignored the pathetic pleas of help from Thomas Kenny.

Other faces, many unknown, flitted by in a chaos of images and glimpses, none of them now able to halt her progress. Even the awful site of slain children who wandered across her way failed to stop her. Within her, Megan felt the movement of the darkness she carried exploring her body, drawing on all memories, thoughts and fears. By the time the last doorway had faded before her, an increased sharpening of her senses had become noticeable as the landing came into view and she stepped through a thin, eerie mist before coming to a halt at the top of the stairway.

'So there you are, you troublesome bitch,' Collette sneered whilst approaching the bottom of the staircase. Raising the handgun directly at Megan, Collette considered for a second why Megan had decided to appear now. Collette had no idea what had happened to the rest of the assault team, and as she placed a foot on the bottom step, she almost expected one or more of them to appear. None did. While she had been taking tentative steps forward, O'Donnell and Walters had positioned themselves on either side of Collette, both showing more apprehension. All this time, Megan remained still.

'I'm surprised you're still here,' Megan said.

'What? Go without you, my freaky darling?' Collette queried mockingly. 'That's not going to happen; you of all people should know that.'

Megan raised one of her arms, making both O'Donnell and Walters flinch nervously. Had they not had specific instructions that Megan was to remain unharmed, both could easily have fired at the unwelcome movement. As it was, Megan simply pushed back her hair, revealing her face fully. Her eyes seemed almost lost in the black shadows surrounding them. A small amount of blood had dried above her left eyebrow, whilst her bottom lip showed evidence of swelling on one side following her fall.

'You know, I was wrong about here,' Megan told Collette, 'wrong about so much.'

'You could add stupid to that too,' Collette suggested as she began to climb the stairs slowly. 'I saw through your little plan far too easily.'

'That's because it was meant to be easy. Even Toby knew that.'

The mention of Toby took Collette by surprise. She paused in her ascent, swallowing deeply to try and keep her breathing under control.

'You see, Collette,' Megan continued, 'you were not the only one who was using Toby. At first, he was all too flattered by the attention. Of course, I could never compete with you on the looks and body front, but ask me to find a point on his body that pleased him, or excited him, well, that was far too easy. A surprising energy level for someone so weak looking.'

'Lying cow!' Collette hissed at her.

'In some ways, you're actually right,' Megan agreed. 'I've lied to so many people. Lied pretty bad, and did some things that disgusted me before I could find a way through his apparent fool proof system and… well, you know the rest.'

Anger surged through Collette, her body temperature becoming almost unbearable.

'But I knew that you had come across my escape plan,' Megan continued, her voice still sounding slightly deeper than normal, 'and knew about the alterations you ended up doing.' Megan looked down at her feet for a moment, using one of them to kick away a couple pieces of glass close to her. When she looked back at Collette, there were signs of relief showing on her face. 'The funny thing is, in the end it all helped.'

'Where are the files that Toby said were missing?' Collette asked, so tired of listening to her taunts and lies.

'What, the information files or your money files?' Megan mocked.

Collette was struggling to keep hold of her anger. She wanted nothing more than to surge at the stupid retard and wipe the smug look off her face. Her finger was aching from holding the trigger for so long, making her wonder how long she could keep hold of her growing temper.

'All the files,' she told her, now only a dozen or so steps from Megan. Behind her, O'Donnell now asked her to step aside and let them take hold of Megan, but Collette told them to remain exactly where they were.

'Gone. Wiped. Disappeared. Every last one of them,' Megan told her, a slight childlike laugh escaping her.

'That's not possible!' Collette screamed at her, pulling hard on the trigger whilst aiming the weapon above Megan. The window above Megan took the fired shot, sections of shattered glass soon falling onto the landing behind her.

'In the end, none of it matters, Collette. Nothing. Thomas was right, nothing m… m… matters.' A much stronger giggle escaped her before she added, 'It doesn't matter, as no-one is going to get out of here in the end. The house will take everyone. Did you not hear what I said about me being wrong?'

Collette again paused, so wanting to shoot Megan now to end her annoying ways. Even though her anger was threatening to explode out of her, the chill she felt around the staircase now was so noticeable that she could feel a cold sheen of perspiration across her face and neck.

'Most of all, Collette, I was wrong about the power here.' Megan added, 'It's far too great, far too powerful.'

'I don't give a shit about this place or your deluded ideas of power,' Collette told her as the two armed men beside her began to notice the change in atmosphere. Blood had again begun running down Walter's neck, the ringing in his slightly good ear masking most of what the girl who was scaring the crap out of him was saying.

'You should go,' Megan told her, pushing back her hair again, 'because you should never have come in here.'

'I needed you,' Collette reminded her, growing wearier by the minute.

'What we need and what we get are often so different,' Megan almost whispered as she lowered her head slightly, allowing her hair to fall forward. Without actually seeming to move, O'Donnell noticed that Megan was now somehow further back. He moved forward against the bannister but found his legs so weak it took all his effort to remain upright. He could see the wall behind the girl shimmering as though heat was being generated somehow, even though the air around him felt so cold. Casting a glance across at Walters, he could see what appeared to be silent words being mouthed by him. Collette herself now stood transfixed as Megan's head slowly rose. Through ragged, dishevelled hair, Megan's eyes showed an intensity of blue that seemed almost blinding. A maniacal grin stretched across her face, which only broke when she finally spoke, the voice so low now that it sounded alien to Collette. It held a tone that bore into her very soul, sending a tremor throughout her entire body.

'Too late, Collette. It's far, far too late.'

As Collette raised the handgun once more, the shimmering around Megan intensified. Collette's anger then burst from her and she fired indiscriminately, even though there was no trace of where Megan had once stood. The shattered remains of the landing window could no longer be seen, and the entire area at the top of the stairway was now completely different.

Chapter 70

Neither O'Donnell nor Walters could think of anything to say to each other by the time they began searching the two upper corridors for Megan. Nothing seemed to be making any sense. Collette followed Walters as her instincts told her that Megan was still close to where she had disappeared, having managed to somehow slip through a hidden panel somewhere. The length of the corridor was impossible for her to tell due to the poor light, the gloom only partially penetrated by the weak light fittings that ran down one side. There also appeared to be no doorways or entrances, nothing but marks and traces of where pictures had once hung and heavy furniture had, over time, indented the carpet. Keen to hurry up the operation, Walters increased his pace, perspiration now coating his face even though his body temperature felt low. As he passed another light fitting, he felt a tremor run through the wooden floorboards beneath him.

O'Donnell had decided that he was going to take the young girl down at the first opportunity. One or more shots to her legs should do it, to stop the silly cow from running away. The thought of running seemed almost idyllic to him now, finding a sense of freedom and escape never more appealing. He then recalled the country lane near where he had first met his greatest love, Jackie Marten. God, the simple thought of her now made the apprehension he felt about the house disappear. Why on earth she hadn't waited for him when he had worked abroad for twelve months, he had no idea. Returning to find her engaged to someone she had known for barely a few months had hurt him deeply, yet for some reason he now felt a form of understanding towards her actions. He needed to see her. He needed to let her know that things could be so different between them now. Who cared about this house and the girl he was supposed to be helping to find? He smiled to himself with the thought that he now had a planned thought in his mind while ignoring the increasing blackness that lined the corridor wall beside him. He even cared little that the corridor in front of him had now come to an end.

There was a framed picture on the wall hanging at a slight angle. The image within the decorative frame was unclear, but the angle was enough for O'Donnell to stop and want to straighten it. Lowering the automatic weapon, he ran the back of his hand across his face, clearing the perspiration then licking his top lip before hanging the weapon over his shoulder.

With the picture straightened he stepped back, almost admiring his simple action. He caught the scent of Jackie's distinctive perfume, felt the way she used to like to stand behind him and rest her head on his shoulder while snaking an arm around his waist. The touch was reassuring, as welcome as anything he had felt in such a long time. When her hair brushed against his cheek, he turned to face her, needing to feel the touch of her lips against his own. The weapon fell to the floor as he turned, his broad smile fading as he found himself looking at a swirling mass of darkness. The density was as unknown to him as was the purpose of it being there. A series of tremors were then felt running along the corridor, making him look down as if for some reason or explanation. He saw nothing untoward, and rocked backwards and forwards on his heels as though unsure of the floor beneath him. Looking back up, he found to his surprise, there was no trace of the darkness that had confronted him. The corridor just ran ahead as it had done before. Still, O'Donnell stared as though almost expecting something to happen. Out of the gloom, a figure approached, the reduced light making it difficult for him to see who it was.

'Jackie?' he asked as the figure began to come into view.

Her hair was longer than he recalled and her style of clothing appeared to have changed. The long coat gave her an added height, or was it the fact that she had lost so much weight since he had last seen her. Passing one of the light fittings, her face became more evident, allowing him to see not only the intensity of her blue eyes but also the expression of anger etched across her face.

The tremors increased further, causing the floorboards between them to jolt under the force. O'Donnell's mouth fell open as he realised the mistake he had made in recognising the figure. A ringing sound began in his ear, its pitch increasing rapidly, causing the injury within to protest loudly. In front of the approaching figure, the floorboards began to lift and separate, fixing nails were effortlessly ripped loose as countless splinters of wood flew upwards as each was ripped from its fixing. In the exposed space beneath, a sea of darkness swarmed. Thick strands of smoke-like tentacles stretched out, each pulsing strongly as the rest of the floorboards began to lift as though a great force was approaching.

'Oh, jesus!' O'Donnell managed to cry out as he frantically scrambled in the shadows below him for his discarded weapon. Twice he almost grasped it, almost felt the reassurance the weapon gave him. Crying out in fear as much as frustration, he scrambled his hands around on the floor, eventually finding the gun as his cries turned to weak laughter. The strap became entangled around his trembling fingers as he struggled to take hold of the weight. Ahead, he could make out the strange blue light from Megan's eyes had intensified to a point where it became almost blinding. O'Donnell backed away as he finally managed to raise the weapon, barely a dozen floorboards remaining untouched between them. His head felt as though it was about to explode by the time he managed to start firing, his vision was barely enough for him to see that no floor existed beneath him now as the air filled with thousands of wooden splinters that silently raked his body. An immeasurable level of pain engulfed him moments before his vision finally failed.

The loud gunfire made Walters and Collette retrace their steps. They had to have been at least a hundred feet down the corridor, maybe more, when they heard shooting. Despite the fact that their headsets hadn't worked since entering the house, Walters called out repeatedly for his colleague to answer him. When the sound of gunfire ended, Walters surprisingly felt worse. He ran as fast as he could, realising with fear that he may now be alone, disregarding the cries of Collette behind him. As the corridor reached the place where the two of them had separated he slowed, trying to understand why the opposite corridor had now vanished. He appeared to be looking at a darkened tunnel, the edges of which flowed like water even though he knew that was impossible. Turning his eyes away, they were drawn to the stairway, which, for some reason, had become much narrower than before. He contemplated fleeing down them, but the sound of shouting caught his attention.

Collette failed to see why Walters hadn't reacted. Somehow he had gotten well ahead of her, even though she felt that she had kept up with him as they had raced to find the source of the noise they had heard. Raising the handgun, she used her free hand to help maintain her aim as she fired repeatedly.

'She's behind you, you stupid bastard!' she cried out as she watched Megan slowly approaching out of the darkness behind him. Caring little now whether one of her shots hit either of them, she repeatedly fired until the hammer struck down on an empty chamber, knowing deep inside her that she wouldn't make it in time. She saw Walters begin to look away from her and called out again, the panic in her voice finally showing. The movement of whatever came out of the darkness was so great that she failed to see the point of contact. On either side of her the walls shook violently, the pulse running through the aged building making sections of the wall's plaster break free along the length of the corridor that she ran down, thousands of tiny flecks swirling all around her like gentle snow. When she moved to the spot where Walters and Megan had originally stood, her heart thumped hard against her ribcage, making her breath coming in short bursts. She blinked hard, trying to improve her vision, wondering how on earth she now found herself facing a solid wall. Thinking it was merely an illusion, she thrust a hand out, the pain of impact against her hand surprising her.

To both sides of her now she could see walls that gave her the impression she was now within the confines of a small room. Above her, a discoloured ceiling reflected the pale glow of the light fitting that, when she turned, she could see hanging from the ceiling. The sound of movement came to her ear, and as her eyes began to adjust to the light, she could now make out a doorway in the centre of the wall opposite. There appeared to be no other doorways or windows to the box-like room, and her breath caught as the door began opening. To help her hold onto some form of control, she gripped hard on the handgun she still held. Even though she knew the small magazine was empty, she remained motionless as two figures entered the room. The features of both still unclear to her, yet the sound of a key turning in the door was as clear as anything Collette Logan had ever heard in her life.

A slight snigger escaped one of the figures as he placed the door key in the pocket of his sweat-stained shirt, the sound of his laughter chilling Collette to the bone. The movement of the two figures caused Collette to raise the handgun whilst beginning to move further back. The glow from the overhead light caught the edge of the long blade that the thinner of the two figures held, the sight making Collette pointlessly squeeze hard on the trigger again. She felt a warm trickle run down the inside of her legs as tears began to form in her eyes when the handgun struck again and again against an empty chamber. The sound seemed to echo around the small room, making both Henry Talbot and Thomas Kenny laugh as they slowly approached.

Chapter 71

Quite how long Page Darrow had wept for, he had no idea. At times it felt as though he had slipped in and out of consciousness, but the visions and images that filled his mind had given him the impression that at some point he must have slept. All the memories he had recalled in those moments felt as though they had been subject to the same violation as he had himself. The feeling that his very soul had been walked upon, that his whole life had been open for all to see and judge, and that nothing he could hold close and dear to him could ever feel the same again. Still huddled in the foetal position that ironically gave him the most comfort, Page felt a stinging sensation across his eyes when he opened them, even though he looked into near darkness.

All concept of time now appeared lost, and the urge to drift away into the darkness remained strong as he began forcing himself to sit up. Every part of his body seemed to protest at the movement, the pain in his temples making him cradle his head as he finally sat. When he put a hand down to help support his weak body, he felt small sections of glass upon the floor, their source unknown to him. Page pulled his hand back instinctively, feeling a touch of moisture on the tips of his fingers when he rubbed them together. He then raised one to his mouth, soon tasting the traces of blood upon it. When a trickling sensation ran down the wrist of his arm, he lowered it gingerly, realising then that the blood had come from somewhere on his arm. On the sleeve of his jacket he felt a gap in the material, and the pain which followed his touch made him realise he had somehow injured himself. Despite the pain, Page clenched the fist on his injured arm and pressed his other hand against the wound. Hoping his grip would help stem the blood flow, he grimaced at the discomfort he soon felt.

Around him, his vision had improved, mainly due to the small amount of light given off from light fittings that lined the corridor he faced when he managed to stand. Attempting to gain some form of control and sense, Page began walking forward, all the time becoming aware of a trembling sensation running around him. By the time the corridor had opened up, he found to his relief that he had reached the top of the main stairway for the house. The crunching sound of glass under his feet made him pause and look up to see the window above the landing. Traces of a cool breeze caught his face, making him realise that the glass was broken. For some reason he called out, hoping that someone would respond to the feeling of solitude that was overcoming him. As he thought about where Megan could now be, a sudden tremor ran through the house, strong enough to knock him off his feet. The lights along the corridor he had walked down now dimmed. Then out of the increasing darkness around him came whispering.

The voices were unclear to him when he attempted to look around him for the source. Instinctively reaching inside his jacket, his hand found only the empty holster, the whereabouts of his handgun now unknown. The gentle breeze that had moments before touched his face became a sudden blast of air as an unseen force swept through the house. As though blown backwards by a gale force wind, Page attempted to stand, but the force was far too powerful. Above him, he could make out what appeared to be black smoke streaming along the ceiling. As if joining the unfolding spectacle above him, the tremors underneath him now became so violent that his body was repeatedly jolted. As the tremors continued, the wind that tore through the house still prevented him from standing. Another pulse seemed to run right through the wall beside him, opening up a broad split, causing sections of plaster and panelling to fall away. Drawing on what little strength his body still had left, Page finally managed to stand and he began making his way as best as he could to the top of the stairway. A deafening crash of noise made him raise an arm to protect his head as high above, part of the ceiling fell in. When part of it struck his wounded arm, Page cried out in pain, with the wind buffeting him from side to side as he attempted to descend the stairway. Streams of the black substance that now smothered most of the walls of the hallway formed strand-like tentacles that swirled around the large chandelier which somehow still illuminated the lower half of the hall. The force of whatever power encircled it caused it to shake violently in its fitting, small sections of the glasswork falling to the floor to join others below. Page clutched at the ornate bannister as repeated tremors shook the building to its foundation. All around him, the house appeared to be disintegrating as he was forced to lower his body to enable him to move against the storm raging around him.

What pieces of glass remained in the window above the stairway now erupted from the frame as the wall around it imploded. Across the rooftops of Ravenscroft, most of the chimneys began to sway as their weakened fixings could no longer hold, sections of displaced roof slates falling down all around the house. The most potent tremor Page had felt so far, brought down part of the ceiling in both corridors, as well as above the stairway. A bizarre mixture of glass and stonework rained down on Page as he forced himself into a misguided run that the wind soon took hold of. In the moment of his stumbling, he felt an intense longing for his mother, for the peace and security that he had known within her for so many months. He longed to have known the love of a father, forever unknown to him, to feel the guidance that his life had always lacked, the advice that he had both wanted and failed to give to Emma. Images of his wife and daughter filled his mind as he recalled a photograph of the three of them alongside a tree-lined road that he had always hoped would have been the road to the happiness he had so craved.

As he finally fell, a large section of the falling ceiling struck against the side of his head, spinning his body around, the wound across the point of impact soon opening up as his grip with the reality around him was lost. Page saw his hands reaching out to him, saw the tenderness and redness of his new-born skin in sharp contrast to the blackness that pulsed and swirled above him. All sound faded away until only the sound of his own heartbeat could be heard, the harshness, coldness and cruelty of life at that moment blissfully unknown to him.

Chapter 72

The sunlight slowly etched its way across the Ravenscroft Estate. Remnants of early morning mist now only clung to the woodland areas. What warmth the sun held was unnoticed by Peter Hamilton, who wiped moisture from his face as he crouched beside the helmet he had recently removed. He rotated his neck slowly in an attempt to clear the dull ache that had resided there all morning. His vehicle had been the first of four fire engines that had attended the scene shortly after 11 pm the night before. The appliance now stood beside two police cars whose blue lights had finally been switched off.

His team leader could be seen nearby, talking to two plain clothed police officers. The crime scene tape, cordoning off the area around the Coach House, fluttered as figures in white overalls passed underneath it. Peter wondered what their findings were going to reveal as he stood and replaced his yellow helmet. He nodded at a colleague who passed, the tiredness showing on his face, also no doubt grateful as well that the breathing equipment they had been using for most of the night was now securely back in their appliance.

The initial act on arriving at the Ravenscroft Estate had been to extinguish the still shouldering helicopter wreckage, clear access to the central fire having been needed. Peter had a decent knowledge of aircraft having spent many years visiting air shows with his father, but the make of this one eluded him. The fire in the main house seemed to have taken hold of what they now knew was the western side of the building. The intensity had taken time to control, their skill and expertise, as always, unseen by an audience. As dawn broke, the extent of damage caused soon became apparent.

Part of the structure where the fire had raged remained erect, but it was the rest of the former building that couldn't help but draw his and others' attention. The house looked as though it had somehow folded in on itself. The debris around the scene was limited given the scale of the destruction. A few dozen pieces of rubble and the remains of one of the chimney stacks caught the eye, but the fire hadn't touched three-quarters of the property. Still, the chances of anyone getting out of the place looked pretty slim.

The sound of someone approaching from behind caused the fireman to turn and face the man he had spoken with earlier.

'The place didn't look much better before,' Charles McAndrew solemnly said, the uniformed officer beside him remaining silent.

'Curious how the fire didn't spread,' Peter replied, 'although the rest of the house appears to have fared worse.'

McAndrew nodded but didn't reply as he moved silently away, his hands deep in the pockets of the overcoat he wore. He had received a phone call from the police close to midnight, shortly after retiring for the night. The afternoon had been spent at the hospital getting checked over following the traffic accident. The long sleep he had craved by staying over at Anthony Rowlance's home soon interrupted. A dressing across McAndrew's right temple was the only visible sign of injury.

Bruising to his ribs added discomfort as he moved. Insisting that his friend get some sleep, he had arrived at the Ravenscroft Estate to find a scene he could barely believe. Flame and smoke continued to billow from the main house, the flashing blue lights of the emergency vehicles adding an extra dimension to the bizarre scene. The acrid smell of smoke still lingered in the air as he made his way over to the sectioned off area of the Coach House.

The scene of crime officers still worked within the building. Their painstaking work would no doubt reveal more and more of the horrors inside. Charles's shock of finding out that one of the six bodies found so far was a woman, remained stronger than that felt for the dead security team members. He had asked the police to show him those who had been recovered from the house and had cried out in pain when the pulled back sheet had revealed Charlotte Wareham's features.

Looking at the Coach House now, it seemed as bleak as the former main house. Most of the upper floor windows were broken, no doubt by the force of the helicopter explosion or crash. McAndrew felt a deep ache in his heart as he contemplated explaining the events to his friend, Anthony. He had given him a call earlier to provide initial details, but how would he tell him of Charlotte's loss? That needed telling face to face as more grief was added to his life. He turned his gaze away from the building, no longer able to look upon it. As he returned to the group of people he had spoken with earlier at work on the investigation, he couldn't help but notice how silent the place had become. No birdsong could be heard, the branches of nearby trees unmoving as though held in silence. *Out of respect*, he thought, *or out of fear?*

Chapter 73

Anthony Rowlance lifted the crystal tumbler and studied the contents within, the darkness of the liquid not lost on him. The ice cubes clinked against the side of the glass as he took a deep taste of the drink, wincing as it burned its way down his throat.

He had been studying the Manchester skyline for over an hour now, his thoughts as sombre as the rain that sheeted its way across the city. How the view had changed in the ten years or so that his company had owned the upper floors of the Arlington Hotel. He wondered how much wealth of the new Hilton and Shard buildings reached those far below who huddled for warmth in shop doorways and alleyways. Draining the contents of his glass, he laughed inwardly at his newly found compassion.

It had been a week since Charlotte's funeral, a week that had been harder than when he had lost his wife. Even on the morning that his only child was being put to rest, the police had been to see him, asking further questions about the events at the Ravenscroft Estate. Anthony had wondered even to himself how much of the version he had given them was accurate. His explanation as to why they had been working close to a half-derelict property was not scrutinised initially, not as much as he thought it would have been, as the range of locations the company worked on and were based in, were varied.

Aside from his daughter's murder, there were seven dead A. R. Solutions employees, all with wounds from so far untraceable weapons. With each passing hour, his mind raised further questions, which refused to go away. He knew the theory of a competitor to blame was not being taken seriously by the police, but it was a straw which Anthony still chose to clutch.

The burnt out wreckage of the helicopter had been traced to a company in Libya, but they had strenuously denied any involvement, so the investigation carried on alongside the mourning. If Collette Logan could be found, then the authorities could be diverted in her direction. The systematic search of the collapsed building had so far revealed no answers. What happened that night remained a mystery to all, especially Rowlance and McAndrew. The immediate concerns of the company's issues had taken priority, the false data and programs which corrupted many of their systems had now been removed. Thankfully, the damage was limited to the North Atlantic projects. Anthony Rowlance knew his well-paid accountants could, in time, recover the losses of money, and the business he had worked so hard to build would recover. But to what value when those closest to him had been lost? Like the police, Rowlance had questions for Toby Connor as well. What part did he have to play in this? Was his disappearance linked with that of Collette Logan? These and so many other questions walked like unwelcome guests through his mind.

The sound of sirens somewhere across the city could faintly be heard as he ran a finger around the edge of his glass. Turning, he sat down on the sofa of his luxury apartment and exhaled. Guilt would accompany him as he contemplated another night here, but the silence was more deafening at his home, as the flowers around Charlotte's grave slowly faded.

The thought that now filled his mind as darkness fell was of Megan. She had failed to be mentioned in any part of the police investigation, nor in any of the endless questions asked so far, a ghost in the machine. Her services and abilities were as secretive as the girl herself. No trace of her was recorded in any form by the company.

Had she been lost within the house like all the others he had brought to Ravenscroft? In some ways he prayed that she had, and the house that he had come to loath would hold onto whatever secrets it held.

As he had woken that morning, he had decided to erase Megan from his mind, to allow work and purpose to be his guide, but as he stood he cursed for allowing himself to be manipulated by the mystery of Ravenscroft. Never again would he let his judgement become so misguided, so clouded. He walked over to where the open whisky bottle remained, his anger rising within him as he poured another large measure, anger that demanded answers and cried out for someone to pay for his losses.

Chapter 74

It was the third successive evening that the cormorant had flown across the bay. Its shape and regular movement were now quite distinctive. The slow, yet steady rate that its wings flapped at seemingly inappropriate for the speed at which it flew.

Megan was unsure of whether its movements so late in the day were due to a search for food, or when she would eventually lose sight of the bird, it had finally decided to settle down for the night.

The sunlight sparkled upon the surface of the stretch of water she looked across, the cormorant silhouetted for a second against a section of sepia toned sky before being lost in the brightness upon the far horizon.

The rain which had fallen earlier had begun clearing late in the afternoon, just as it had done on previous days, leaving behind mottled brown clouds which now appeared to be melting away before her. Megan sat with her legs drawn up before her on top of a large rock which jutted out from the water's edge.

Her hands were hidden inside the sleeves of the grey fleece she wore, which, as ever, was due to her thin frame, looked slightly too big on her. The full tide lay deep to both sides of where she had perched herself just over eight feet from the surface of the ocean.

For the past two hours, she had sat silently watched the tide come in. With hardly a breath of wind, the huge force of the ocean had been subdued, the gradual encroachment on land almost unnoticed. At first, Megan had charted its slow progress along the shoreline where the mixture of white sand and small pebbles had felt soft under each step. The olive green seaweed that coated many of the rocks slowly transformed into a swaying forest of life as it became once more submerged below the surface. As the tide reached its peak, Megan had clambered up onto the large rock and sat alone, lost in her thoughts.

It had been almost three months now since they had arrived at the cottage. When Megan looked over her shoulder, the white painted walls of the single building still held the last remnants of sunlight, keeping a pinkish tinge which seemed more prominent set against the grey slate roof.

A 'safe place' Charlotte had called it. *Not safe enough for her,* thought Megan as she began to feel slightly cold as a single tear welled in her right eye. It fell down her cheek as the aching for her lost friend surfaced again. Since she had escaped from Ravenscroft, Megan had doubted whether she was going to be able to cope without her. For now, her purpose seemed uncertain and without any form of order, the guidance and direction that Charlotte had always given her now lost forever.

The place Megan now mourned at was only known to her and Charlotte, somewhere Charlotte had found by herself, hoping she would never have to use it. Frightened by her father's increasing control over her, coupled with the increasing doubt over her strained marriage, had made Charlotte look for an escape route should she ever have needed it. Somewhere she could start afresh. Megan hoped that her friend knew why she had come here and that she would understand that the place was still hers and always would be, even though she would never get to step foot in it.

In each of the times that Megan had cleansed her mind, her thoughts had brought her to this place, the feelings she felt were stronger than she could understand. She had only seen it in a couple of photos that Charlotte had shown her, and she had not been prepared for the sheer beauty of the place. The range of mountains, which held colours that she could scarcely believe, appeared to shield the cottage and bay. The expanse of ocean that her tears fell close to seemed to put an incredible distance between worlds which she barely understood. She now used each incoming tide to cleanse herself, attempting to take hurt and memories away as each one retreated.

Raising herself onto her feet, Megan climbed down along the tapered edge of the rock and began making her way across the bay. A lone gull cried out, making her look up, but she failed to catch sight of it even though she continued to hear its cries.

The walls of the cottage had now turned a paler pink as the sky began to clear to a red ochre colour, giving her hope that the weather would soon become more settled. In the seat close to the cottage entrance, Megan could now see a figure sitting, looking towards her.

Page Darrow wore the black fleece as he had done for the past week. Only having had the clothes that they had arrived in, Megan was grateful to find a box of random clothing in one of the cottage's bedrooms. None of the clothes fitted particularly well, but neither of them was going to complain about it. Within the comfort provided by the fleece, Page sat with his arms wrapped around himself as though the remains of the sun's warmth had failed to reach him. His unkempt hair still masked part of his face, and when he didn't respond to her gesture, Megan believed that he had just not seen her. She was about to wave again when she saw him raise a hand, revealing the dressing above his right eye. The wound across his forehead had been deep and had needed stitching, as had the deep gouge on his left arm, but Megan knew that both would have to wait as she had bundled him into the back seat of the first car she had come across as they fled Ravenscroft. The car they had taken had been Charlotte's. A zip-up bag, a leather jacket and a small umbrella still lay on the floor behind the driver's seat of the Ford Focus the only evidence, now no longer of need.

The few driving lessons that Charlotte had given her had been more than enough for her to be able to manoeuvre the vehicle away from the disintegrating estate. As she had driven on, her confidence in driving had grown and she began to lose the fear of being stopped. They passed several roadside services before she was confident that they were not being followed. Megan used some of the five hundred pounds which she had found in the zip up bag to buy antiseptic wipes and dressings for Page's wounds. Delirious and incoherent, he had resisted her help at first, whatever horror he had witnessed still evident in his eyes. The head wound had been the worst to tend, and she had bound adhesive tape around his head in an attempt to stop the bleeding. Page had slipped into a deep sleep, which Megan feared was unconsciousness. Too tired to keep on driving, she had pulled the car over into a lay-by behind two parked trucks and slept herself.

Rain had fallen steadily the next morning when, still in the darkness, she had filled a box in the boot of the car with food and drinks bought from a 24 hour superstore in the last town they had passed before they hit the open country. All this time, Page had slipped in and out of sleep, only the thought of the white cottage beside the blue-grey ocean was driving her on. She drove for over four hundred miles, following pulses of colour that showed at various junctions, along with tremors and changes in both pressure and colour before they reached the island. Megan had had no idea that the place she would eventually arrive at would be an island, the white road bridge being the only attachment to the mainland. It seemed to mark the boundary of her fears, with the open expanses around her helping to clear her thoughts. Despite the strength of the wind, Megan had wound the window beside her down, allowing the swirling breeze to cool her. As the roadway narrowed and began to descend, the expanse of the ocean before her took her breath away. Tears fell freely as she took the winding road down to the small cottage close to where the roadway came to an end.

The two of them had remained sitting in the car for nearly three hours, the reality of how far she had driven finally hitting home. Getting the still disorientated Page over to the cottage had been difficult. His unsteady body forced her to actually drag him over the final few feet. Page Darrow cared little about the reasons for them being there in those first few hours; he sought only the escape that sleep could bring him.

After three days of sleep and recovery, Megan told him not only about the events of the last few hours at Ravenscroft, but also about Charlotte's death. The loss of Charlotte seemed to numb him further.

For the next few days he had attempted to get Megan to return with him to try and explain what had happened, but she had repeatedly lost her temper with him and refused to disclose the location of the keys to the Ford. His attempts to force them from her only stopped when the pain from his wounds returned.

But who could they tell, who could help them? she had asked him as he slowly began to calm down, *and what steps were already being taken by A. R. Solutions to cover any incident up*?

In the small garden of the cottage where a single tree misshapen by winter storms had stood, they had placed a white stone with the letter 'C' marked upon it. After they both said a few words privately in her memory, Megan had laid a bunch of wildflowers that she managed to find on a nearby hillside. Megan continued with her walk where the sand and pebbles gave way to the low wall of a former stone jetty. She stepped upon it and looked across to the rock where she had been sitting. Behind it, the light was fading in the distant mountains, the purple colour now moving to a more russet shade. She wondered how long they could stay there. How long before the small amount of money they had ran out? And how about the story they would have to invent to answer questions by local people in what she imagined was a tightly knit community, even though the properties were few and far between.

The edges of the sporadically placed trees would soon show the first signs of autumn approaching, the green colour of the nearby bracken would then shift closer to shades of brown. When the storms of winter came, she prayed that they would act as cover for them and give them the isolation and quiet that they needed to heal. The trail of false leads and chaos she had left for her former employees would only keep them occupied for so long. She wondered what had become of the main house at Ravenscroft and what the reaction had been when the extent of the carnage was discovered. When no trace of hers or Page's bodies were found, she knew that those behind A. R. Solutions would put the pieces together and in time come looking for them. The full extent and power of the company she kept from Page, hoping that her senses would let her know of any threats. Each morning Megan sat alone and slowly opened her mind to see if she could sense any danger. None came, but still, her mistrust remained. Since arriving at the cottage, she had refused to use any other of her abilities, still unable to believe what she had done to gain her freedom.

The nights on the coastline were the darkest she had ever experienced in her short life, the canopy of countless stars the only disruption she could see. The form of darkness that had held her in fear for so, so long now failed to find her.

Page was waiting for her by the time she returned to the cottage. He did his best to appear brighter to her over the past few days, but his eyes still held the haunted look that unnerved her at times. The former lives that both of them had left were now over in all senses, the future for them unknown and uncharted. Megan shivered involuntarily and smiled at him as he passed her one of two hot drinks he had made. They sat on a wooden bench close to where the garden's lone tree stood. Nearby, Charlotte's stone looked on, wrapped now in the cloth friendship bracelets given to her by her one true friend as the two of them sat in silence for a while, watching the sun finally drop over the other smaller islands out to sea.

'Looks like it could be a better day tomorrow,' Page suggested as he watched her take a drink from her mug. 'Red sky at night, as they say.'

'You could well be right,' she replied as she rested her head on his shoulder and closed her eyes, feeling her body relax a little, enjoying the warmth his body generated next to hers. Megan smiled as he put an arm around her and held her still.

'Are we okay?' she asked softly, her eyes remaining closed as she wondered whether the cormorant had itself finally found its nesting point now that night had fallen.

'We will be,' he promised her, 'we will be.' His words sounded hopeful, if only to himself.

'Take me to the island, I'll show you all I've never told you.
The boy I never showed you, more than I gave in my life.
Take me by the hand, you'll either kill me or you'll save me,
take me to the island, show me what might be real life...'

Marillion - Fantastic Place

About the Author

Travis Little was born and raised in Cheshire. During his childhood, he spent time in a haunted house, which he believes started his fascination with ghosts.

He uses experiences in his life, along with childhood memories, for his ideas and stories. Travis has a deep love for the Lake District and hopes to live and write there one day.

For now, he lives in Northern England with his wife and a vivid imagination.

41971891R00218

Printed in Poland
by Amazon Fulfillment
Poland Sp. z o.o., Wrocław